Down Sand Mountain

STEVE WATKINS

CANDLEWICK PRESS

Copyright © 2008 by Steve Watkins

First paperback edition 2011

The Library of Congress has cataloged the hardcover edition as follows:

Watkins, Steve, date.
Down Sand Mountain / Steve Watkins — 1st ed.
p.   cm.
Summary: In a small Florida mining town in 1966, twelve-year-old Dewey faces one worst-day-ever after another, but comes to know that the issues he faces about bullies, girls, race, and identity are part of the adult world, as well.
ISBN 978-0-7636-3839-9 (hardcover)
[1. Family life — Florida — Fiction. 2. Schools — Fiction. 3. Self-actualization (Psychology) — Fiction. 4. Race relations — Fiction. 5. Bullies — Fiction.
6. Florida — History — 20th century — Fiction.]   I. Title.
PZ7.W3213Dow 2008
[Fic] — dc22   2007052159

"R-O-T-A-R-Y, That Spells Rotary" from the Rotary songbook by Norris C. Morgan. Copyright © 1923 by the Rotary Club of Wilmington, DE. Reprinted by permission of the Rotary Club of Wilmington, DE.

While every effort has been made to obtain permission to reprint copyrighted material, there may be cases where we have been unable to trace a copyright holder. The publisher will be happy to correct any omission in future printings.

ISBN 978-0-7636-4835-0 (paperback)

10 11 12 13 14 15 BVG 10 9 8 7 6 5 4 3 2 1

Printed in Berryville, VA, U.S.A.

This book was typeset in Berkeley.

Candlewick Press
99 Dover Street
Somerville, Massachusetts 02144

visit us at www.candlewick.com

For Janet

And for Mom and Dad and Wayne and Jo

Chapter One

IT WAS THE MIDDLE OF AUGUST 1966, and me and Wayne and Dad and about two hundred people were sweating and stinking in the auditorium of the Sand Mountain High School, home of the Mighty Mighty Miners. We were there for the Rotary Club Minstrel Show, but Wayne fell asleep after fifteen minutes. When he did that in church, Mom always said it was because of his hay fever and let him alone. That night of the minstrel show, I stayed awake with Dad, who was the treasurer of the Rotary Club, although as it turned out, he fell asleep, too. I sometimes wished I had hay fever like them so I could fall asleep anywhere. I also wished I had a bag of marbles with me, since the auditorium floor was slanted and if you dropped them on the hardwood floor, they would probably roll all the way down to the stage. Not that I wouldn't about die if I ever did that and got caught.

Dad couldn't carry a tune—that's what my mom said. I remember the day she said it, I asked her, "Carry it where?" and she said, "Oh boy, here we go again." Anyway, that's why he wasn't in the minstrel show but down in the audience with us. They started up with a prayer, "Lord bless us and keep us," then the Pledge of Allegiance, then the Rotary Club song—"R-O-T-A-R-Y, that spells Rotary. R-O-T-A-R-Y is known on land and sea. From north to south, and east to west, He profits most who serves the best." After that a guy sang "Old Man River," then a kid I knew shuffled onto the stage and it was Boopie Larent, who was twelve, the same as me, and used to be a friend of mine. We were in the same kid choir at the Methodist Church. He wore a white bow tie, which I bet somebody tied for him, and white gloves, and big white lips, and his face was shoe-polish black, not like real colored people. He sang "Chattanooga Shoe-Shine Boy," which was about a very happy colored boy who shined people's shoes and made them happy, too.

Boopie carried a shoe-shine kit and danced soft-shoe. That's what my dad told me it was. It just looked like sliding around to me, then some leaning way forward, and some running in place to keep from pitching over on his face while he windmilled his arms. The only other kids I ever saw dance before that were the twins Darla and Darwin Turkel, who always tap-danced at County Fair, where my dad worked in the Rotary Club corn-dog booth. Darla and Darwin were all dressed up with their mom a couple of rows in front of us that night at the minstrel show. Their mom used to wear a mermaid costume and do underwater ballets and stuff over at Weeki Wachee Springs by the Gulf of Mexico. Now she taught dancing lessons sometimes. Darla had fifty-two ringlets in her hair, just like Shirley Temple, or that was the story, anyway. Everybody said to stay away from Darwin—he was worse than a girl.

I realized something about halfway through Boopie doing the "Chattanooga Shoe-Shine Boy." "Is that my shoe-shine kit?" I asked my dad. I was holding his hand, feeling his calluses. I was too old to be holding his hand—when you get to be twelve, you're too old for a lot of things—but I did it anyway and he let me when it was dark like that in the auditorium and nobody could see. I liked how it felt from him working at the phosphate mine where he was an engineer, only not the kind that drove a train.

I thought maybe my dad was listening to the show and that's why he didn't answer, so I asked him again. "Is that the shoe-shine kit you bought me, Dad?" I don't know why it made me mad. But if it was my shoe-shine kit, I thought I ought to get to be the Chattanooga Shoe-Shine Boy. Everybody was laughing at old Boopie up there, and the harder they laughed, the more I wished it was me. I wanted to be funny like that, and dance, and sing, and wear a white tie and white gloves and white lips and shoe-shine face darker than the colored people.

"Dad!" I said again. He was asleep like Wayne, like it was

Sunday and we were in church. He opened his eyes and I asked him once more.

"Hush, Dewey," he said. "I let them borrow it. They needed it for Boopie's routine." Boopie dropped down on one knee about then. A fat man came onstage and stepped his shoe on the slanted footrest on top of the kit so Boopie could buff it with a shine rag. That was my job on Sunday mornings, shining my dad's shoes and then my own shoes before we went to Sunday school. Wayne had to do his own.

Boopie finally quit singing and buffing. It was the end of the "Chattanooga Shoe-Shine Boy," and him and the fat guy danced off the stage. Only as soon as they disappeared, they ran back with all the other men in their minstrel show costumes, more fat men in black suits and black painted faces, until they stopped and spread their arms out and sang really fast out of their big white lips:

Swanee, how I love you, how I love you, my dear old Swanee.
I'd give the world to be among the folks in D-I-X-I-E-ven now.

After that it was Mister Bones and Mister Interloculator, with colored faces like the rest of the others. Mister Bones looked like the choir director at our church. Mister Interloculator looked like Boopie's dad.

"Mister Bones?"

"Why, yes, Mister Interloculator."

"Did I hear correctly that you asked your wife if she believed in the Hereafter?"

"'Deed I did, Mister Interloculator. 'Deed I did."

"And why come you did such a thing as that, Mister Bones?"

"Well, you see, Mister Interloculator, it happened thisaway. I comes home and I says to my wife, 'Wife, does you believe in the Hereafter?' and she says, 'What you talking? You knows I do.' So I says to her, 'That's good, honey, that's mighty good, on account of I is *here,* and you knows what I is *after.*'"

I didn't get it, exactly, and asked Dad what the heck that was all about. He said he'd explain later, but he never did.

On the way out after the minstrel show, we saw a real colored man, Chollie the janitor, pushing his mop and bucket in to clean up. My dad said, "Good evening, Chollie," and Chollie said, "How are you, Mr. Turner?" Somebody else walking out behind us said really loud, "Mistuh Chollie!" It was Mr. Hollis Wratchford, who ran the produce market downtown, under the Skeleton Hotel. He said Chollie's name a couple of more times, like he enjoyed the sound of it. Then he said, "You're the expert, Chollie. What is your assessment on the minstrels this year?"

Chollie nodded and nodded and worked his mop handle back and forth as if the answer might come out of the soapy water in his pail, but also as if he'd rather not answer at all. My dad had told me Chollie lost his job at the mine after the strike last year and Dad helped him to get on at the high school. Chollie looked at Mr. Wratchford's feet. "Yes, sir," he finally said, still nodding. "I believe the jury coming in with a guilty verdict on that one, Mr. Wratchford. The gentlemen of the Rotary Club might of out-colored the colored folk tonight."

Mr. Wratchford laughed and slapped Chollie on the shoulder and gave him a dollar, then he repeated what Chollie said to everybody else all the way down the stairs, laughing every time, and I heard him until we got outside, where there was a bunch of people looking up at something on the roof and laughing, too. Me and Dad and Wayne stepped farther away toward First Street and then we saw it—an old, wood outhouse with a crescent moon somebody must have hauled up on top of the high school. There was a sign on the door, but the words were too small to read from where we were. The high-school boys were always doing funny stuff like that. Wayne told me that the seniors caught every seventh-grader during the first month of school, all the boys, and held them down, pulled up their shirts, and gave them red bellies, which I was very nervous about and which was why I didn't want to start the seventh grade. I wished we had a junior high at Sand Mountain, but I guess the town was too small for something like that.

After a while we went home and told my mom. She said, "Oh, for goodness sake, what's wrong with these people?" The way she said it made me think she didn't just mean why would they haul an outhouse on top of the high school. They had a picture of the outhouse in the *Sand Mountain Citizen* a couple of days later, which was the only newspaper we got except for the Sunday

Tampa Tribune my dad bought so he could sleep with it over his face while he watched football on TV after church. The sign wasn't in the picture, though. Wayne, who was going into eighth grade that year, told me it had said COLORED PEOPLE GO TO THE BATHROOM HERE, only the newspaper got rid of it before they took the picture, and it didn't say COLORED PEOPLE, and it didn't say GO TO THE BATHROOM, either. I don't know how Wayne knew that stuff. I guess when you're older like him you just do.

I asked him why anybody wanted the colored people to use an outhouse on the roof, and he said, "They don't want them to go to school there." I said, "But the colored people *don't* go to school there, just white people," and he said, "Well, they don't want the government to make them let them go to school there." I still didn't get it. But that's the way things always were in my family, and in the whole town as far as I could tell. You asked a million questions but you never knew what was really going on.

Chapter Two

I WENT OVER TO BOOPIE LARENT'S HOUSE the next day, which was Saturday, to get my shoe-shine kit back. He was in his garage, bouncing on his pogo stick, trying to set a new world record. His sister, Dottie, was counting, but really she was watching to make sure he didn't have another accident. When Boopie first got his pogo stick, he was bouncing in the garage at their house and chewing a big wad of bubble gum and he slipped off and hit his chin on the pogo stick handle and bit all the way through his bottom lip. The blood splattered all over his face and his shirt and the floor of the garage, and when Dottie heard him and came running outside, the first thing she saw was him spitting out this big bloody thing that she thought was his tongue he must have bit off and she screamed and screamed but it turned out it was only his bubble gum. He got stitches in his lip and Dr. Rexroat had to give Dottie nerve medicine to calm her down.

So now whenever Boopie got on the pogo stick or rode his unicycle or did about anything, Dottie watched him just so she'd always know what was what.

I picked up my shoe-shine kit, which was just sitting there in the garage like nobody even cared whose it was, and said, "If you borrow something from somebody, you're supposed to ask them first."

Boopie kept bouncing, and said, "My dad got it from your dad."

I said everybody knew it belonged to me, so he should have asked me.

He said, "Sorry, Your Highness."

I wanted to ask him how he got to be the Chattanooga Shoe-Shine Boy, and how he learned soft-shoe, and how he got his face painted black with the big white lips, and where he got the suit and the top hat and the gloves he wore in the minstrel show. But I wasn't about to give him the satisfaction of thinking he had anything I wanted. Dottie was on three hundred and twenty-nine then, and I started counting with her: "Three hundred and thirty, thirty-one, thirty-two, thirty-three, twenty-two, twenty-three, two hundred and eleven, twelve—"

She tried to count louder, but I just counted louder, too: "One hundred and one, one hundred and two, three thousand and nine," until she finally yelled at me to shut up and go home and leave them alone, but when she did, Boopie yelled at her, "Don't listen to him; don't stop counting," but it was too late, she had already lost the count, and I yelled back at both of them why didn't they just start over since they didn't know what number they were on, then I pushed Boopie off the pogo stick and ran home.

The next night, I asked Dad if I could be the Chattanooga Shoe-Shine Boy in next year's minstrel show. Me and Wayne and our little sister, Tink, were lying on the floor in the living room after Sunday night church, watching the Disney show *Wonderful World of Color,* only it wasn't color because we only had our black-and-white. Dad didn't believe in color TV, plus he said we couldn't afford it.

I said, "Can I, Dad?" but he wasn't in the mood to talk about it, because he said what grown-ups always say when they're not in the mood to talk about it: "We'll see." That meant I was supposed to be quiet, but he had only said it once, so I tried again. "When will you see, Dad?" I said. "Does that mean you have to ask somebody? Who do you have to ask? When can you ask them?"

He said, "I said we'll see, and we'll see. A year is a long time. You could be too big by then. They only want small boys." A commercial came on and he went into the kitchen to eat his cold consommé out of a can.

What he said just about made me happy, though. I was the third smallest boy in my class and had been since second grade, and I was pretty sure I wasn't going to grow anytime soon. There was Ronnie Lott, who was always spitting, and picking his under-wear out of his butt. Then there was Richard Speight, who everybody said was a dwarf but I think there was just something wrong about his back. Then there was me. I had a twenty-five-dollar bet with Dad about whether I would still be shorter than Wayne when I turned eighteen. I know he only made the bet because he felt sorry for me. I probably shouldn't have bet against myself, because it might jinx me from growing, but twenty-five dollars was a lot of money, especially when your allowance was only a quarter a week.

I gave up on the *Wonderful World of Color* and went into mine and Wayne's bedroom and got out my shoe-shine kit and looked through it until I found the flat round can of Kiwi black. I twisted the top off and rubbed some on my arm to see how it looked. We had brown, too, which looked like it might be more the color of real colored people, but from what I'd seen at the minstrel show, I thought maybe I ought to go with the black.

It took me about half an hour to get my whole face painted with the shoe polish. The smell of it made me dizzy even though I didn't do any right around the edge of my nostrils or right around my eyes, which left little pink rings there, like a pig snout, and like I-don't-know-what eyes. My ears were a problem, too, because I didn't want to get the polish up inside where it might be too near to my brain, so it was just black around the big part of the ear. Some got up in my hair where my crew cut stuck up in front, and when it dried, it was harder than Brylcreem. My lips looked stupid because they were pink but they were supposed to be white, only we didn't have any white Kiwi since who wore white shoes except a nurse?

I thought I looked good enough, though, better than Boopie Larent, anyway, and I stood up and waved my arms around like Boopie did, like windmills, and I did my legs and my hips like Elvis. That stuff, that Kiwi, I don't know what was in it but the next thing I knew I was singing pretty loud and it sounded good to me, too—also better than Boopie—and I must have got louder and louder the more I sang of those songs from the minstrel show.

My arms, I was cranking them faster and faster like I could just about take off at any minute, and I believe if Elvis had seen me, he would have been proud to call me son, and I could have danced and sang like that all night, probably, except I heard something at the door and it was Wayne, standing with his mouth open and full of a bite of one of his usual peanut-butter-and-banana sandwiches. I could see the mash of it in his mouth all the way from where I was in the middle of the room and it was disgusting, also like usual. Next to him was Tink, looking scared about something, so I turned around to look behind me to see if there was something by the window, because you never know, there could have been.

I stopped singing by then, of course, and I also wasn't dancing like the King anymore, or like anybody, but I was still dizzy and my head felt like it was still dancing, only I couldn't breathe too well. Also I didn't feel my legs too well, either, so I decided to sit down and so I dropped from standing up directly to my butt on the floor. I heard Wayne tell Tink, "Go get Mom," but I don't remember between that and Mom holding my face in her hands and saying, "Dewey? Dewey? Answer me."

From a long ways away I said, "Yes, ma'am." I didn't know why I was so dizzy then, or why my tailbone hurt. I must have already forgotten about the shoe polish and sitting down from standing up. I heard her say, "Go get your father and tell him to bring some turpentine and a rag," and Wayne said, "He's not going to like this," and Tink said, "He thinks he's the Chattanooga Shoe-Shine Boy but he's not," and Mom said, "Go watch TV," and Tink said, "I don't have to," and Mom said, "Excuse me, Young Lady?" Tink ran back to the living room and I must have been laughing at something because Mom said, "I don't see what's so funny, Mister." When she started calling us Young Lady and Mister, it meant we were in a lot of trouble but I couldn't stop laughing and she said, "You better stop laughing, this is serious. Do you have any idea what you did to yourself?" only something didn't sound the way it was supposed to and I realized it was because she was laughing, too, and I thought everything was going to be all right even though I still couldn't feel my legs. I hadn't heard my mom laugh in so long, probably since before President Kennedy died, that I'd forgotten how happy it made me, but that was just until my dad came in and he started cussing, which my mom always called Mine Talk, which he wasn't supposed to do around us kids. Mom always told him if he was mad to just say "Good garden peas!" instead, and he said that now, too, which just made me laugh more, and I think made Mom laugh, too. I slapped my hands down on the floor over and over like a seal at a zoo until Dad grabbed me by the back of the neck and lit into my face with a rag soaked in turpentine that felt like a Brillo pad. Then I really couldn't breathe and I wasn't laughing and slapping the floor like a seal anymore, I was bawling like a calf like they had out at Mr. Juddy's farm, who was a dragline operator from the mines. Dad scrubbed and scrubbed the skin off my face with that rag and I tried to tell him I couldn't breathe but he wasn't listening, and I don't think Mom was laughing anymore by that time, either; she was saying, "You don't have to do it so hard," and he said, "If I don't do it hard, it won't come off. Look, look, it's not coming off. There's going to be a stain that won't come off, and how in tarnation is he going to go to school like this? Oh, good garden peas."

Chapter Three

MY FACE WAS STILL STAINED KIWI BLACK when Mom pulled off the covers to make me get up the next morning, which was the first day of school. I checked right away in the mirror. I have this part of my brain that makes stuff up when somebody asks me a question but I don't know the answer. It makes them think I'm smarter than I really am, which is OK, but it also makes *me* think I'm smarter than I really am, which can be a problem. Anyway, that part of my brain took over, and what it did was convince the rest of me that I looked tan. Maybe not regular tan, but tan the way those kids whose families have cottages out at Snake Lake are tan because they spend the whole summer with their boats and their rich families and their friends going water-skiing. A lot of people called them Colored-People Tans, except they used the other word for it.

Unfortunately, my tan idea didn't last long. "He still looks like a colored boy," Tink said when I finally came into the kitchen for breakfast.

Wayne said, "Mom, you can't let the freak go to school like that. Not with me. He'll embarrass me."

I said, "You told me you were a Lone Wolf."

Wayne did one of his giant sighs, then he said, "That was last year. This year is different. I'm going out for JV football and don't need a freak brother, a *freaktoid*, to mess everything up." The way he said all that, it wasn't like he was talking to me. In fact, it wasn't like I was even there.

Tink jumped up on her chair. "What's a freaktoid? Does it mean colored?" I told her to shut up and she said, "You can't make me."

Mom had cooked grilled cheese sandwiches and tomato soup and stewed prunes because it was a special morning, and *Good Housekeeping* said lunch for breakfast once in a while kept a family from falling in a rut. I poked my finger in the middle of Tink's grilled cheese because I knew she hated anybody to touch her food.

Mom waved her spatula at me. "Dewey, that is unacceptable." She grabbed my plate and set it down in front of Tink. "Here you go, Tink. You can eat your brother's."

"Good," I said. "I'm not going to eat it, anyway."

Wayne shoved the rest of his sandwich in his mouth and grabbed his new notebooks and pens and lunch money that Mom had lined up on the counter. He would have just left but Mom said, "Aren't you forgetting something?" and he said could he please be excused, please, and thanks for the breakfast.

Mom said, "Wait for your brother," then she wrapped another grilled cheese in a paper towel and handed it to me. She told me I could eat it on the way to school, and I wasn't a freak, I looked fine, I was a very handsome boy. Then she stopped.

"Where is your new shirt?"

"What new shirt?" I said, though I knew exactly what she was talking about because it was still hanging on the back of a chair in my bedroom. It was something called Ban-Lon. Mom said it didn't hold water, just sort of shed it, so instead of hanging it on the line to dry, all you had to do was wring it out. And it was wrinkleproof, too, so no ironing ever. I went back to the bedroom, knowing it was no use arguing, and looked at the shirt. It was orange. It had three buttons and a collar. It smelled like the chemical plant at the phosphate mine. In elementary school I only wore T-shirts, and they were always cotton, but my mom said, "This is high school and things are going to be different around here, Mister, so you better get used to it."

I pulled on the Ban-Lon and right away my skin went crazy. I think the cells on the outside were trying to crawl behind the ones underneath, a worse torture than getting tied down in the desert on an ant bed with honey smeared all over your body. I tugged at the neck and sleeves, trying to stretch it every way I could, but nothing worked, plus I started to sweat right away. If

Wayne ever pulled it over my head, he could suffocate me with it. I was so miserable, I thought about suffocating myself. Our dog, Suzy, a half beagle–half basset, had followed me to the bedroom, and I was pretty sure she was shaking her head.

When Tink saw me come out of the bedroom in the Ban-Lon, she blew tomato soup out of her nose and said, "Colored boy freaktoid." I stuck my finger in her other grilled cheese, then ran out the door. I could hear Tink crying and Mom yelling until I was halfway down the block.

Wayne was all the way over on Orange Avenue at David Tremblay's house at the corner of Orange and Second Street by then. They'd been best friends since about first grade, so I guessed if Wayne was a Lone Wolf last year, then him and David must have been Lone Wolfs together. I walked toward them, trying to act like I wasn't worried about anything, when the fact was that I was worried about everything: the Ban-Lon, the shoe polish, remembering my locker combination, the red bellies the seniors gave the new seventh-graders. When I got to the corner, Wayne and David Tremblay were already walking up Second Street. David Tremblay turned around with his Elvis hair and his eyes got big when he saw me and he laughed like a girl until Wayne punched him on the arm and he punched Wayne on *his* arm, and they ran on up Second toward the high school.

I decided I was mad at everybody, especially Wayne, who'd called me a freaktoid and wouldn't wait for me even though he knew, because I had told him in secret, how scared I was about high school and the red bellies and remembering my locker combination and all. I wished I could be a Lone Wolf the way he was last year, only he had *wanted* to do that—chew on toothpicks and stand on one leg against the wall with his arms crossed and his other leg pulled up so his foot was braced against the wall behind him, which left a dirty shoe print, which was part of being a Lone Wolf. For me, though, I'd have been a Lone Wolf if it meant kids wouldn't make fun of me anymore, but I'd rather everybody just liked me instead.

I slowed down walking and finally just stopped there in the middle of the street.

The Ban-Lon must have affected my brain, or maybe it was the chemicals from the shoe polish, but it finally got through my thick skull that there wasn't any way anybody who didn't like me before was going to start liking me now, on account of how colored I looked, and as bad as it was with Wayne and Tink at home, it was going to be a million times worse at high school. The seniors would probably give me a red belly so hard it would rupture my kidney or spleen or something, which was how the Great Houdini died. A guy showed up at Houdini's dressing room and said he'd heard Houdini could tense his stomach muscles to take any blow no matter how hard and was that true and could he try it? Houdini was lying on a couch, talking to his admirers, and maybe grunted but didn't really pay any attention, so he wasn't ready when the guy hauled off and socked him in the gut. I was a big fan of the Great Houdini except for the part where he died the agonizing death. It was the one thing he couldn't ever escape.

So I didn't go to school. Where I went instead was the doghouse in W.J. Weller's backyard so I could hide with W.J.'s old bassett hound, Lightning, until everybody was gone to school, then sneak down to Bowlegs Creek until I wasn't colored anymore, or at least until three o'clock, when the bell rang at the end of school.

I didn't stay in the doghouse too long, though, because Lightning wouldn't move over and give me any room. Also, they must have been feeding him on a lot of beans.

It took me about an hour to get to Bowlegs because every time I heard a car I had to jump in the bushes, plus it was three miles south of the Sand Mountain city limits. Bowlegs Creek was where the Indian outlaw Billy Bowlegs hid in the old days, I think when they chased him out of the Everglades. My mom said the army caught all the Miccosukee Indians and put them on a train to somewhere, and Billy Bowlegs was the only one they couldn't find.

Bowlegs Creek twists around the woods under cypress trees so thick you can't see the sky, so it's cool and dark all the time, and they say Billy Bowlegs's ghost might be living under one of those cypresses, hidden behind the cypress knees or in a hollow place carved up under the bank like the alligator nests that aren't supposed to be there, either.

One day back in July, we found five colored boys there. I don't think anybody said anything for a couple of minutes, because we had never seen colored boys anywhere we played and couldn't believe they would come to Bowlegs Creek, which everybody knew was ours, not the colored people's.

We stared at them on the one bank; they stared back at us on the other. We were barefoot; they were barefoot. We wore cutoffs; they wore cutoffs. We had inner tubes; they didn't have anything but the mud, so of course somebody must have said something and next thing you know we were all pulling up our own mud and throwing it at them, getting hit by theirs, trying to dodge the big clods coming at our heads, and when it got in your eyes, you had to slide down the bank to the creek to get it out in the water, only you were closer there and you got hit even more. There were six of us, but one didn't count and that was this kid named Connolly Voss, the biggest yellowbelly in Sand Mountain, who pretty soon ran off from the big fight. Wayne, who couldn't stand Connolly Voss anyway, fired one that hit Connolly on the butt, which wasn't easy since Connolly was about as wide as a stick, not to mention he had a pencil neck, and that even made the colored boys laugh. But they didn't have time to laugh long, because we had been having a lot more mud wars there than them, plus we had David Tremblay, who could probably throw harder than anybody in the state. One of theirs, and then another one of theirs, went like Connolly Voss up the bank toward the bridge and out of range. We thought they were gone but one of them must have picked up a rock from the side of the road because the next thing you know I felt something hard on the back of my head and then felt back there with my hand and there was blood.

The colored boys all ran away, which was a good thing because when word got around about what happened, some of the dads—not ours, but some of the others—went looking for them. Wayne especially was worried about what might happen if the dads ever did catch up with the colored boys. I wasn't worried so much about that, though. What I was worried about was that I only got one stitch in my head when Mom drove us to Dr. Rexroat's, and I knew people would make fun of me if they knew that, because if you just got one stitch, you probably didn't even need any and I wanted people to think I was really hurt so they would feel sorry for me and not say you'd get Deweyitis anymore if you touched me on accident.

When I finally made it to Bowlegs Creek, I went down the trail from the road to the deepest part of the woods to a beach at a bend in the creek everybody called Sand Head because it looked like a head with a big nose and was all sand, no trees. It should have been a great hiding place, and at first I thought I would stay there and draw pictures in my new notebooks, eat the grilled cheese sandwich before it got limp, and then make up my story about what happened the first day of school.

But after a while I got worried about Billy Bowlegs's ghost, and the half man–half gator they were always talking about that also hung out around there. I started hearing stuff, too. Leaves crackling, twigs snapping, a breeze stirring things up, a bird, a splash in the water. Something growled, which might have been my stomach, but also might have been that half man–half gator, and that did it. I grabbed everything and ran back up the path out of the woods to the bridge, which was out in the sunshine and not as scary. By the time I got there, I was sweating like a fat monkey because of that Ban-Lon shirt. August in Florida is 99 degrees and 99 percent humidity, so I pulled the Ban-Lon off and got my magnifying glass I always carried in case I needed to look for clues about mysteries I might have to solve, although there hadn't been too many of those yet but you never know. I aimed the lens at the Ban-Lon the way you do the sun to start a fire, and the shirt started smoking orange smoke, but instead of igniting and burning up, it just melted a hole. I couldn't believe it. I melted a couple of more holes but it took too long, so finally I just dug a hole in the bank under the bridge and buried it.

The good thing about Bowlegs Creek was that you couldn't see down there from the road unless you got right to the edge of the bridge and leaned way over, plus hardly any cars went down that far because there weren't any citrus groves or cattle ranches out that way, just scrub brush and scraggly trees and palmettos and moss and sandy soil and ant beds and sandspurs and maybe gator lairs, and cattails, and turnarounds where people dumped old mattresses and clothes washers and leaky bags of trash, and old dogs or puppies that never lived very long so you were always finding their bones if you weren't careful.

Since nobody could see me, anyway, and since I knew everybody who might come down to Bowlegs Creek was in school except me, I took all the rest of my clothes off, because I didn't want them to get dirty or wet, except my underwear. Then I climbed down the bank to where we had the mud wars and started digging another hole, actually a cave like the ones the Vietcong lived in, with their miles of tunnels. They had a color picture in the Tampa paper one time of a cross section of the tunnels. It looked like this ant farm I used to have until Tink felt so sorry for them that she let them go.

I dug in the bank of Bowlegs Creek all the rest of the day. When my hands got too sore and my fingers numb, I found a stick, and when the stick broke, I found a hubcap, and when the hubcap got too big for the tight space in the back of the cave, I used my hands again until the cave was wide enough and deep enough for me to crawl inside. And even then I kept digging. I dug out a shelf to put stuff on, and then the start of a second hole off to the side in case I wanted to add another room. I thought I could even live there.

When the afternoon rain came, I brought my clothes and notebooks inside and put them on the shelf and sat there for a long time, still in my underwear, watching it pour down outside.

The rain smelled like mold at first, then like dirt, then just like the clean water they had in the North Carolina mountains where we went camping at Deep Creek. That was nice—that smell, and thinking about Deep Creek, where we met our cousins and saw bears. I thought about that for a while and the rain kept coming down, buckets of rain, and I also thought about being in my own bed some nights with clean sheets still crunchy from drying on the clothesline, stretching my legs and yawning and hearing Wayne snore on the bottom bunk and Mom and Dad watching something on TV in the living room, the blue light from the TV coming in the edge of the bedroom door. They might laugh, or say something I couldn't understand, just their voices coming through the door, too, like the blue light, and then the night summer rain starting, tapping, then drumming, then roaring on our tin roof while I was deep under the sheets pulled up to my mouth and the pillow over my eyes so just my nose stuck out so I could breathe. That was like a cave, too, actually better than a cave because it occurred to me that the one I was in right then at Bowlegs Creek had turned cold, and my underwear was wet, and the rain had shifted and was blowing in on me. The water from the road and the trees ran down the bank and into the cave so that pretty soon I was sitting in a puddle, and the rain was still pouring down outside, and the edge of the cave washed away, then more of it, then more—

Everything happened so fast, I hardly remember anything except that I jumped out just in time before it collapsed, and slid down the bank into the creek. Then I was under the water and it was rushing hard over my head and there was nothing to grab on to and I swallowed and coughed and felt the bottom and kicked back up so I could breathe, and the current dragged me halfway under the bridge before I could even think about swimming to the side. Once I did, I just shivered there for a while so I could catch my breath, then I crawled back over through the mudslide, but too late: my notebooks and pants and shoes, even the grilled cheese sandwich from breakfast that I never ate, were all buried and I was too tired and scared and wet and cold to dig them out. I just sat there, my feet sinking in the mud, until I had to do something, so I crawled back under the bridge and dug up the Ban-Lon. It was probably going to rain forever, and I didn't have anything else to wear.

Chapter Four

IT WAS AN HOUR LATER AND STILL RAINING and I was hiding at the edge of the bridge only in just my underwear and the Ban-Lon shirt with the holes. The rain had already raised the level of Bowlegs Creek up over where my cave used to be, and I wasn't sure what I was going to do except wait until it got dark and then sneak back home. I wished my mom would come looking for me and I said a couple of prayers for that, but nothing happened except finally this guy Walter Wratchford showed up in his car.

Everybody knew Walter Wratchford, because his dad was Mr. Hollis Wratchford that ran the farmer's market under the Skeleton Hotel, and that gave Chollie the janitor a dollar after the minstrel show. Walter Wratchford had been in the Vietnam War but was back now. I guess he did a lot of just driving around sometimes.

I saw him from a long ways off, coming real slow from the direction of the old Turkey Creek Mine that was about ten miles south of town and nobody ever went there anymore. The car was an old blue Ford Fairlane with red doors, and it got slower and slower until it finally kind of glided to a stop there next to me like maybe it had run out of gas. There was a rope holding the passenger door shut, and I guess Walter Wratchford untied it from inside because in about a minute the door swung open and there he was, sitting inside smoking a cigarette. His hair was long and stringy, which you didn't see much around Sand Mountain, and he had on his old army jacket. I ducked down some more but then figured he must have already seen me or why else would he have stopped, so I lifted my head up.

He just looked at me like he saw stuff like that all the time, and he said, "Well, are you getting in or not?" I nodded and pulled my Ban-Lon shirt as far down as I could, almost to my knees, so he wouldn't see that I didn't have any pants on. Once I slid in the seat, he grabbed some old yellow newspaper, which I started to lay over me.

"No, no, put it under you first," he said. "I don't want my car all wet." Then he said, "Dang."

So I put some down under me and he handed me the piece of rope and said for me to loop it over the door handle outside and then tie it inside wherever I could find a place. Before I hardly even got started, he put the car in gear and crawled back out on the road toward Sand Mountain. I had to reach all the way to the back door handle to find a place to tie off the rope, and when I did I saw this big carved wood hand he had from Vietnam, about two feet tall—actually a fist with the middle finger shooting the you-know-what. It was laying there on the backseat. Wayne told me that Walter Wratchford took it with him down to The Springs, where they sell the liquor on the county side of the Peace River bridge, and he sat by himself with that big finger in the middle of the table in front of him and got in fights if anybody said anything about it. Wayne heard that from David Tremblay, who heard it from his stepdad, Bud Teeter, who was always down at The Springs drinking, too.

I'd seen the finger myself one time before, at a Veterans Day Salute at the high-school auditorium, where Walter Wratchford was supposed to make a speech to represent the Vietnam veterans. When they introduced him, he pulled it out of a bag he was carrying and balanced it on the lectern. At first he didn't say anything and you could hear people whispering what's wrong with this crazy nut, and then he did say something. He said, "If Vietnam was a woman, I'd marry her in a second." Then he picked up his carved hand with the finger and said, "Anytime any of you want to borrow this, you're welcome to borrow it. It's all right by me." And that was all, except that he said "borry" instead of "borrow." I thought that was pretty funny.

Walter Wratchford lit a new cigarette from the butt of the one he had been smoking, then wiped his forehead on the sleeve of his army jacket. The windshield was fogged up and he wiped that with his sleeve, too, but it didn't much matter because the smoke from his cigarette filled up the car so fast you could hardly see through that, anyway. Every time we hit a bump, the passenger side door swung open a little bit and the rain came in, or maybe it was the water from the tires. I guess I hadn't tied it tight enough. I kept getting wetter even though I was already soaking wet, and the inside of Walter Wratchford's car kept getting wetter, too.

"You want me to take you down to the Boogerbottom?" Walter Wratchford said. His voice even sounded like cigarettes.

I shook my head and said no, just on up Orange Avenue.

"Colored don't live on Orange Avenue," he said.

I didn't know what to say. I didn't want to make him mad or anything, but the last place I wanted to go was the Boogerbottom. "I just need to go home," I said. I was about to cry.

He snorted. "I know you're not colored. I was just kidding you." He offered me a cigarette but I shook my head again. Then he asked me what was the story with my face and all and how come I looked that way. I just told him *shoe polish* and he nodded like he heard that sort of thing all the time, too.

"I been around a lot of colored guys," he said like that's what we'd been talking about all along. "They got a lot of them in the army now. I even had a friend in the army that was colored. That boy was one dumb son of a you-know-what."

My teeth were chattering even though I wasn't cold, just wet. Walter Wratchford wiped the windshield again and turned on the heater. He was grinning, but not in the way somebody grins if they think something's funny. "You know what they got over there? Over in the war? They got these things—they call them Bouncing Betties—where when you hit the trip wire, they don't just blow up and take your foot off or your leg off. Them bombs bounce up in the air so you can see them right in front of you for about a second. Not even a second, but a second of a second. And that's the last second of a second you ever get. Then it blows your dang head off."

He didn't say hardly anything after that, and I didn't know what to say back, either. I was too scared to ask him much even though there were about a million questions I wished I could have asked about Vietnam since I was pretty sure I would go over there to be in the war once I was old enough. I read about it all the time in the *Tampa Tribune*. In Vacation Bible School the summer before last when they had us write down who was the most important person in our lives not counting our moms and dads, I wrote General Westmoreland. That turned out to be the wrong answer, though. The Vacation Bible School lady said it was Jesus, and how come nobody wrote down Jesus, and she was very disappointed in us for not a single one of us saying Jesus. That got us in a big argument about whether Jesus was actually even a *person*. A lot of the kids thought he was more like Superman, with his super powers of turning wine into water and feeding the multitudes with the fishes and the loaves and bringing back Lazarus from the dead and walking on water. The Vacation Bible School lady said those were miracles, not super powers, and she rolled her eyes and said, "Land of Goshen," the same way my dad said, "Good garden peas."

It didn't take long before we got to town. Walter Wratchford didn't ask me anything about where to go; he just drove on across First Street and on down Orange Avenue toward my house. I hadn't even told him where I lived, but Sand Mountain was such a little place, he must have just known somehow. Maybe he knew my dad. A lot of people knew my dad from the phosphate mine, or the Rotary Club, or the Methodist Church, where he was on the board of trustees, or him running for city council a bunch of times only never getting elected.

"I wish I could remember what that colored boy's name was," Walter Wratchford said. He shook his head pretty hard like he had water in his ear and was trying to get it out.

I thanked him when I got out of the car. He said, "Don't even mention it."

Chapter Five

THE WAY I FELT WHEN I WALKED IN THE DOOR was like I'd been gone a week, but it turned out to only be about two o'clock. Mom wasn't home. Nobody was. I went in the bathroom and sat on the toilet backward the way I used to when I was little. Back then I did it so I could play with my army men on the toilet tank while I was doing a Big Job—that's what Mom called it—only this time I didn't play anything, but just laid my cheek on the cool porcelain tank until I was done.

Wayne was the first one home. I was at the kitchen table eating crackers and rat cheese—Dad said that; Mom just said "cheddar"—but he didn't say much of anything, just went straight to the refrigerator and took a big swig of milk from the carton. Then he burped my name: "Hey, Dewey." It was disgusting, but also maybe a little funny. I don't think he even noticed that I hadn't been in school. That made me kind of mad, but also made me think that if Wayne hadn't noticed, then maybe nobody else did, either. He fixed two peanut-butter-and-jelly sandwiches and took off for JV football practice. I followed him to the front door. David Tremblay was waiting out front, sitting on his bicycle and holding Wayne's. They traded: Wayne gave him one of the sandwiches and David handed over the bike. I could see Wayne already had a gob of jelly on the front of his shirt—that happened about every time he ate anything. David pointed at it and laughed. Wayne lifted up his shirt and licked it off, but it left a big grape stain. I would have been embarrassed about something like that, but you could just tell Wayne didn't care.

Mom and Tink showed up right then. I watched them all through the front window but couldn't hear anything. Mom probably asked if they had a good first day of school. Then she probably asked if they had time for a snack, and when would they be home—even though David didn't live with us, of course—and would they please, please promise to drink plenty of water at their football practice?

Then she must have asked about me, because suddenly everybody turned to look at the house, even Tink, who had been leaning over, talking to the sidewalk, maybe to a line of ants or something. I should have waved at them—they must have seen me—but instead I ducked below the window and then crawled out of the living room and down the hall to my bedroom. I don't know why exactly.

I was hiding under the bed—another dumb thing to do—when Tink found me.

"Here he is!" she yelled, even though Mom was standing right beside her. "He's hiding under the bed!"

I tried to kick her. "No, I'm not." I said. "I'm looking for something."

Tink said, "What? Like a dust bunny?"

Mom told her to never-you-mind, then said that I needed to come out from under there right now because I had some serious explaining to do. So I crawled out.

She was holding the orange Ban-Lon shirt like it was a dead cat. I had stuck it in the dirty-clothes basket, under a towel, when I got home, hoping she would just wash it and not notice the mud and the holes I had burned with my magnifying glass. I don't know how she found it so fast.

Mom shook it. "What is the meaning of this?"

The phone rang before I could tell her anything, or make something up.

It was the school.

When Dad came home, he asked if I had anything to say for myself before punishment. He had talked to Mom, so of course he knew everything by then already. He still had on his steel-toed work boots and his khaki pants, which had a mud stain on one of the knees, and a short-sleeved shirt but no tie. When he looked like that, it meant he had been out with the survey crew, and if he'd been out with the survey crew, it usually meant he was tired and hungry when he got off work, and not in too good of a mood if something was keeping us from sitting down to dinner right away.

I said, "No, sir. Just that they were making fun of me about being colored."

He was already unbuckling his belt. "Who? Who was making fun?"

I told him Wayne and David. He said he'd speak to them later, but that that didn't excuse what I did, and did I understand what Big Trouble I was in? I knew I was supposed to answer with "Yes, sir," but I couldn't say anything because my mouth was too dry. I hated even *looking* at Dad's belt. He hadn't used it on us in about a year, since a time me and Wayne socked each other on the arm during church. I didn't think it was fair that time, because not only did Wayne hit me first, but also a lot harder. I didn't think it was fair this time, either, because Dad also put me on restrictions, and with a lot of extra chores.

I could barely sit down to dinner afterward and asked if I could bring in a pillow. Mom always felt bad whenever Dad spanked us like that and so she said yes. We were having pork chops and potatoes au gratin. Tink thought it was called "potatoes *hog rotten*," and everybody else thought that was pretty funny but I didn't.

■　■　■

I still looked colored the next day, but at least I didn't have to wear Ban-Lon. Nobody said anything when I walked into homeroom, but I guess that was only because it was me and I'm usually not somebody that kids notice all that much to begin with, plus I looked down at the floor the whole time so it was hard for anybody to see my face too well.

I headed for a desk in the back. I had math class in this same room first period, which was good because since I'd lost my notebooks at Bowlegs Creek all I had to write on was some of Dad's graph paper from his work. I hoped we would get to use it, because I liked writing on graph paper and making charts and graphs and stuff. The teacher was Mr. Phinney, who was about a hundred years old and wore his pants up to his ribs and tucked in the end of his tie.

The PA buzzed and clicked. The principal read the announcements. Mighty Miners home game Friday. Key Club car wash Saturday. A scratchy record played "The Lord's Prayer" and we all stood up for that. Then it was the Pledge of Allegiance, and then "God Bless America."

The girl in the back row—her name was Mary Dunn and she was about a foot taller than me—she started staring at me halfway through the Pledge. It was the kind of way you look at somebody that has something really wrong with them, like a big neck goiter, or a glass eye that falls out, which Dad told me happened one time to a guy at the mine. Once the record was over and everybody else sat down, she went up to Mr. Phinney and said something, and when he looked back at me, the whole class did, too.

Everybody laughed pretty good for a while. I stared down at my graph paper and wrote my name over and over until they stopped, or until Mr. Phinney made them stop. Then Mary Dunn got all her stuff and moved to a different desk near the front, so I was the only one left in the back row after that. I tried really hard not to cry or anything, but I might have gotten kind of a runny nose, sitting there the rest of math class.

Mr. Phinney stopped me on the way out of class. He hiked his pants up a little bit higher, and tucked his tie in a little bit deeper, and I thought if he kept it up, the two things together might pull him over so far that he finally just folded himself in half.

One of his furry caterpillar eyebrows went up and the other went down, and he asked me if I was some kind of a joke boy and did I think I could get away with funny business in his class.

I told him, "No, sir. It's no funny business. I just had an accident with shoe polish. That's how come I missed the first day of school yesterday."

"Shoe-polish accident?"

"Yes, sir."

The caterpillars were on the move again, the way they did when Mr. Phinney explained math problems on the board. "Try turpentine?"

I nodded. "But my mom didn't want to get it too close to my eyes and mouth and nose."

He said, "Well, all right then," but that I had to stay sitting in the back row because he didn't want me disturbing the class anymore. And if I wasn't telling him the truth, he said, I better believe he'd find out about it, one way or another.

The second-period kids were crowding past us by that time, and I knew I was going to be late for my next class, which was what happened: I got a tardy for English, plus a whole other bunch of kids laughing once I came in after the late bell. Somebody said, "Hey, Sambo," when I squeezed down the aisle between two rows of desks to the one empty one.

Nothing much else too bad happened, though, and by the end of the day, I thought maybe it would all fade away—the shoe polish and the getting laughed at and the having to sit in the back of the class. I hoped it would, anyway.

Chapter Six

FRIDAY NIGHT CAME BUT I WASN'T allowed to go to the
Mighty Miners game with Dad and Mom and them. I was feeling
better about looking colored, I guess, but still didn't mind not
going. Mom had come into the bedroom the night before, when I
couldn't sleep, and rubbed my back until I finally did. Maybe she
said something to Dad, because just before they left for the game,
he let up on the restrictions some and said I could ride my bike,
but only around the neighborhood. So that's what I did—I rode
about ten times around the perimeter.

I had read about perimeters in the Tampa paper, and if I ever
talked to that Walter Wratchford again, I thought I might ask him
about it. They said that that was the most dangerous job in the
war—patrolling the perimeter. That and walking point, although
one officer they interviewed said it wasn't the guy walking point
that got shot usually, it was the guy behind him, so I didn't want

to walk point or be the guy behind him, but I figured if the Vietcong opened up on me while I was patrolling the perimeter, I could either ride away fast or jump into a ditch. I practiced both for a while until I thought I had my technique down—up on the balls of my feet on the pedals so I could go directly into a sprint or jump off. It always worked better in my mind than it did when I actually tried it, though. Once when I jumped off I conked my head on a tree root and my bike rolled into a stop sign. Another time my foot slipped off the pedal and I landed face-first and got grass and dirt in my mouth.

Dusk is the most dangerous part of the day, and the time when you have to be the most vigilant on patrol because the changing light and the shadows can play tricks on you. It's when the Vietcong can sneak up on your perimeter the easiest, and that's what happened. This one was a girl: Darla Turkel. By the time I saw her, it was already too late.

I don't know how I could have missed her. She was sitting on a pink PF Flyer on the other side of Green Street. The sun was low behind her, a red ball that made her blond Shirley Temple hair look pink, like the bike. I figured my only hope was to be friendly: Hi, bye, gotta fly.

"Hey, Darla," I said.

She looked surprised. "Who are you?"

"Dewey Turner." There were only about a thousand people in all of Sand Mountain, plus we were in a couple of the same classes at school. How could she not know who I was?

"Oh. I thought you were a colored boy. What's the matter with your face?"

I had avoided the question all week, because after they all finished laughing, mostly people just stared at me and maybe whispered something to somebody else, and maybe called me Sambo, but that was about all.

"It's just the makeup they use for the minstrel show," I said to Darla, lying like crazy. "They picked me to be the Chattanooga Shoe-Shine Boy next year. It doesn't come off too good."

Now there was a sour look on her face. "They just had the minstrel show."

"Yeah, but it takes a lot of practice," I said. "You practice for a whole year for that."

She looked like if she hadn't been a girl she would have spit right on the ground. "I saw that minstrel show, and I don't think that boy they had this year practiced so much. He couldn't even dance. They should have asked my brother, Darwin. My mom's pretty mad. She's really going to be mad now that you're already it for next year."

I felt bad for Darwin and her mom, and said I was sorry. Then I told her I was taking dance lessons.

"Oh, yeah? Where?"

"I meant I'm *going* to take dance lessons," I said.

She told me I ought to go to her mom because she was a great dance teacher, and I said that yeah, I would probably do that, I'd been thinking about it and all, I just hadn't had time yet. We were both quiet for a minute. The sun was almost down and the street-lights made circles of light in little pools on every corner. You could hear the crowd all the way over by the Peace River at the football field.

Darla was staring, I guess at me. She said, "I know where this old lady lives that has a parrot that sings 'When the Roll Is Called Up Yonder.' You can see it through the kitchen window. You want to ride over there? It's on Sixth Street."

That kind of surprised me. I had thought she was mad or something before, and now she wanted me to go spying with her.

"I can't," I said. "I'm on restrictions. This is as far as I can go right here." Then—why, I don't know—I said, "But you can come over here and we could ride around."

"I can't, either," she said. "I'm on restrictions, too. This is as far as I'm allowed to go."

"What are you on restrictions for?"

She blinked a couple of times. "I'm not allowed to tell."

"You're not allowed to *tell*?" I'd never heard of that before. I thought you *had* to tell, anytime anybody asked, so people would know how awful you were. It was part of the punishment.

"No," she said. "I'm not. Besides, everybody already thinks they know, anyway, so I won't dignify their gossip by defending myself."

"You sound like my mom," I said.

She rolled her eyes. Then she did a strange thing. She said, "Watch this," then got off her bike and pushed it out of the circle of light, and when she stepped back into the light she started singing like Shirley Temple. "Put another nickel in, in the nickelodeon, all I want is lovin' you and music, music, music, music." As she sang, she also danced like Shirley Temple, which involved a lot of skipping and bouncing her hair and throwing her arms open like she was trying to hug everything in the world. I had never seen anybody open their mouth so wide, except to eat something really big. This went on for quite a while. She sang a couple more songs. She did "Mares Eat Oats and Does Eat Oats and Little Lambs Eat Ivy." She also did "High Hopes," about an ant that ate a rubber-tree plant.

I guess I was hypnotized or something, watching her and listening, because I hardly noticed when she finally stopped. She was panting. A drop of perspiration rolled along the side of her face and down her cheek.

"You can close your mouth now," Darla said. "You're attracting flies."

Green Street, at that minute, looked wider than the Peace River. The crowd roared from far away. "Somebody must of scored a touchdown," I said.

Darla said, "Yeah, I guess."

On weekends at our house, everybody had to pull two pieces of paper out of the job jar and then do the chores they picked: clean the bathroom, vacuum the house, beat the rugs, wash the garbage cans, sweep the carport, edge the sidewalk. One slip of paper said

"FREE," and another said "25¢," and if you ever got both of those, you jumped on your bike and tore out of there because if you stayed around the house doing nothing—even though you had a right to—you ended up doing chores, anyway.

I got Wayne to tell me the Darla story later that Friday night, but it cost me two weeks' worth of his chores from the job jar. He was lying in bed, on the bottom bunk, with his hands behind his head. I was leaning over the edge of the top bunk barely able to see him in the dark. "If I get the FREE or the money, that doesn't count," he said. "Maybe you better put that in writing."

"I will tomorrow," I said. "Just tell me about Darla."

The more I wanted to know, the more he was going to make me wait. "What do you care, anyway?" he said.

"I just do. Now tell me."

"First you have to say you want to marry her."

"OK. You want to marry her."

"Not me. You."

"OK," I said again. "You want to marry her."

Wayne snorted. "I guess you don't really want to hear this, then."

"I already said I would do your chores," I said. "We have a deal. You have to tell me." I swung my pillow down at him but he grabbed it and pulled it out of my hands.

"Violence will get you nowhere, Mister Sambo."

"Shut up, *Wiener*," I said back. That was the nickname he had that he hated.

"Sambo."

"Wiener."

He jumped out of bed and started whacking me with my own pillow, and I didn't have anything to defend myself with except the wood bar that kept you from rolling off the bunk bed. I nearly hit him in the head with it and then the light came on. It was Dad. We froze. He glared at Wayne, standing in his underwear holding my pillow, then at me on my knees up on the top bunk holding the bar.

"Do we need to have a conversation?" he said.

"No, sir." Wayne handed me back the pillow.

"No, sir." I put the bar in its place.

The room was darker than before when he left and shut the door, partly because he turned off the hall light and partly because it always takes your eyes time to adjust. Things were quiet for a while. Then Wayne started talking.

"The police caught her setting off firecrackers in the cemetery, is what I heard. Somebody that lives by there called the cops and when they came, she tried to run away across Riverside Road into the woods. They chased her down a path and finally caught her. She was lying on the ground with her feet stuck up in the air, laughing like a Laughing Hyena."

"She was laughing? How come? And how come her feet were in the air?"

"Because she was *drunk*." I could tell Wayne had been saving that part.

I said "No, she wasn't," and he laughed at me and said, "Yes, she was. And that isn't all."

"What else?" I don't even know why I asked him, because I didn't believe any of it.

Now came the part he had *really* been saving. "She was with a colored boy."

I was already lying on my back, but it felt like all the air went out of my body. "A colored boy?"

"Yep," he said. "A colored boy."

When I started breathing again, I asked Wayne what happened to the colored boy and Wayne said he got away but they were still looking for him, and still trying to make Darla tell them his name and what all really happened after he gave her the liquor and where he got the firecrackers.

"What do you think they'll do to him?" I said.

Wayne said you couldn't be too sure. Put him in jail maybe. Or cut his you-know-whats off. If they put him in jail first, they might not do the other one; but if they did the other one first, they would still put him in jail.

"What about Darla?" I said.

His bed springs creaked. "Nothing, I guess. Nobody's going to talk to her is all."

"*I'll* talk to her," I said, which surprised me on account of I about always tried to do what everybody else was doing, because I wanted to fit in and have people like me—something that was getting harder ever since I turned colored, of course.

I thought Wayne would make fun of me for saying that—go on some more about how I loved her, or say I was Little Black Sambo.

But he didn't. He didn't say anything else, and I didn't ask him anything else. It took a long time for my mind to be quiet, thinking about Darla and the colored boy and the cemetery and everything else. When I finally fell asleep, I dreamed about that half man–half gator down at Bowlegs Creek, and that wasn't any better, either.

Chapter Seven

THE SENIORS AT SAND MOUNTAIN HIGH SCHOOL had a list of all the seventh-grade boys according to height, and they were going for the tallest ones first with the red-belly attacks, then working their way down. That's what I heard, anyway. That should have meant I was third to last, before Ronnie Lott and Richard Speight, although some people had the idea that they might spare Richard Speight because he was a dwarf. But that's not how it worked out. Ronnie Lott and Richard Speight both got theirs on the second Monday of school.

I saw Richard Speight after he got his in gym. There were big red handprints all over his belly that were already turning purple. Plus he didn't have any shoes on. I asked where they were and he pointed over to the power line next to the outdoor basketball courts.

"You're never gonna get those down," I said. I meant it to sound sympathetic, but Richard didn't want sympathy; he just wanted somebody to be mad at.

"Yeah," he said. "But that's nothing compared to what they're gonna do to you."

"What?" I said, still thinking me and him were on the same side.

He tucked in his shirt. "All I know is I'd move to a different town if I was you. You're gonna wish you was dead. I just hope I get to see it."

I decided I hated Richard Speight. "Oh, just shut up, midget," I said.

I had forgotten that Richard Speight was pretty strong even if he was so short. He could also move pretty quick when he wanted to. He jumped up and grabbed me around the head and just about wrestled me to the floor, when one of the coaches came out of his office. Richard Speight scooted off but the coach grabbed my collar before I could get away, too.

"You ought to be ashamed of yourself, picking on a boy like that," he said. "Do you want detention?"

I said, "No, sir." He shook me around and said that I better watch my step and mind my p's and q's, Buster Brown.

Things got even worse after that. On Tuesday somebody put a WHITES ONLY sign on all the boys' bathroom doors, and when I tried to go in, two seniors blocked the way. One of them was a guy they called Head because of his big head. He should have been a football player, but they didn't have any helmet that fit him. The other one looked like Moe of the Three Stooges.

"Hey, Little Black Sambo, can't you read?" Moe said.

Head snickered and pointed to the sign. "Whities only."

"Not 'whities only,'" Moe corrected him. "*Whites* only."

"Yeah, *whites* only," Head said.

I didn't start crying but I almost did. They laughed pretty hard when I went away. I heard them all the way down the hall. I guess they must have taken the other stairs, because when I tried to go in the bathroom on the second floor, Head and Moe were already there, too.

I don't know what they talked about in second-period English, because I had to pee so bad. I even asked Mr. Crow for a hall pass, but when he asked me what for and I told him, he said, "There's a reason you have five minutes between classes, young man. You're not in elementary school anymore. I suggest you budget your time more wisely."

So I didn't go. Not then, not before the next period, not until lunchtime, when I ran outside and peed behind the building. It hurt so much I did cry then, only nobody saw me except Chollie the janitor, who was mowing, but I ran back inside before he could come over and get me in trouble. I didn't drink anything at lunch or the rest of the day, and I made it home before I had to pee again, but just barely. I stayed in the bathroom a long time because when I finished peeing it felt like I had to go again right away, and I was afraid maybe I broke something holding it in so long. After a while I got so tired of standing to pee that I sat down backward again so I could put my head down on my arms because I had a giant headache, and I decided I was never going back to school ever and they couldn't make me. In sixth grade it had been Deweyitis. Now it was Black Sambo and Whites Only, and maybe a red belly and maybe something worse. I also still sometimes forgot my locker combination, so I had to write it on my arm.

The idea I came up with was military school. They had one over near Tampa. Of course, I would miss my family, but they could write me letters, and call, and send packages, and probably realize what a great guy I was once I wasn't around, and feel bad about the way they had treated me, and try to make it up to me when I came home on leave or over breaks. I could wear my uniform around town, and if I saw Darla Turkel again at Green Street, I could explain my officer's stripes and badges. I would be tough but fair. They'd call me sir, but when they talked about me when I wasn't around they'd call me Dew-Man or something like that. Like, "The Dew-Man sure can handle his weapon. He had eight bull's-eyes at target practice." That sort of thing. Or maybe I wouldn't use Dewey anymore once I got there. My middle name would be better—Markham. That was my mom's last name before she married Dad. They could call me Markham because Mark-*ham* sounded like Marks-*man*, as in Expert Marks*man*. I planned to be very good with a rifle.

Dad listened pretty nice while I told him my plan. We were out back in his work shed, where he was always making stuff and where he also kept his survey equipment. He used to go out there to smoke cigarettes, until John Wayne got lung cancer. John Wayne announced that he was planning to lick the Big C, which of course he did, but Dad probably figured he wouldn't be so lucky. My dad smoked Chesterfield Kings, and he used to hide a pack in one of his nail jars. He did this thing where he nailed the lids of all his nail jars to a board that he then nailed to one of the beams over his workbench. When he needed a particular jar with a certain nail or screw or Chesterfield, he just reached up, unscrewed it, got what he wanted, then screwed the jar back in.

My dad kept everything neat like that, and as I explained about going to military school over in Tampa, I made sure to tell him how neat and orderly they did things, and how it would teach me to be neat and orderly, too. Plus probably lead to a career in the military. Plus I was already the best around at shining shoes, which they made you do a lot of, for parades and stuff.

When I finished, he looked up at the nail jars like maybe he wished there was still a pack of Chesterfields tucked up there in one of them. There was a light on over the workbench, a naked bulb, and the sun came in through the one little window, and through the double doors, which he always left open. But mostly it was dark. He said, "So what brought all this on?"

"I don't know," I said. "I just don't think it's a good idea for me to go back to school here anymore."

Dad said, "Did something happen at school you should tell me about?"

I shook my head. There were the WHITES ONLY signs, and not getting to go to the bathroom, and Little Black Sambo. And there was the Deweyitis, though that was last year. But how could I talk about any of that? Besides, he was probably still mad at me for the shoe polish and skipping school and losing my clothes at Bowlegs Creek. Which left just the one thing.

"Did they have red bellies when you were my age, Dad?"

He nodded. "I believe they probably did, sport. Is that was this is about? What the seniors do to the new boys?"

"Yes, sir," I said, although I left out the part about everybody already getting theirs except me. I knew my dad liked that kind of problem, anyway, because he always had a story he could tell me about when he was a kid, and he always knew what to do, and he always had good advice that made a lot of sense, the same way scouting stuff made so much sense when you read about it in *Boys Life,* even though it never worked too well when you tried it yourself. But it *sounded* good. Usually I guess it didn't work for me because the problem Dad thought we were talking about wasn't really the problem because I had to leave too much stuff out.

One time I asked Dad what I should do if a guy wanted to fight me, because if I was in a fight, I always got in trouble not only with the principal, but with Dad, too. That was back in elementary school. What Dad said was I should pray for help in those situations, and ask God for the strength to resist, and turn the other cheek. I said, But the other guy could hit me when my eyes were closed and Dad said it was OK to pray with your eyes open; just pray in your mind. He said you didn't have to get down on your knees or bow your head or fold your hands or close your eyes.

"Or get in a closet?" I said. We had a Sunday school teacher that year who told us the Bible said you were supposed to go into a closet when you wanted to pray. Dad said, "That's right—or get in a closet," but he also had this exasperated look he got when he tried to explain something to me but I kept missing the point.

That business about praying—I guess it was good advice, and I did try it one time, but the problem was I usually did something myself to get in the fight in the first place so what I should have been doing was maybe praying to not be so stupid all the time.

Dad had been working on an old lamp while we talked—one of those lamps where the shade spins slowly around so it looks like water crashing over Niagara Falls. It hadn't worked in about a million years, and I didn't know why he was trying to fix it now, since Mom didn't like it and he would just have to sell it or give it away. But that never mattered to Dad. He just figured if something was broke, you fixed it and that was the end of that. I watched him with the rewiring and the splicing, and I handed him a new bulb that he screwed in, and then he remounted the shade and plugged the lamp into his extension cord. It hummed and the shade turned and the light swam around the walls.

"The best thing is probably to tough it out on this red-belly business," Dad said. "Sometimes bigger boys just need to prove how big they think they are, and they pick on smaller boys like the seventh-graders. If it gets out of hand, you let me know and I'll speak to the principal. But what they want you to do is be scared, and if you show them you're scared, that's how they win. Just act like you don't care what they're up to. They might not leave you alone, but you'll have your dignity, and that's the most important thing in all of this. Your dignity. Nobody can take that away from you unless you let them."

He stopped then and looked at me, and I wondered if he remembered who he was talking to—a boy who stained his face black with Kiwi shoe polish, and burned holes in his Ban-Lon shirt with a magnifying glass, and had to sneak home in the burnt shirt and his underwear.

"I understand, Dad," I said, and I did—about the dignity, and about the toughing it out, and about the bigger boys and the smaller boys.

"Great, son," he said.

"But Dad—"

"Yeah, sport. What is it?"

"Well, I was still wondering—you didn't say yet about the military school, about can I go."

He looked back up at those nail jars and I *know* he wished he still had some Chesterfields then. He didn't answer. Or maybe he had already answered and I just hadn't heard right. I don't know. The lamp was still on and the shade was still turning and the river was still running like it was carrying me and him and the shed and everything closer to the falls. All he said was didn't I have some homework I needed to do for school tomorrow, and shouldn't I head on back to the house to do it? I wanted to say, "Wait, Dad, there's more, a hundred things more, a hundred reasons for me to go off to military school that I haven't told you yet, and never go back to Sand Mountain High School or stay in Sand Mountain," but the words wouldn't come out of my mouth, so I just said, "Yes, sir."

Chapter Eight

I WAS STILL ON RESTRICTIONS THE NEXT FRIDAY, but I didn't want to go to the football game, anyway. I was barely colored anymore, but that didn't stop kids from still teasing me about it at school. After Mom and Dad and Wayne and Tink left, I lay on the rug in the living room for a while burping—we had fried liver that night for dinner—but you can get tired of that after a while, so I eventually got up and rode my bike over to the corner of Second and Green Streets to see Darla Turkel again. I don't know why I thought she would be there except that she had been the week before.

I waited about ten minutes for her to show up, then got back on my bike and rode around for a while, trying to do all the same things I had done the Friday before—the patrolling the perimeter, the jumping off into ditches, the sprinting to get away from the Vietcong—but afterward Darla still wasn't there in that circle of streetlight on Green Street on her pink PF Flyer with her Shirley Temple hair, so I went back home and lay down on the rug again in the living room and did some more burping and watched some TV.

Darwin Turkel answered the door when I showed up at their house the next day after the job-jar chores and Dad lifted my restrictions.

"They're not here," he said, even though I hadn't said anything, including who I was there to see. "They're out and they're not back yet." He folded his arms and didn't move over to invite me in, so I just stood on the front porch and looked at his lips, which were the reddest I ever saw on a boy, almost like he wore lipstick. I could tell he didn't, though, because he had a habit of licking his bottom lip with his tongue back and forth very fast. Not all the time, but every once in a while: his tongue shot out of the hole like a rabbit or a gopher, turned both ways, then popped back down. He also wore a red Ban-Lon shirt buttoned all the way up to the neck. I didn't know how he could even breathe with that shirt on, or why he would wear it when he didn't have to, like on a Saturday afternoon, which this was.

I tugged on the collar of my T-shirt to stretch it out some more.

"Well?" he said.

"Well what?"

"Well, are you going to come inside and wait?"

I said I guessed so and started to come in, only he stopped me.

"You have to go around to the back door," he said. "That's the servants' entrance and where we take deliveries."

"What are you talking about?" I said. "You don't have servants. And what deliveries?"

He rolled his eyes. "Well, aren't you supposed to be colored?"

I told him, "Heck no," but he just smiled and closed the door. I heard his voice again, though. "See you around ba-ack." He kind of sang it at me, and for some reason I went around the house to the servants' entrance like he said, although I almost couldn't find the door there was so much junk on the back porch, including an old washing machine that was green with algae or something, wet boxes full of magazines that you knew if you tried to pick them up the bottoms would fall out, bags of stuff, a couple of rolled-up carpets, toys and board games like Chutes and Ladders for kids a lot littler than Darla and Darwin, two big dolls without heads, some empty orange crates, a chair with three legs, the heads of the two dolls—a Raggedy Ann and a Raggedy Andy—stuck on the ends of two poles.

"*Entrez vous,*" Darwin said, holding open the screen door. It was French and meant "Come in, you."

"I'm *not* colored," I said again. He shrugged and said, "Well, all right, then," and opened the door wider, and even though I sort of didn't want to, I followed him inside.

The house was dark and Darwin told me I had to be very quiet because his grandfather was taking a nap. We went upstairs to Darwin's bedroom. He shut the door behind us.

"So you're the boy in the minstrel show," he said.

I said, "Not this year," but that next year maybe I would be.

He smoothed down the front of his Ban-Lon shirt, then stuck his hands in the pockets of his Bermuda shorts. I looked down at his shoes. He was wearing penny loafers without socks. "I was told you were already the one," he said. "Can you dance? Let's see you dance. I won't even ask you to sing."

I said I didn't have to show him anything. Then I asked when were Darla and their mom coming back, anyway? Then I said I was leaving. He scooted over to block the door.

"Don't go," he said. "Never mind. Just kidding. You don't have to dance. I don't care, anyway. You can be in the minstrel show. Why should I care? We're moving to Hollywood as soon as we get out of here and I'll probably be in the movies."

I said, "Maybe Hollywood, *Florida*," which was down near Miami.

He started to say something and I could tell it was going to be prissy, but he stopped himself and asked me if I wanted to play a game. "They'll be back in a little while. Darla went to ride her stupid pony. We can just play until they get back. You have to play."

I wasn't used to somebody wanting me to be around like this, even if it was somebody so weird like Darwin Turkel. "OK," I said. "What?"

"It's a game I made up called Turn Off the Lights."

"That's a dumb name."

"Well," he said, "if you win, you can make up a new name that I'm sure will be better."

The game was that we closed the blinds and turned off the lights, and one of us tied up the other one and blindfolded him. The one that was tied up had to sit on the floor, and no matter what happened he wasn't allowed to say anything for five minutes. If he did, he lost. If he didn't, he won. It sounded pretty stupid to me.

By the time he finished tying me up, I couldn't see anything, even when I opened my eyes under the blindfold. I heard a scratching sound, which was a record player, then the Beatles' "She Loves You." I heard Darwin's voice singing the "yeah, yeah, yeah" part, and his feet every now and then creaking a loose floorboard. I was sitting in the middle of a big rug and figured once he was on it, I wouldn't be able to hear him, which turned out to be true, because when he poked me in the ribs the first time, I just about jumped up off the floor.

Now it was just the Beatles singing.

He poked me again, this time in the stomach, and then he grabbed both of my sides and tickled me. I squirmed to get away from him, but clamped my jaw tight to keep from making any noise. I wanted to win so I could rename the game "This Is Stupid."

I felt something on the back of my neck, I think a feather.

Then something in my ear, which must have been the feather again. That didn't tickle so much. I couldn't believe how black it was under the blindfold, and I got that kind of panicky feeling of being claustrophobic. I wanted to ask him how I was supposed to know when five minutes were up, but figured that was probably a trick of his to get me to say that so he would win.

He grabbed one of my shoes and pulled it off, and I almost said, "Give it back," but didn't. He grabbed the other shoe, too, and then I felt the feather again, this time across my face. At first I twisted away but it actually felt kind of good, so after a while I quit trying to move away. He did the feather for a long time after that, across my forehead, down the side of my face, over my ear, across my mouth. He did it around my neck, too, really slow. Then my mouth again, which felt funny the more he did it. Then down my arm, then my other arm, to my hands, which were sitting in my lap. Across my knuckles, up my arm, around my neck, across my mouth, over my ears, down my arms again. The song had stopped and the needle was just going round and round on the last groove on the record. He needed to stop it but maybe he didn't notice, and I didn't say anything because of the game. The feather ran over my legs some, my arms, everything. And then disappeared. I hardly noticed when it did, except that I felt his hands on my arms instead, not squeezing, just holding my arms for a minute moving up and down, then one of his hands was on my shirt kind of rubbing on my belly. I held my breath when he did that, just for a second, or maybe longer than a second, I'm not sure. It sure was dark.

Then I finally said something. I said, "Five minutes is over; now untie me," and I rolled away from where I thought he was and didn't feel his hand anymore.

"Untie me," I said again. "I won. It's five minutes. Untie me." I began to get panicky under the blindfold and with my hands tied, and didn't know how I had made it that long because of the claustrophobia. "Untie me!" I yelled. "You better untie me!" I could hear Darwin breathing a little ways away.

I started yanking really hard on the ropes and got one of my hands free and right away pulled off the blindfold. Darwin helped me get the other knots out.

Then it was his turn.

I knew some knots from Scouts and used every one I could think of when I tied him up: the sheepshank, the half hitch, the square knot, plus a few I probably made up. I kept tying until I ran out of rope. Then the blindfold—I pulled that tight until he said "Ow," then I pulled it even tighter. He said it was about to make his eyeballs pop, and I said he wasn't allowed to talk for five minutes, remember?

He hadn't said much after he let me go, and I hadn't said much, either. I pushed him down to a sitting position on the rug, turned off the light, turned it back on again so I could find my shoes, which he had tossed under his disgusting bed, which hadn't been made up and which had sheets that were yellow, not that that was their real color. I would have thought a guy that wore Ban-Lon on a Saturday would have a much neater room, but I guess not.

I still felt pretty funny about the game but didn't know what to say about any of it, so once I found my shoes, I licked my finger really good and stuck it in Darwin's ear. "The new name of this game is Wet Willie," I said, then I tiptoed over to the door, turned off the light, threw a book against the wall to distract him, and made my getaway.

I didn't get too far, though, because Darla and her mom walked in the front door about the time I got to the bottom of the stairs. They were both wearing big riding boots and matching pink pants and T-shirts. Darla's hair was still perfect, like Shirley Temple. Her mom's hair was red and piled up on top of her head like Jackie Kennedy, only her face was harder.

"Call the police, sugar," Mrs. Turkel said. "It's a midget burglar." She laughed at her own joke and winked at me. "You must be one of Darwin's little friends. What's your name? And where is he, anyway? And where's my papa? He's not still asleep, is he? That man would spend his entire life in bed if you let him, I swear. Well, it's time to get him up. Darla, sugar, I'm going to get Papa up. You hold on to this boy and go count the silverware. Check his pockets. Ha-ha. You are the cutest little thing, I swear."

She went on like that with the "Where's Papa?" and the "I swear" and the "Darwin's little friend," even when she stomped away down the hall in her riding boots, leaving a trail of mud prints that nobody seemed to notice but me. If it had been at my house, my mom would have handed somebody the broom and dustpan and stood there pointing at the mess or just looking at it until it got cleaned up.

Darla's pony was named Bojangles after Bill Bojangles Robinson, a colored man Shirley Temple danced with in some movies. We were riding our bikes when she told me this, because I had said I had a sore leg and couldn't stay at her house for a dance lesson, but really I was nervous about Darwin tied up upstairs and wanted to get out of there before he started yelling or something. Darla said she would go with me, and just followed outside and hopped on her pink PF Flyer, even though I hadn't asked her. We were a ways down Orange Avenue when she told me about the pony. I wondered why if she could afford a pony they couldn't clean off their back porch, too, but I didn't ask.

"Why'd you name him Bojangles, besides that?" I said.

"Well, why do you think?" she said.

I said I guessed because he was a colored horse.

She pedaled up next to me. "Not colored. He's a *black* horse. And anyway, he's a pony. His mane is black, his tail is black, his coat is black, his eyes are black."

I said colored people weren't black, they were brown. She said she wasn't talking about colored people, she was talking about her pony. I said I thought she was talking about why she named him after Bill Bojangles Robinson, and she said, "I *was*." She studied me pretty hard for a minute, still pedaling, and said, "You're not slow, are you?"

I said, "You mean like retarded?"

"I mean like slow," she said.

I shook my head. "I make all *A*'s usually."

"Well, good, then," she shouted. "That's very, very, very good."

We kept riding all the way to Bowlegs Creek, and I decided I didn't understand much about talking to girls. But then again Darla didn't seem like any regular girl, just like her mom didn't seem like a regular mom, and her brother sure didn't seem like a regular boy. Which reminded me—

"Can I tell you something? And don't get mad at me," I said.

Her cheeks were red from riding, and her blond hair back off her face from the wind and the perspiration. "What?"

"Your brother, he's all tied up in the bedroom with a lot of knots in a rope, and the lights are off, and he's also blindfolded."

Darla blinked at me. We had gotten to Bowlegs by then and were putting down our kickstands. She said, "So?" like she thought I was accusing her of doing it.

"So I might of been the one that tied the knots and all."

"I don't care," she said. "He can just stay there all day. He probably likes it."

"Oh," I said, thinking no conversation I'd ever had with Darla so far ended up the way I thought it would.

We sat on the stone wall of the bridge for a while, flicking sticks in the water and watching them disappear under us with the current, and I told her about the time I dug a giant cave in the bank and lived in it for a while until it collapsed on me and I had to claw my way out. It was kind of a miracle I survived. I would have been fine probably except for a storm that came up—I thought it might have been a hurricane—that was what washed the cave away. She asked what I lived on and had I run away from home and did my family give me up for dead—practical questions that I appreciated, and nothing that went in the direction of Ban-Lon and underwear.

I spit down in the creek and she said she hated it when people spit, and I said I usually never did that but a gnat must have flown in my mouth, I was sorry. She said she thought you should always be a gentleman, no matter how old a boy you were. That seemed pretty hard to me, to not be able to spit, or burp even if you ate liver and cabbage, or cut one, but I would try around her. I suddenly had about a million questions I wanted to ask her—about the cemetery and what happened there, and how long her mom could actually hold her breath underwater when she was a mermaid, and what about Darwin—and a million things I wanted to say to her, too, but I was also afraid of talking too much, of saying something too stupid, so I kept my mouth shut after that and we just sat there in the afternoon. She sang a couple of songs just because she wanted, I guess. Bowlegs gurgled along under us, and two cars passed a half hour apart, but it was quiet mostly, and that was nice, too.

Chapter Nine

DAD SAID GRACE THAT NIGHT AT SUPPER the way he always did—*Dear Lord, bless this food You have set before us that it may nourish our bodies so we may better serve Thee, amen*—then announced he was running for the Sand Mountain city council. Again. It would be his third time. As soon as he said it, I lost my appetite even though we were having macaroni and cheese. Tink asked if he would be the mayor. Dad rubbed her head. "No, sweetie. But you never know in the future. Anything can happen." Wayne seemed to always be hungry from the JV football practices and was shoveling in the macaroni. I stared down at my plate because I knew what was coming next.

"I'm going to need a lot of help with this campaign," Dad said. "And I'm going to be relying on you boys. We'll divide up the neighborhoods so you can get the flyers out. We're going to have to be very organized about this."

Wayne groaned but kept eating. Tink said she would pass out flyers at school, but Dad said since kids weren't allowed to vote that might not be the best use of our campaign resources. He had a special job for Tink, though. He needed somebody reliable to answer the phone and take messages, and could she handle that? She ran from the table into her bedroom, then came back a second later with a little notebook with hearts on it. "Can this be the message book I use?" she said. Mom and Dad both smiled, and Dad rubbed her head again. It was all so cute I thought I was going to vomit.

I hated doing the flyers because I had to hand them out to people I didn't know, which meant I had to talk to them, although I usually tried to sneak up to their door, knock so soft nobody could possibly hear me, then stuff the flyer somewhere and run back to my bike. And I hated for my dad to run for city council again because it was a big waste of time since he always lost.

Dad said it was still a few weeks before we'd be passing out the flyers because the election wasn't until November, but he'd already been working on his platform, which he said was what they called your campaign promises and what you would do if you got elected. One of the first things Dad wanted to do was have them tear down the old Skeleton Hotel, which he said was an eyesore to the town.

I got nervous right away. The Skeleton Hotel scared me

because everybody said it was haunted, but at the same time I couldn't imagine downtown Sand Mountain without it being there. They started building it before I was even born—four stories high in a town that had only one two-story building and just a couple of two-story houses, including Darla's. Only something happened when a colored man got killed at the work site, and they never finished it but just left the steel frame, with the floors and the old elevator to the roof, but no walls or windows or rooms or anything except a farmer's market that Mr. Hollis Wratchford ran on the ground floor underneath—the same Mr. Wratchford that had started to build the Skeleton Hotel, so I guessed he still owned what was there.

Dad said another thing that ought to happen—and he'd make sure of it once he got elected—was annexation of the east side of the Peace River so they could shut down the one bar in the area, or at least the one white bar, that place called The Springs, which was built up on concrete blocks over a deepwater spring right next to the Peace River bridge. It was where David Tremblay's stepdad went on the weekends, and of course Walter Wratchford with his carved wood fist with the finger, and where they said guys were all the time throwing their bottles in the water or falling in or drowning in or driving their cars in.

Tink was too little to know any of that, though, and she asked what was The Springs. Wayne said, "It's where you get your liquor."

Tink stood up on her chair, which she always did when she got mad. "I don't drink liquor," she said, loud. Wayne laughed at her and Mom told him to quit teasing his sister, and she told Tink to get down this instant, Young Lady. I still hadn't said a word.

The last thing that Dad said would be on his platform was a promise to pave some of the streets down in the Boogerbottom. "Those people are citizens," he said, "and it's not right they were left out of the comprehensive paving plan."

Mom had been spooning Tink another helping of macaroni even though Tink hadn't eaten her spinach yet, which wasn't fair. She asked Dad if that was his big plan to get the Negro vote and Dad said that yeah, he guessed it was, and that he had already been talking to Chollie, the janitor down at the high school, about helping him spread the word down in the Boogerbottom and to go talk to the colored churches around town.

I had a bunch of questions, like how come Dad needed a Negro vote, and did people know about him talking to a colored man about the campaign, and were me and Wayne going to be the ones putting all those flyers on the doors of the houses in the Boogerbottom. But I didn't want to give Dad any ideas, so I didn't say anything.

I could tell Mom wasn't happy about any of this, either. She kept asking Dad if he was sure. About the tenth time she said it Dad kind of snapped at her and then dinner was over.

Mom stood up from the table. "Take your plates into the kitchen," she told us. "It's Dewey's turn to wash. Tink dries. Wayne puts away." Dad picked up the newspaper and asked if there was any coffee. Mom asked was instant OK?

Sometimes me and Wayne talked at night when we were in bed and neither one could sleep. That was about the only time we talked, really, especially since the start of school last year, when Wayne turned into a Lone Wolf. When we were little, I would get scared on the top bunk, and to get him to let me in the bottom bunk I would have to tell him stories. I made up all this crazy stuff about two boys who were mole rats, which I had read about somewhere in a library book. They were blind like all the mole rats, and rolled in their own poop so they could tell one another apart by smell like all the mole rats, but had super mole powers. They lived their whole lives underground with no light at all, and they fought a lot of snakes that tried to invade their tunnels, which in the stories were like the Vietcong tunnels that had rooms and places to store food and weapons and everything. Wayne didn't like to sleep side by side because he said there wasn't room for his elbows, so we always went head to feet, which sort of worked because there was room for all of our elbows, but sort of didn't work because of the cover situation. I told him that was how the mole rats slept, too, only they had a whole bunch of them lined up like that, head to toe, head to toe, so they could fit more in a room.

I didn't know if he was awake that night, but I thought he was and maybe we could talk, though I doubted he would let me in bed with him or anything, and he probably didn't care about the mole rat stories anymore, either.

I hung partly over the edge of the top bunk. "Wayne?" I couldn't see him in the dark.

"Hmm."

"Wayne?"

"What?"

"Are you asleep?"

"Yes."

"No, you're not."

"OK, I'm not."

"What are you doing?"

"Trying to get to sleep."

"Can I come down there and sleep with you?"

"No."

"Why not?"

"Because. You're too big."

"I'll lay the opposite of you, head to feet."

"No."

"Why not?"

"You have toe jam and your feet stink and you chew your toenails."

"Please?"

"Why are you such a baby?"

"I'm not. I just can't get to sleep, either. I keep thinking."

"Well, I'm thinking, too, so leave me alone."

"About what?"

"About stuff."

"About going down to the Boogerbottom to pass out the fly-ers for Dad?"

"No."

"About school stuff?"

"No."

"About a girl?"

"No."

"About your peter?"

"Shut up. No."

"About the JV team?"

"Maybe."

"About what position you play?"

"No."

"What position *do* you play? Are you the quarterback or is David Tremblay?"

"David Tremblay. He's always the quarterback."

"What are you?"

"Guard."

"First string?"

"Second."

"Is there a third string?"

"No."

"Oh."

"What do you mean, 'Oh'? I'd like to see *you* out there."

"I didn't mean it like that. I just thought you should be first string."

"Well, I'm not."

"Why not?"

"I'm not good enough. Coach says I'm not focused."

"What does that mean?"

"It means when he's explaining the next play we're supposed to learn, I'm standing over there thinking about some song on the radio in my head."

"Oh."

"And then they give me a hard time because my brother thinks he's a Negro."

"Oh. What do you say back?"

"Nothing. I tell them to shut up."

"Do you really tell them to shut up?"

"Yes. Of course. What did you think I would say?"

"I don't know. Hey, Wayne."

"What? Jeezum Crow, what is this—a hundred questions?"

"They didn't give me my red belly yet."

"Don't worry. Just when you least expect it, they'll get you."

"I don't think so. They won't let me go to the bathroom."

"Well, that's what you get for going to school looking like a Negro."

"Why do you keep saying 'Negro'? You sound like Mom."

"It's what you're supposed to call them, that's why."

"Since when?"

"Since this year."

"Says who?"

"Says LBJ."

"Well, anyway, they won't let me go to the bathroom."

"So just go outside."

"I do, but I might get caught."

"Then do what Tink did."

What he was talking about was when Tink was in first grade, two years ago, she was very nervous, and so for about a week she took a cigar box to school with her. Everybody thought she had her supplies in there, but instead what she was doing was using it to put her poop in if she had to go when she was at school so she could bring it home and flush it in our own toilet and say goodbye to it there and watch it go down the way little kids like to do. For some reason that made her less nervous.

All of a sudden I felt very tired—mostly tired of talking to Wayne. He used to be a lot nicer to me back when he was a Lone Wolf, before I started seventh grade and he went into the eighth and became a big hotshot second-string guard on the JV football team, even if he wasn't focused. I thought about telling him that, but what was the use?

The funny thing was, when I decided to quit talking to Wayne, he started talking to me. Mostly it was about football stuff, like how he couldn't do any of the blocking right, and he was always getting holding calls on him in drills, and they had this one drill where it was just a lineman and a running back, and the running back was supposed to run straight into a lineman and through him, and the lineman was supposed to not let him and was supposed to tackle him instead. Wayne said he always got run through. I guess he really meant run *over*, but that was the way they talked in football.

Another thing he told me was a lot of the guys chewed tobacco on the team, and you knew it because they spit their Red Man on the field and it got all over everybody's practice jerseys and pants and helmets. One guy even swallowed his and they had to call his dad. So Wayne got Mom to buy raisins, which he would cram all in his cheek when nobody was looking so it looked like he was chewing tobacco, too. "It looks just like tobacco juice when you spit it between your teeth," he said, "but it doesn't hurt you if you accidentally swallow some."

That made me laugh, but Wayne got quiet after that and pretty soon I was back to worrying. I thought about having to ride my bike around the whole town delivering campaign flyers to everybody, and maybe even in the Boogerbottom, and that game of Turn Out the Lights with Darwin Turkel that I still hadn't told anybody about, and what they planned to do to me at school instead of a red belly, and people thinking I wanted to be colored, and me wanting to be the Chattanooga Shoe-Shine Boy but not have people think that that just proved I wanted to be colored, and what Darla Turkel was doing in the cemetery with that colored boy, or if that was even true, and atomic bombs, and not being big enough for sports, and the Vietcong, and all of communism, and Dad tearing down the Skeleton Hotel, and the half man–half gators all over the place, apparently, and Ban-Lon, Ban-Lon, Ban-Lon, Ban-Lon, what if they decided to make all the clothes in the world out of Ban-Lon?

"Wayne!" I knew I woke him up that time. He'd been snoring. "Please can I come down there?"

He grunted something and I decided that meant yes, so I crawled down to the bottom bunk and got in. It was very crowded, but I brought my own blanket and pillow.

"Do you ever worry about everything the way I do?" I asked him. His feet were next to my face and I said it at them like they were a microphone.

He was already snoring again, though, plus his feet smelled like tennis shoes, so I pulled the pillow over my face and pretended I was a mole rat and me and Wayne were in our nest underground. That kind of cheered me up after a while—I don't know why—and I finally fell asleep.

Chapter Ten

I HAD MY FIRST DANCE LESSON with Mrs. Turkel on Monday, after school. Darla had asked her for me because I was too nervous to ask her myself. Mrs. Turkel charged me twenty-five cents, which was my whole allowance for the week, but she didn't mess around. Right away she laid cardboard feet down on the floor for me to step on so I could learn the fox-trot. I didn't know why they called it that. It didn't look anything to me like a fox trotting.

"Sweetie pie," Mrs. Turkel said, "you're going to have to pay more attention if you're ever going to learn these steps. You're shuffling your shoes and kicking these instruction steps all over the place. Now I want you to forget all about them. I'm going to tape them to the floor so they'll just be here, but instead of looking down at them, I want you to try it this time with Darla—"

She crooked her finger at Darla, who had been sitting in a chair by the wall in their dining room, which was where we all were. The way Darla sat, with her feet flat on the floor, and her back straight, and with her hands folded in her lap, you would have thought she had been sitting there all that time at a fancy ball, like Cinderella waiting for a boy to come by and ask her to dance, instead of just watching me and her mom. Darla had on saddle shoes, bobby socks, a pleated skirt, and a button-up blouse with a Peter Pan collar, and except for her Shirley Temple ringlets, she almost looked like a regular girl.

Darla floated over and curtsied and lifted one hand so that when her mom pushed me toward her, my shoulder fit exactly under it. Darla stretched out her other arm and turned her hand palm down, just sort of hanging out there in space until her mom took my arm and pulled it out in the direction of Darla's and laid Darla's hand in mine, almost like it was a bird and I had caught it. She pulled on my other hand to stick it to Darla's side. Then Mrs. Turkel went back to the old scratchy record player, which must have been the one in Darwin's room, and put on a song she said was called "The Blue-Damn-You Waltz." I stomped on Darla's feet for a while, until I thought she was either going to cry or hit me, but then I sort of got it and said so to Darla, who said back, "Well, golly, I guess so, as hard as I'm having to back-lead," and that's when Mrs. Turkel said, "My goodness, look at the time. I do have to get back to work. You children keep practicing, but don't wake up Papa. You know he needs his rest this afternoon; he had a hard night last night."

Darwin, who had been leaning in the doorway watching, snickered and said, "*Hard*-ly." Mrs. Turkel gave him a dirty look and left the room.

Wayne had told me their grandpa was a general in the Second World War and fought the Germans and all—it was another one of those things Wayne just seemed to know—but I didn't believe a general would ever live in a town like ours, plus that didn't explain why he never came downstairs.

"Where does your mom work?" I asked Darla.

She said Dr. Rexroat's office. She was his receptionist. I said, "Oh yeah, I knew that already, I just forgot." Darla said her mom had been there in the morning, but Dr. Rexroat always closed down for a while in the afternoons to take his naps.

Darwin snickered again from the door. "He has to take his naps to sleep off his lunches," he said, and he made a drinking motion and said, "Glug, glug, glug. Like old granddad."

Darla said, "Come on, Dewey. Help me pull these feet up off the floor."

Darwin mimicked her with a fake high voice: "Come on, Dewey, come on, Dewey." Then in his regular voice he said I had to come on with him to help clean his room. I thought about those yellow sheets and his dirty rug and the stuff lying all over, almost as bad as their back porch, and I really didn't want to go with him. And I sure didn't want to play that game again, either.

Darla said I had to help her, and we had to move all the furniture back, too, and anyway, Darwin should have to clean up his own room; she always cleaned up hers by herself. Darwin made scissors with his fingers and said how would she like it if he subtracted a few of those ringlets, Shirley Baby? He said it out of the side of his mouth like a gangster or something, and I couldn't help laughing.

Darla said, "Don't laugh; you'll only encourage him." Darwin made more snipping motions, and said it, too: "Snip, snip, snip." Then he started chasing her around their big dining-room table over by the wall. "Snip, snip, snip. Snip, snip, snip." Darla screamed at him to cut it out and he said oh, he would cut it out all right, and he kept chasing her. I laughed until I had to sit down, and they kept it up until a door slammed somewhere upstairs really loud, and then they stopped like they had just gotten caught in a game of freeze tag. It was dead quiet in there, and I waited to hear footsteps above us, but there was just the echo of the door slamming, or maybe I just imagined there was an echo.

Finally I said I had to go and I would help with everything next time. They didn't even look at me, just stayed frozen like that, waiting, I guess, for their grandfather to come downstairs or whatever, not that I think he ever did.

▪ ▪ ▪

Everybody in seventh grade in the whole state of Florida took the class in Americanism vs. Communism, and nobody ever asked questions there, not even me. Our teacher was Mr. Cheeley, who had been in the South Pacific during World War II, which he kept reminding us, and who had these photos he let us look at— before and after pictures of a prisoner of war being executed: first the guy kneeling with his head on a hay bale and a Jap soldier standing next to him, with his sword raised up, then just the dead guy's body on the floor on one side of the hay bale and his head on the floor on the other side of the hay bale. The quality wasn't all that great, and you couldn't see his face at all in the before picture, but if you looked close, you could see part of his face after they chopped his head off. Some guys said you could tell he had been begging for his life, because his eyes and mouth were wide open in the after picture. I hoped that was wrong and it only looked that way because of the shadows.

Mr. Cheeley got choked up when he showed us the photos, which he said he found left behind when they liberated Midway or Guatemala or Portugal or Iwo Jima from the Japs; I forget which island exactly. He told us the names of all the good men he knew personally who gave their lives for America. He said he could still see the faces of some of them right now if he closed his own eyes, boys not so much older than us at our desks without a care in the world because we were so lucky, and we didn't have any idea or any appreciation for how good we had it, and we didn't know the meaning of the word *sacrifice*—

"And do you think the communists know the meaning of the word *sacrifice*?" he asked us. "Do you think the communists would have crossed Valley Forge in the dead of winter with General Washington, their feet bound up with rags because their shoes were worn out from years of fighting, and their fingers turning black from frostbite, turning black and falling off, but that's what they were willing to put up with for their independence from King George, who would have fit right in with the worst of them—Hirohito, Stalin, that whole murdering bunch?"

Mr. Cheeley said the Japs and the Germans and the Italians were fascists, but everybody else America had to fight was communists, and that included the North Koreans, the Red Chinese, the Vietcong, the Cubans, and of course the Russians, who were behind it all. He also said the trade unions were communist; and the National Association for Colored People, and Martin Luther King Jr.: all communist, all communist.

He didn't like colored people almost as much as he didn't like the communists, and the worst thing you could be, to hear him tell it, was both.

We didn't have much to say in that class. We didn't even take notes. There was a textbook, but what Mr. Cheeley put on the first test was just a single essay question: Did we agree (or disagree) that America should drop the atom bomb on North Vietnam to stop the spread of international communism? When I told my mom about all the stuff from class, she said, "Oh, good Lord."

◆ ◆ ◆

Me and Darla were in three classes together at school, including Americanism vs. Communism, but she never looked at Mr. Cheeley's photos. She always just kept her head down and, as soon as she got them, passed them right on to the next kid. I meant to ask her why, but we didn't talk much at school except in the hall, where we would say hi, and I must have forgot about it whenever I hung out with her riding bikes and having dance lessons and stuff. I guess it wasn't a good idea to talk to girls in front of everybody, because people might laugh or something. It was the same with Darwin, too, except I tried to avoid even running into him at school, especially when he told me that he had handcuffs and did I want to come up to his room and see them.

At lunch all that week I sat with Wayne and the guys from the neighborhood—W.J. Weller, and David Tremblay, and Connolly Voss, and sometimes Boopie Larent, who I guess wasn't too mad anymore about my wrecking his big attempt to set the world record for bouncing on the pogo stick. They didn't exactly talk to me much, but they let me sit there.

And every day either that guy Moe or the other one, Head, stopped at our table and took my roll from my lunch tray, which was usually the only good thing they ever gave you to eat at the cafeteria and was the thing that made you hungry all morning whenever you walked near the cafeteria between classes and smelled the bread baking and the margarine they melted on top of those big trays of bread. I don't know why they did that, or still wouldn't let me go to the WHITES ONLY bathroom, since the shoe polish had faded all the way away a while ago. I guess once they get it in their heads that you're colored, there's nothing you can do but try to stay out of their way.

The neighborhood guys just looked down at their trays when Head or Moe did that, even Wayne, and I couldn't eat afterward, so I usually went to my locker and kind of leaned inside of it with my head in there like I was looking for something. I got to where I wished those seniors would go ahead and give me my red belly and then maybe they might leave me alone to eat my rolls and go to the bathroom.

We all went to Wayne's first JV football game Thursday night— me and Mom and Dad and Tink. Fortunately almost nobody was there except some other parents, and I guess little brothers and sisters of the players. A dozen eighth- and ninth-grade girls were there, too, sitting all together in a big knot. I brought my homework but Dad said I had to pay attention to the game and support my brother, even though I pointed out that Wayne was sitting on the end of the bench just about the whole time. They let him in when they had a kickoff after the Mighty Miners scored a touchdown, but the return went the other way and Wayne was stuck on the wrong side of the field, blocking a guy who was stuck way out there in the middle of nowhere blocking him back. Neither one of them did it very hard, just sort of kept bumping each other like a couple of goats, or not even goats, but maybe sheep. I thought I saw Wayne right in the middle of things look over to see if the coach was watching. It was funny—once the kickoff was over, Wayne went back to his end of the bench on his side of the field, threw his helmet down and kicked it like he was really mad or really fired up or something, and the guy he was blocking went back to *his* end of the bench on his side of the field and threw his helmet down, too. The next time there was a kickoff, the two of them ran around on the wrong side of the field again until they found each other so they could do some more blocking.

It reminded me of this story, or I guess it was an Aesop's fable, where two rams got into a fight and started butting each other, but they were the same size so they kept butting each other and butting each other, neither one getting anywhere, no way either one could win, so they stayed at it all day, all night, the next day, the next night, and so on, wearing themselves down to just about nothing over the days and weeks until they were just the ends of a couple of tails, that was all that was left of them, and they still kept butting into each other until finally a gust of wind just came along and blew them away.

At halftime I got a candy bar with my own money but Dad made me share it with Tink anyway, which wasn't fair, and then he even made me give *him* a bite, which turned out to be the biggest bite in the history of our family.

I was too bored to even pretend to watch the second half of the game. About the only excitement was to see if they put Wayne in any other time besides the kickoffs, which they didn't.

JV football didn't seem like much fun to me, not like when we used to play in the empty lot next to our house. There would always be arguments and fights and stuff, but at least you got to play, even if you weren't any good, like me.

Darwin Turkel even came over one time last year. I think his mom might have made him. He didn't know how to play football, so everybody made fun of him, but he got picked for one of the teams anyway, because we needed one more guy. It turned out he was really fast. He caught up to W.J. Weller running for a touchdown, but instead of tackling him, Darwin grabbed W.J.'s arm and swung him in a circle and then pulled him to the ground. Darwin jumped up and down he was so excited, but W.J. had a broken arm, actually a broken shoulder.

At first a couple of guys defended Darwin and said it was just an accident, but W.J. got madder and madder until after a while we all agreed that Darwin had meant to do it. Nobody talked to him after that at school, and he never tried to get back in the football games. Guys made fun of Darwin for a while—called him Darla instead of Darwin, and Turtle instead of Turkel, and Peter Eater for no reason except we didn't like him. He didn't seem to notice, though. He just did like he always had: sat in the front of the class at school and answered all the questions right if the teacher called on him, but never raised his hand and looked like he was always bored but in a way that made you think he practiced it a lot in front of a mirror. He ate by himself or with one or two other prissy boys in the cafeteria, and never went to the real football games, and tap-danced with Darla when she sang "On the Good Ship Lollipop" at those talent shows at County Fair, and didn't seem to notice how much fun people made of him for that, either.

I was actually glad he was around back then because it meant they were less likely to make fun of me—for being slow, or short, or uncoordinated, or always being the one waving my hand in class to answer the questions, even when I didn't know the right answer. But there was just something inside me that needed to have the right answer, so I guessed at the question, hoping the teacher would give me that smile they always give you when you're right, and nod their head in the way they always do, and cross their arms but with the chalk between two fingers away from their sleeve, and say, "Very good, Dewey, that's correct. I can see someone did the assignment," or did the reading, or did their homework, or came to class prepared, or spent some time thinking about the problem, then, "Now, who can tell me—?"

And I would already have my arm up in the air wanting to answer that next question, too.

The JV team won twenty-one to seven. Tink fell asleep in Mom's lap. Dad ate a hot dog and got mustard on his shirt. I did all my homework, including a letter to General Westmoreland in Vietnam for Americanism vs. Communism, telling him to keep up the good work. I was kind of worried that Wayne would be sad, since he never did get in the game hardly at all, besides four kickoffs and some punts, but when Dad took us and David Tremblay out to the A&W afterward, it was kind of funny: David was in on about every play, of course, but the way Wayne and him talked and talked about the game, you'd have thought Wayne was, too.

Chapter Eleven

AFTER LUNCH ON SUNDAY, I fell asleep on the floor in front of the TV, and when I woke up, everybody was gone except Dad. Wayne was probably somewhere with David Tremblay. Tink and Mom had left a note saying that they were visiting the shut-ins, including this old lady Mrs. Cronk and her parrot, Jehosaphat, the one Darla had wanted me to go spy on with her. Dad was asleep in his easy chair with the newspaper for a blanket and the TV on to a Baltimore Colts game.

I went outside and stood in the sun for a couple of minutes with my eyes closed. Sometimes when you do that and then you open your eyes, everything looks different to you and strange, but not today. It was all still my house and my yard and my street. Still the same Sand Mountain. So I got out my bike and rode over to Darla's.

She wasn't home but Darwin was.

"What is he doing here?" he said in his usual prissy voice when he finally opened the door, like I wasn't standing right there and he wasn't really talking to me. I noticed he had combed his hair over to the side all neat like the Beach Boys. "Oh, wait," he said. "I've got it. He's looking for Darla. He loves Darla. He wants Darla to have a baby with him."

"Just shut up, Darwin," I said.

Darwin looked all around on the porch, everywhere but at me, like he was talking to a crowd of people. "He's upset. You can tell because his cheeks are red. He misses his Darla."

"What are you being so mean for?" I said. "I didn't do anything to you."

"Oh, no!" Darwin panted. "His feelings are hurt. He's going to cry now. Take your seats, everybody. He's going to cry. Here it comes. The dam's about to break. It's going to be a flood. Grab your life preservers. Man the lifeboats. Women and children first."

I called him a turd-knocker and jumped off the porch, not even bothering with the steps, and picked up my bike.

That changed his sorry tune pretty quick. "I was just kidding," he said. "Don't go. They're probably just out riding Darla's old nag. Come on."

I turned around. "Why are you always so mean?"

He said, "I don't know what you're talking about. You're the silliest boy I ever met. Come inside and I'll get you a Coke from the Frigidaire." We never had sodas in our house, so it was hard to turn down a free one at somebody else's. I put down my bike and followed Darwin inside, where it was cool and dark, and down a long hall next to the stairs. At the end of the hall was the kitchen, and it was enough to make you never want to eat again in your entire life. They had dirty dishes and pots and pans and glasses and silverware piled everywhere on the counter, and a trash can without a lid on it and garbage that spilled over on the floor and would have to be cleaned up, but probably not by anybody in the Turkel family except Darla, who had already told me that she was the only neat one in the whole house.

"Where's the Coke?" I said. He opened the Frigidaire, which probably used to be white but was now yellow, like Darwin's sheets. He pulled out a bottle that somebody had already drunk out of and handed it to me. It didn't even have the cap on.

"Last one, and it's all yours," he said, as if I couldn't see what was going on.

"Somebody already drank most of it," I said.

Darwin shrugged. "They must have poured a glass. Probably Darla. She's always doing that. But nobody put their mouth on the bottle, I swear."

I was pretty thirsty, so I took a swig. It was the flattest Coke in the history of the world and I spit it out in their sink, on top of the pile of dishes. The whole thing was disgusting. I thought I saw a palmetto bug in there crawling around on the dirty plates.

"I'm leaving," I said, and I did, even though he offered to fix me a ham sandwich with mustard, then he offered to teach me a boy dance instead of those girl dances of Darla's, then he offered to take me up to his room and show me some new stuff he had gotten recently from his grandfather that he couldn't tell me about, he could only *show* me and I had to come upstairs if I wanted to see it. He was so desperate I started to feel sorry for him, but that just made me want to get out of there faster.

I heard somebody call for him from somewhere upstairs—it must have been his grandfather—and Darwin looked like he would rather be anywhere in the world than where he was. I don't know why Darwin couldn't just leave and go somewhere—go anywhere—but he didn't, and I sure wasn't about to invite him to come with me.

My next stop was Boopie Larent's house. He wasn't home, either, though, just Dottie, and she said her mom didn't want me at their house.

"You're lying," I said to Dottie.

"No, I'm not," she said. "Stick around and I just might have to call the police."

"How about if I spit in your yard?" I said, which was pretty dumb but all I could think of.

She put her hands on her hips like she was her mom and said, "I might have to call the police for that, too."

"On what charge?"

"Trespassing," she said. "And public nuisance. And loitering."

"What's loitering?"

"It's a very serious charge."

"What does it mean? I bet you don't even know."

"Yes, I do."

"Then tell me."

"I don't have to."

"Then I don't have to leave."

"Yes, you do."

"No, I don't."

"Yes, you do."

"No, I don't."

I had to admit I was having fun arguing with Dottie, and I would have been happy to keep doing it for a while. She was in Wayne's grade but it was obvious to anybody that I was a lot smarter than her. But then things got out of hand the way they always do just when you think they're going just fine. She called me Little Black Sambo, which nobody had called me for a couple of weeks and I didn't like, and I called her Fat-stuff, which she *really* didn't like, and she didn't bother with calling the police, she just chased me out of their yard with a rake.

Now I was completely out of anybody to do anything with. No Wayne, no David Tremblay, no Mom or Dad or Tink, no Darla, no Boopie, and *not* Darwin Turkel and *not* Dottie Larent, and I don't think I had any other friends that I knew about. I didn't want to go home yet. I didn't have any money to go to the drugstore to buy a comic book or a milk shake. I guess I could have gone over to Connolly Voss's house, which was just a couple of blocks away from Boopie's, but he was less of anybody's friend than me, just one of those guys who lived in the neighborhood so was always a part of things because of that.

It was late in the afternoon and the streets were so empty you'd have thought they'd had an atom bomb that killed everybody except me. That made me feel pretty lonely, not seeing anybody and not having anybody to see, so I did what I hadn't done in a long time—rode my bike out of the city limits and down Brewster Road a little ways to the turnoff to the W. R. Grace mine, and then down that road, which was a one-lane blacktop with potholes you had to dodge all the time, so it looked like you were drunk, weaving all over, but that was what you had to do to get from Sand Mountain the town to Sand Mountain the mountain, which some people said was the tallest place in Florida and I thought was about the best place in the world.

You couldn't see the mountain when you were in town because of all the trees, unless maybe you were on top of the Skeleton Hotel, where of course nobody ever went since it was haunted. Once you got to Brewster Road you could see just fine, though, because all that land had been mined out and was flat as anything, plus Sand Mountain stood in the middle of a big swamp of nothing and was thirty stories high—that's what Dad told me—and so white that you couldn't hardly look at it in the middle of the day, the sun reflected off of it so bright. The sand got too hot for anybody to play on it then, too, but you could later in the afternoons.

It was the W. R. Grace Company, the company my dad worked for, that made Sand Mountain. They pumped their left-over sand to that one spot in the middle of a swamp from the processing plant after they shook out all the phosphate rock. Most of the mining companies just spread their leftover sand around the old mines—they called it the tailings—but one of the problems with that was sinkholes, and one time W. R. Grace had a sinkhole right in the middle of a mine road and a bulldozer fell in so deep they never got it out.

After ten years they couldn't pump their sand any higher, so they quit making Sand Mountain, and then after they tested to make sure it wasn't going to have avalanches that might kill everybody, they let people climb on it. At first everybody tried to run down from the top, and some still did, or they rolled like crazy maniacs and got sand everywhere in their clothes and their hair and their mouths and their ears. Then one day somebody dragged the first cardboard box to the top and tore it apart and sat on it and lifted up the front end so it wouldn't snag under the sand and rode it all the way down to the bottom going a hundred miles an hour.

It was about five o'clock when I got to Sand Mountain, and I figured I would be able to climb up, which took about a half an hour, and slide back down, which took about thirty seconds, and still make it home for dinner. At first I thought I was the only one there, since I didn't see any cars or trucks or anything. I tried to lean my bike up on the kickstand where everybody parked, but the sand was too soft so I just laid it down, even though I could hear my dad telling me a hundred times never to do that because it would get sand in the chain and the sprocket.

Then I saw a flash of something over in the bushes, some color that wasn't part of the bush, and when I went to investigate, I knew what it was right away, and whose it was, too: red, white, and blue streamers in the handles, playing cards in the spokes, pink banana seat, pink PF Flyer.

That made me pretty happy, and I hurried up and grabbed a big piece of cardboard that somebody had left, and started the long climb to the top, which was slow because my feet sunk in with every step since it wasn't packed sand like at the beach, and because it was so steep, about a forty-five-degree angle. Looking up, I had to squint. You could see for about five whole miles from the top, which meant even though you couldn't see Sand Moun-tain from the *town* of Sand Mountain, you could see all of the *town* of Sand Mountain from Sand Mountain. I am afraid of heights really bad—almost as bad as my claustrophobia—but at the same time, one of the things I like best is being really high up and seeing everything there is to see.

So I kept climbing and sinking and climbing and pulling the

cardboard, which got heavier, especially when I dragged it too low and it cut into the sand and got sand on top of it and I had to drag the weight of that, too. Pretty soon I was sweating from the top of my head to the bottom of my tennis shoes, and wished I had taken them off and left them with my bike, but by the time I thought about that, I was already about a quarter of the way up, so I just kept climbing, plus I didn't want to take too long getting to the top in case Darla might come flying down on her own cardboard right past me and then I'd probably never catch up with her.

But I still had to rest every now and then, Darla or no Darla, and when I did, I got to see the town way down below and how it looked like graph paper the way everything was laid out so neat except for stuff like the field next to my house, a grove behind Nora Barnes's house, the high school and Lewis Elementary, and the Riverside Cemetery, where Darla got in trouble drinking with a colored boy and setting off firecrackers, if you could believe Wayne about anything. Over by the Peace River where the Boogerbottom was it didn't look like graph paper anymore but instead a bunch of gray boxes and winding dirt streets and gray trees and Spanish moss and smoke and a pile of old tires you could see that was about five stories high that a colored man had collected and saved that they called the Tire Tower.

Away from the river, over next to the Bartow Highway, was the Pits, four man-made lakes separated from one another by little dikes you could walk on, left over from one of the first phosphate mines there ever was in Florida. They said the Pits was so deep, nobody had ever touched bottom in the middle, and when somebody drowned, they couldn't ever find the body. When you swam down under where the sun couldn't reach, it was so cold your teeth shook even in the hottest part of summer. My mom, one time when we all climbed to the top of Sand Mountain, pointed to the Pits and said, "Look, Dewey, it's the four chambers of the heart right there—left ventricle, left auricle, right ventricle, right auricle," and I have never been able to look at the Pits since then without thinking about that.

Farther out was Moon's Stable, where Darla kept her horse and where there were some pastures and barns and stuff. I hadn't been out there with her yet, but she kept saying she was going to bring me to ride the horse someday. Mostly up that way it was just old mines that they had left, and it looked like the surface of the moon. West as far as you could see were the mines where they were still digging—miles and miles and miles of mines with their draglines and processing plants and float houses and water cannons and float crews and dams and chemical plants and pipelines and booster pumps and train tracks and open boxcars with the regular phosphate they carried over to the Port of Tampa to ship to where they made fertilizer and stuff, and the special cars for what they called Triple Super Phosphate, which Dad said was what they had when they mixed phosphate with sulfuric acid and which you couldn't have be anywhere in the air or it would explode, so they shipped it in sealed tanks and Dad said it was funny that it was that dangerous, because if you ever saw it, it looked just like honey.

I don't know what Darla was doing up there—probably dancing or something—but I was so tired when I finally made it to the top of Sand Mountain that I just waved to her and then fell right down on my cardboard and lay there looking up at the sky. The flat top of the mountain was about as big as my bedroom, so it was only a couple of seconds before Darla came over and I saw her face staring down at me.

"Are you following me?" she said. "Because if you are, I have a right to know why."

I closed my eyes. When I opened them again, she was still there. "Well?" she said. "Well?"

I didn't know what to say. I thought she'd be happy to see me so I said that: "Aren't you happy to see me?"

Darla crossed her arms. "That depends."

I sat up. "Depends on what?"

"On whether you'll let me bury you."

I said how about if I let her share my cardboard to ride down on instead. Darla sniffed and said she already had her own and did I think she was stupid or something that she would climb all the way to the top of Sand Mountain without her own cardboard, for goodness sake?

"OK," I said. "You can bury me, I guess. But I wasn't following you."

"Oh, sure you weren't," Darla said. Then she said I had to help her dig the hole to bury me in, which I did, and pretty soon I was standing in a four-foot hole and she was covering me up until I just had my head sticking out of the sand. It was hot and sweaty and itchy everywhere, even the deep parts. I held my breath as long as I could while she packed sand up around my neck. I didn't want to get it up my nose and in my mouth. I hadn't even got to stand up and look around yet, but that's just how it was with Darla.

She said, "You know my mom can hold her breath longer than anybody in the world."

I asked how come?

She said because her mom used to be a mermaid at Weeki Wachee Springs, which I already knew, and all the mermaids had to do that, but her mom was the best. She said once her mom held her breath for five whole minutes. I said nobody could hold their breath for five minutes, not even the Great Houdini, who I had read a book about. Darla said did I want her to cover my whole head in sand, too? Then I better take back what I said. I said I wasn't going to take it back and I tried to get my arms out, but she had piled too much sand and I couldn't lift them, and she scooped more sand up to where it was right at the bottom of my lips and just about to go into my mouth.

"OK," I said. "Maybe your mom did."

"Maybe?"

I spit out some sand. "Definitely."

Darla brushed away the sand from my mouth and stood up. "Now, what should I sing?"

I said, "How about 'It's Howdy Doody Time'?"

She gave me a look like I had just said the stupidest thing ever. "Maybe I should bury your head anyway."

"You better not," I said.

Darla said, "Oh, all right," and then she sang the entire song of "Strangers in the Night," while I blinked out grains of sand that kept blowing in my face. Mostly she stayed where I could see her, and she did a little dance while she sang. It was like the whole world was just her and me, or at least my head sticking out of the sand, and the top of Sand Mountain, and the big blue sky.

When Darla stopped singing, she came over and lay down next to me in the sand. "Dewey," she said, "close your eyes." I closed my eyes. She asked did I want her to kiss me? I opened my eyes and she was looking right at me and she was so close I could even smell her. She smelled like chocolate. "Well, do you?" she asked. I hadn't ever kissed a girl before, and I thought about her with the colored boy in the cemetery and wondered if she kissed him, and I thought about Darwin and his Turn Out the Lights game and wondered why they were always tying people up and burying them in that family, and I got nervous, and she asked, "Do you?" one more time, and I just said, "Heck no."

Darla stood straight up when I said that, which of course kicked a bunch of sand right in my face. Then she tore on out of there and didn't say anything else: not good-bye, or more about kissing, or anything—just grabbed her sled and disappeared down the mountain.

It must have taken me a whole other half hour to finally dig myself loose, but at least she left me my cardboard so I could slide down, too. I should have known that was what would happen when I said the "Heck no," I guess, but I hadn't ever been around girls too much before, and never anybody like Darla.

Chapter Twelve

IT TOOK ME A COUPLE OF DAYS to get Darla to talk to me again. On Monday when I saw her at school, she acted like Darwin did that one time and said stuff about me like I wasn't even there. I really hated that. I said I was sorry I didn't want her to kiss me up on Sand Mountain, and she just looked up at the sky and said, "Some boys are so conceited, they actually think some girls want to kiss them, when that's just the biggest lie." Then she walked away real fast like she was busy. It wasn't fair that I was the one to apologize, of course, but saying sorry wasn't too hard—I'd had so much practice that it sort of came natural.

On Tuesday night I made Tink watch that old movie *Heidi* with me on TV that had Shirley Temple in it, so I could try to talk to Darla about it since I knew she was so crazy about Shirley Temple and all, but that didn't work, either. When I saw her the next day, she just looked up at the sky that time, too, and said, "I think I see Superman." It was the dumbest trick in the world but I fell for it, and when I looked up, she ran away and jumped on her bike.

My mom told me she read in the paper that Shirley Temple had gotten married and I tried to talk to Darla about that on Thursday, but she just said everybody already knew that old news, for goodness sake. I could tell I was making progress, though, because at least she said it *to* me and not just sort of *about* me.

Finally on Friday she decided we could be friends again, I guess, because she showed up at my house after school—or rather she sat on her bike across the street from our house until I finally happened to go outside and see her. She said why didn't we go back to that old bridge at Bowlegs Creek, so we did and she showed me some of her tap steps, with our feet hanging over the edge so I could do it along with her without getting my feet twisted up and falling down and hurting myself. We were kind of in a rhythm—kick, tap, step, slide, kick, tap, step, slide, tappa-tappa-tappa-tappa—and since I wasn't sure what else to talk about, I told her that my dad planned to knock down the Skeleton Hotel as part of his campaign promises.

Darla pointed her toes way out and rolled her feet down like they were bananas, which she had told me was what ballerinas did. She said, "You know it's haunted, don't you?"

I said sure I did. Everybody knew it was haunted from when they were building it and two guys up on the top got knocked off a girder. One fell straight down and broke all his bones but he lived. The other one—a colored guy—grabbed on to a rope and hung on there for a long time. At first he yelled for help, then he cried, then he got quiet, then his hands and him just slipped away. They said he didn't make a sound the whole way down. Just fell and died.

Darla asked me if I'd ever heard him.

"Heard the ghost?" I said.

She sniffed. "Heard the *Howler*."

I asked her what was the Howler and she kicked me. "It's who howls on the top of the Skeleton Hotel. It's what makes it haunted. What did you think it was—a dumb dog?"

I said no, I thought it was that colored guy, but I didn't think he would howl or anything like that. I started to explain about him not making a sound at the end and when he fell, so it didn't make sense for him to start howling now, ten years later.

Darla folded her arms and sniffed again.

"Well, I heard it, so I ought to know."

I didn't actually believe her for a second, but she said it was true, and then she told me this story about how one time her family was driving home from Tampa and got back to Sand Mountain at midnight and their car stalled at the one stoplight in town. Nobody was anywhere, but Darla's mom figured the police had to drive by sometime, so they just waited in the road. It was dead quiet, not even a dog, not even another car, nothing. Just the Sinclair station on one corner, City Hall on another corner, the new 7-Eleven on the other, and the Skeleton Hotel on the other, with the tarps rolled down on the sides of the ground floor where they had the farmers' market.

Darwin fell asleep. Their mom fell asleep. Their grandfather had already been asleep and never even woke up when the car died. After a while Darla got out. She thought it was funny to be there in the middle of the road, just stopped under the light. She practiced her tap dancing. When she got tired, she lay down in the road, right directly under the stoplight. The road was still warm even though the sun had gone down a long time before. Green-yellow-red, green-yellow-red. She tried to see if she could hold her breath through the whole of green-yellow-red. She did that for a while and so admitted to me that maybe she was dizzy from a lack of oxygen, but that was when she heard the howling from the top of the Skeleton Hotel. It scared her so bad she said she thought she was going to soil herself, which I didn't know what that meant but pretended I did.

Anyway, when she heard that stuff, Darla jumped back in her car and screamed and woke everybody up. Her mom didn't know what was going on and for some reason just turned the key in the ignition and the car started right up. Darla kept screaming and was too scared to talk when her mom asked her what was the matter, why was she screaming, so her mom slapped Darla in the face to make her stop, but that just made Darla keep screaming, so her mom put her hand over Darla's mouth and kept it there and drove on home with one hand.

She finally calmed down and told her mom about what she heard at the Skeleton Hotel, and her mom told her to just hush and never mind what she heard, she was a girl with too much imagination and it was going to get her in trouble someday and she should quit making up stories, that it was probably a dog somewhere and she was confused and she was old enough that she shouldn't get so hysterical about things.

"But I really heard it," Darla told me. "Nobody believes me, but I really heard it."

Her voice turned into a whisper. "So I think we should go back there before your dad tears it down."

I said, "What do you mean?" even though I already knew, and she started talking about the Howler of the Skeleton Hotel like it was a Nancy Drew book, which she had obviously read a lot of, and since I had read all the Hardy Boys, I said "Sure," like I did that sort of thing all the time. I thought about telling her I had a magnifying glass we could use, although I had no idea how that would help, but you never knew. But then I thought maybe that was something I ought to keep to myself.

I said maybe we could buy a special notebook and see if we could find some invisible ink to write everything down, and have a secret meeting back at Bowlegs Creek to plan out what we were going to do, and I could bring some sandwiches if Darla brought something for us to drink. She nodded a lot, like what I was saying made plenty of sense, but once I shut up, she just said, "We better go tonight." I told her they didn't have the election until November and this was still September, and my Dad wouldn't win, anyway, because he never won, and probably nobody else wanted to tear down the Skeleton Hotel, but Darla said we couldn't be sure.

"Once an idea gets around, people believe it just because somebody said it was a good idea," she said. "It's the same as gossip and the way people believe all of that. And I can't stand gossip. Not one little bit."

She looked at me hard, then she added, "The thing I like about you is you're not a big fat gossip like some people." Her face was all red when she finished, and I thought maybe it had something to do with what happened in the cemetery with the colored boy, which I still hadn't ever asked her about.

I had to go — it was Friday afternoon and my dad was making me go with them to the varsity game that night — but before I did, Darla told me the trick to making yourself wake up at a certain time was to repeat that time over and over in your mind as you were falling asleep and then you'd automatically wake up when you wanted to. So when we got back home after the game and finally went to bed, I said, "Midnight, midnight, midnight, midnight," until Wayne started snoring on the bottom bunk, and then I said, "Shut up, shut up, shut up," but he wouldn't until finally I whacked him with my pillow.

At 12:30 somebody woke me up scratching at the window, or I dreamed about somebody scratching at the window. I sat up with my heart running so fast I thought it would explode, then I remembered.

"You were supposed to meet me at midnight," Darla said once I got outside, which took about ten hours because the floor creaked every time I took a step, and I kept thinking I heard somebody else getting out of bed, and the window got stuck when I tried to open it, and the screen fell out when I pushed it.

I said I was sorry, it was Wayne's fault, which was the only phony excuse I could come up with, and it wasn't really an excuse, just blaming somebody else, but Darla didn't catch me on it; she just said, "Who's Wayne?"

I couldn't tell if she was being serious or not, but I guess she was. She was always surprising me like that, making a big issue out of not knowing things I just assumed she knew because it was stuff everybody just knew. "He's my brother," I said. "You know—Wayne Turner? My brother? *Wayne?*"

She said, "Oh, big deal, so you have a brother, I have a brother, everybody has a brother, so what about it?"

I said, "So nothing about it, but you asked was all." It was turning into another one of *those* conversations with Darla, which never made sense to me, and made even less sense the more I tried to make it make sense, but it did help me get over being so nervous, I guess, and by the time I decided to give up on the whole dumb conversation, we were all the way down Orange to Second, and a little ways down Second toward downtown.

I stopped.

"What?" Darla said. "Why'd you do that?"

I said I was listening. I wanted to see if I heard anything. She said, "Good idea," and we both froze, standing on the edge of David Tremblay's yard under their oak tree where it bent low to the ground. I heard her breathing and I heard myself breathing. I smelled her, too. She had on perfume. And she was wearing jeans rolled up really high, which I had never seen before, like she was expecting a flood, and a black T-shirt that was big on her, and tennis shoes. You never knew with Darla what she would look like, except for her hair, which was always the same. I said, "Let's go," but she said to wait; she thought she heard something. I listened some more but didn't hear anything, so we took off again.

A block later she grabbed my arm. "I heard it again," she said. I asked her what and she said footsteps. I started to say something else but she squeezed my arm and said, "Be quiet," and this time I heard something for real, too, and when I looked back where Darla was looking, I saw the shape of somebody in the shadows just off the street about half a block away.

"Run," I whispered.

"No," she said. "Let's keep going and see if he follows us."

"OK," I said. So we walked a ways and stopped. He walked a ways and stopped. We walked some more. He walked some more. I could hardly breathe and neither could Darla, judging by her hiccups. It was dark as anything for most of the block, and even darker under the trees. There were clouds, so no stars or moon,

114 •

so the only light just about anywhere was the streetlights at the end of the block. When we got to the next corner, we ran across it and into the shadows again and then waited to see who it was when he got in the light, but I was shaking so hard everything looked blurry to me. Darla was shaking, too. "I have to pee," she said, which surprised me since I had never heard her talk like that before. For a second it almost made me forget somebody was following us.

Who, it turned out, was just Wayne.

Chapter Thirteen

WAYNE WAS GRINNING LIKE SUZY, our dog. I had never seen him like that before. He wanted to know everything about everything: Who was this I was with, where were we going, was Darla that girl that sang and danced at the county fairs, didn't she have a brother who did that, too, how come he never saw her around anywhere? I couldn't believe all the big baloney. If Wayne knew about Darla being drunk with a colored boy, I figured he must have known all that other stuff already, too.

He kept pushing his hair off his forehead the whole time he talked, even though his hair wasn't *on* his forehead. It took me a second but I finally figured out what was going on, which was that Wayne was *flirting*. Darla hardly looked at him, which I was happy about, but at the same time I noticed she didn't seem to exactly mind answering his nosy questions. I asked him what was the deal with him following us, and he put his arm around my shoulders and said, "You made so much noise, I'm surprised the whole family didn't follow you. I tell you, if you're thinking about being a cat burglar, you better not quit your day job."

Darla actually laughed when he said that. I couldn't believe it. I pushed his arm off of me and decided I didn't know who this guy was, but he sure as heck wasn't Wayne. Wayne had never put his arm around my shoulders in his whole life.

"Just come on," I said. "It's way past midnight and we probably already missed it."

"Missed what?" Wayne said—to Darla. She kicked at something in the street, which I couldn't see—a microscopic pebble, I guess—and she said, "We just thought there might be a ghost at the Skeleton Hotel, that's all."

I couldn't believe this either. "What are you talking about?" I said to Darla. "You heard it, remember?"

Wayne said it was a good thing he decided to come along, then.

So we all three went. For the next couple of blocks I let them know I was annoyed, and I gave them all sorts of directions— "Don't walk so loud," and "We're almost there," and "OK, this way." Then I said, "Maybe we should practice jumping into a ditch in case somebody comes along," and I heard Wayne whispering something to Darla that made her laugh again, but I couldn't tell what it was.

After about eight blocks we got past most of the houses and then the row of churches that all faced on to First Street. We could see the backs of them from where we were on Second Street—the First Baptist, the First Methodist, and the First Presbyterian, each one of them taking up a block all on its own. Then there were a couple of houses again. We cut through a yard, then down a street, then through an alley and then we were there, at the corner of First Street and Bartow Highway. The Sinclair station was closed and dark, so we snuck up onto the concrete island with the three pumps, where we could see everything but nobody could see us unless they drove all the way in under the little roof and pointed their light directly at us. Sinclair was my favorite gasoline because of the dinosaur. They had a station over at Weeki Wachee Springs that my dad took me to one time that actually *was* a dinosaur—a giant concrete brontosaurus painted bright green, standing over the pumps.

To the right of us, on the other side of the highway, was City Hall with its one yellow light on at the top of the steps. Kitty-corner across the intersection was the new 7-Eleven, which was closed and dark like the Sinclair station. And directly across First Street, in the middle of a big dirt parking lot, was the Skeleton Hotel.

Looking up at it, I got kind of scared all of a sudden, I don't know why, and I said, "God."

Darla said that I shouldn't take the Lord's name in vain. I said, "I didn't say God *damn it;* I just said *God.*" And she said, "Well, it's still taking the Lord's name in vain." I said I was a Methodist and we didn't believe that, even though I thought she might be right, but what I wanted to do was remind her that she was supposed to be my friend, and when did she all of a sudden get to be such a great pal of Wayne's? I didn't, though, and I sure didn't tell her the other thing I had been thinking a lot about, which was kissing. Ever since she had asked me if I wanted her to on top of Sand Mountain when I was buried, I had been thinking about it, and I had sort of thought maybe tonight, except now here was Wayne butting in.

I realized I was hugging one of the gas pumps, so I quit and said, "I thought we were here to see about the Skeleton Hotel. What happened to that big plan?" Darla said the big plan was we should listen and see if we heard anything, so we all sat down on the island, her and Wayne squeezed between two of the pumps, and me between the others. None of us said anything else for a while and it got really really quiet and you could tell from how quiet it was how much noise we must have been making before.

I stuck my hands in my pockets. One had a hole, so I poked a finger in and worked it around until pretty soon I could just about put my whole hand through. I scratched my leg and thought how strange it was to be so scared tonight when I must have gone by the Skeleton Hotel about a million times and hardly even noticed it. When we went with Mom to the farmers' market, I usually forgot that I was even under a building or anything, it was just there up above, the red steel and wood scaffolding and a construction elevator and unfinished stairs that stopped before they even made it to the second floor.

I looked over at Wayne and Darla and wished they were sitting with me, even if they were only a little ways away. I wanted to go ahead and hear the howling that Darla said she had heard that night with her family. If I heard that, and they heard it, too, that would be enough for one night. We didn't actually have to go over there. We could come back another time to check it out up close. Plus it was getting so late. What if Dad came in our room to check on us and we weren't there and he thought we'd been kidnapped? I bet Mom would be really upset, and I never liked for that to happen. If you got Dad upset, he would yell at you or pull out the belt, or do something like call the police right away if he thought you'd been kidnapped, but Mom was different, and I didn't want to think about how disappointed she would be in me and Wayne once she found out we'd just snuck out of the house instead of being held for ransom.

Something banged into something behind the Sinclair station and made me jump. I was feeling nervous, anyway, I guess, and maybe that was why I stood up, but it was a bad idea no matter why I did it, because of course there came the one lousy cop car in the whole town right then, cruising up First Street toward the light.

Probably if I hadn't moved again, just stood there by the pumps in the dark, in the shadows of the Sinclair station, the cop wouldn't have seen me. I tried holding my breath but I was too scared, and I knew Wayne and Darla were scared, too, because they were even holding hands and when I saw that, I started to hyperventilate, and that sounded louder than anything, and then I thought I heard Wayne say something and that did it. I yelled, "Run!" and took off around the back of the Sinclair station. I didn't know my legs could go that fast—like the Flash in comic books—but they had to keep up with how fast my heart was beating, and once I got going at that speed I couldn't slow down much because my heart wouldn't have anywhere to send all that blood and something bad might happen, like maybe my arteries and veins would swell up and explode.

A siren whooped behind me—maybe the cop was whipping through the Sinclair to chase us—so I cut down an alley, then a street, then through a backyard, then past the First Presbyterian church, then behind the First Methodist. That's about where I realized that my legs and heart might be going as fast as the Flash, but the thing slowing me down was my lungs turning into sandpaper, which I bet never happened to the Flash, so I ducked behind the trash cans, and only then realized that Wayne and Darla hadn't followed me and weren't anywhere around.

I was still hyperventilating, which I always did when I got too excited. My mom always brought out a paper bag when that happened and crumpled it together at the opening and told me to breathe in it, but I didn't have my mom there. I didn't have a paper bag; I didn't have anything. I was about to cry, actually, because I was so scared and because I didn't know what happened to Wayne and Darla.

Then it got worse: the cop car turned down Second Street, his blue light blipping round and round but his siren not on. He was crawling along about six inches every minute or so with his searchlight aimed at the backs of the houses two blocks up, but even going that slow he kept getting closer and closer. I couldn't move. He inched past the block with the houses and moved on to the Presbyterian Church, one block up, where they had their trash cans out back just like the Methodists. He might have even stopped there and I thought about taking the opportunity to take off running again, but then I kicked something behind me and knew right away what it was because I'd snuck through it a million times before, playing hide-and-seek—a door into the ground for the church's fallout shelter, which was never locked because if you locked it, then how would people ever get in if the Russians dropped the bomb in the middle of Sunday service, which as Mr. Cheeley had told us was exactly when communists *would* drop the bomb.

I didn't even think about it. I just pulled hard and the door scraped open and I climbed down inside and shut the door behind me. Just in time.

You can think about a lot of things when you're sitting in a bomb shelter in the middle of the night and it's so black you can't see your hand, and you're scared of the dark and you're claustrophobic and the cops are after you so you can't do anything about any of those things except try not to hyperventilate again. I sat there on a step like a blind man to wait until the cop was gone and I could finally go home, only how was I going to know the coast was clear without going back outside where the cop might be waiting? I listened as hard as I could but the only thing I heard was my own sandpaper breathing, which got quieter after a while but still echoed. I tried holding my breath to see if I could hear any better but got nothing with that, either. And I was shaking about a hundred times worse than I ever did in my life, and my mind was racing around a track like a greyhound dog. Where were Wayne and Darla? What happened to them? What if they got caught? What if it was my fault?

I decided I'd better pray awhile, so I started in on the Lord's Prayer but that sounded too lonely, so I sang it the way we did in school when they played it over the PA system after the Pledge of Allegiance and before the announcements:

> *Our Fa-ther*
> *Who art in hea-ven*
> *Hallow-ed be thy name.*

For some reason, even as scared as I was, that got me thinking about how everybody said I had a pretty voice when they made us sing in the vesper choir at church—actually me and Boopie Larent—they said we were better sopranos than the girls, only I didn't want to sing like girls, and I also hated Mr. Rupert, the choir director, who was always grabbing your leg when you messed up and squeezing your thigh real hard and saying, "Boy, you want to see how the horse eats corn?" I guess his hand was supposed to be the horse's mouth, and your leg was the corn.

I don't know how long I sat there thinking about dumb stuff like that, but I finally had to come out. My claustrophobia got so bad I thought there were things in there touching me that I couldn't see, plus I couldn't breathe, either, and I got panicked that I might be running out of air. What I wanted to do was run home, but after I peeked out for a while and didn't see the cop, and then climbed out and just stood there for a couple of minutes until I could stop shaking so bad, I made myself go back downtown to look for Wayne and Darla.

As far as I went was the dark side of the Sinclair station. At first I just looked around, but when I didn't see any sign of them or of the police car, I tried whispering their names as loud as I could, which when you're whispering isn't very loud, of course. Nobody said anything back, even though I listened so hard it made my ears hurt.

And then I heard something else: not the cop again, but the little elevator on the Skeleton Hotel that nobody even knew could work—the freight elevator, which was just a pallet and cables. I couldn't actually see anything, but it must have been at the top of the Skeleton Hotel and then brought somebody to the ground floor, which was just the farmers' market, because a minute later somebody came out of there and walked across the road right toward the Sinclair station, then right on by, not even noticing me in the shadows because I didn't move and didn't breathe and didn't make a single solitary sound.

It was a lady with a long coat and a hood, or else the ghost of a lady—I couldn't tell because she went by so fast, plus I was so scared I squeezed my eyes shut until she was gone.

That right there would have been enough of a shock to me, but I never got to think about it too much because a minute later, after the lady got out of sight, I heard something howling from the top of the Skeleton Hotel and that was it for me. I got out of there as fast as I could and didn't stop running until I got all the way home, and crawled in the window, and saw that Wayne wasn't home, and threw my clothes in the dirty-clothes pile, and crawled up in the bunk bed. When my heart stopped galloping, I said my prayers, which I hadn't done earlier when I went to bed the first time, before sneaking out. I prayed that nothing had followed me, and prayed about where the heck was Wayne, anyway, and what happened to Darla, too, and I kept praying like that until don't ask me how but I fell asleep.

Chapter Fourteen

"RISE AND SHINE, BOYS. Fence won't paint itself and breakfast is waiting."

That's what Dad said when he came banging into our bedroom the next morning. He yanked open the blinds and turned on the overhead light and said it was eight o'clock already, and Saturday morning, and time to get cracking. I felt like crying but sat up because I knew it wasn't any use. Saturday was chore day and we always had to get up early, but nobody had said anything about us having to paint the fence. Wayne just kept snoring on the bottom bunk until Dad pulled down the covers and dumped him on the floor in his underwear.

"Let's go," Dad said. I couldn't believe how happy he was when me and Wayne were so tired and miserable, but he didn't seem to notice. I wondered if he knew we had snuck out and all, and maybe that's why he was going to make us paint the fence, but if so he didn't say anything about it, but just finally left. "Breakfast is on the table," he yelled back at us, and I knew what that meant. I crawled off the top bunk.

Wayne was trying to cover himself on the floor with the rug. "Where *were* you last night?" I said, but he didn't answer.

"Well?" I said, but got nothing except he groaned under the rug. I accidentally kicked him on my way out of the bedroom and forgot to say I was sorry.

The kitchen table was loaded with everything you might need to get ready for chores: scrambled eggs, cheese grits, orange juice, halves of grapefruits with sugar, pancakes and syrup, even a box of Krispy Kremes. Tink had a glazed doughnut in each hand and looked as happy as Dad. First she took a bite from one, then a bite from the other. She parked them on her index fingers like giant rings and did some nibbling.

"I told Tink she could go on ahead since the boys were taking so long," Mom said from the stove, where she was cooking about twenty pounds of bacon. She looked around when she heard me fall onto the old church pew that we used for a bench at the kitchen table and said, "Dewey, you look like you haven't even slept. Tink, pour him a glass of orange juice right now and see if that won't revive him. And where is your brother?" Mom was happy that morning, too, and I wondered if her and Dad were up to something, only I couldn't figure out what that might be. Mom yelled for Wayne and it gave me a headache: "Wayne Turner, you have until I count to three to get in here. One. Two. Two and a half—"

Tink took over: "Two and three quarters, two and four quarters, two and five quarters. THREE."

Wayne dragged himself in and plopped down next to me. Dad folded up his newspaper, clapped his hands together, and said why didn't we sing "Johnny Appleseed" this morning instead of saying grace, which was something he never did, because he couldn't hold a tune. Wayne put his head down in his hands. I just stared at my plate. The pattern around the edge, I think it was green vines, looked like it was swimming.

Tink dropped her doughnuts and said, "Everybody hold hands," so Wayne had to lift his head and I had to touch his pinkie with my pinkie, then Tink started singing the grace. Mom and Dad sang too, all the way through to the end.

Wayne's eyes were closing back up and my mouth barely could form the words, but Tink wasn't through yet: "Amen, brother Ben, shot a rooster, killed a hen. Hen died, rooster cried, poor old Ben committed suicide."

Mom popped Tink on top of the head with a serving spoon and said, "That will be all, Young Lady." But she smiled. "Now everybody dig in. There's plenty."

Half an hour later me and Wayne were standing outside at the end of the driveway at the start of the two-rail fence that ran the length of our yard and separated it from Turners Field. Dad handed us each a giant paintbrush and a bucket of white fence paint. "Let me know if you run out," he said, still happy. "And nothing sloppy. I don't want to see any paint on my grass."

"OK, Dad," I said, looking at all that fence, which went so far back in the yard that I couldn't even see the end of it, although actually I couldn't see the end not because the yard was so long— it was just half an acre—but because, halfway down, there was a stand of bamboo that grew through the fence. The bamboo section was the hardest to get at because whichever one of us was on the field side had to hold the bamboo away while the other one painted, and then had to make sure the bamboo didn't swing back over and mess up the wet paint.

"This is going to take all day," Wayne croaked. Then he started bossing me around. "I'll take this side," he said, waving his brush toward the yard. "You go over there."

"I don't think so," I said. "I want the yard side. You got the yard side last time."

"No, I didn't," Wayne said.

"Oh, just shut up." I was too tired to get worked up about how unfair everything was, the way I could usually, so I went around to the field side but made sure I splattered paint on Wayne the first chance I got. He splattered me back, but at least I got him first. Dad came back after not too long to point out all the spots we had missed and to ask if we happened to know how come the screen was out of our bedroom window. Wayne said,

"No, sir." He guessed it must have just fallen out or something, but he was asleep and had no idea, and did Dad want us to get the ladder and hang it back up?

Dad said no, that was all right, he already put it back up himself, just thought he'd ask was all, and wasn't it a great day to be painting? He said he figured if we really worked hard, we'd be done by that afternoon.

After he left, I was just about to tell Wayne what happened the night before—about the bomb shelter and the lady and the Howler—and also ask him again what the heck happened to him and Darla. I didn't get the chance, though, because right about then we heard a squeaky bicycle and somebody singing an Elvis song coming up Orange Avenue and it was David Tremblay.

David hated his own house—or hated his stepdad, so he hated being there—so he came over to our house a lot of Saturday mornings, especially after they shipped his older brother, Ricky, off to reform school. When Mom saw him hanging out, she always told him the same thing: "David, there's no standing around. If you're going to be over here when the boys are working, you're going to have to pitch in, too." David smiled when she said that, and said, "Yes, ma'am." And then he worked about twice as hard as me or Wayne. He always stayed for lunch, and probably would have moved in with us if he could.

Today he was riding with no hands like he owned the whole road and like if any cars came along they could just drive through people's yards for all he cared. He had his hair done up like Elvis with a gallon of Brylcreem, about half of which you could see had already dripped down the back of his T-shirt.

He didn't bother with the kickstand, but just dropped his bike in the grass by the fence.

"Whatchyall doing?"

He always asked that, no matter what. Then he pulled his giant comb out of his jeans pocket to touch things up a little bit with the hair.

"Digging a hole," Wayne said, wagging his brush like he might flick paint on David Tremblay.

"Doesn't look very deep to me," David said, wiping his comb on his pants leg and leaving a big oil smear.

"It would if you climbed down in and looked up," Wayne said.

"After you." David did a sort of a bow and stuck his comb back in his pocket.

"No, no," Wayne said. "Ladies first."

David looked around slow, like there was a big crowd of people he had to examine, then back at Wayne. "I don't see no ladies here. Maybe you were talking about yourself."

"Not me. I thought maybe you just came back from the beauty parlor, and because of how bad that hairdo looks, I thought you might want to crawl in this hole for a while and hide."

The way they kept talking about a hole this and a hole that, I finally glanced around to see if maybe there really was a hole that somebody dug when I wasn't there or something. But there wasn't. Just the fence.

After that Wayne and David moved a little ways off in the yard and leaned their heads together. Wayne's brush dripped on the grass. He had his back to me but I could still tell he was whispering stuff to David. I leaned over the fence and yelled at them that I wasn't going to paint all by myself and Wayne better come back or I was going to tell Dad. They kept whispering, though, and laughed a couple of times, and I heard David say, "Holy moly!" That's when I knew they must be talking about last night. I yelled at them again. "Hey! We are supposed to be painting the fence or did you forget? You better get back over here or I mean it—I'm telling."

Wayne looked over his shoulder and told me to shut up, then he turned back to David for more whispering. I yelled at *him* to shut up, but he ignored me and they laughed some more and so I got madder and madder. I figured what they were talking about was probably Darla, too, which I didn't even want to think about, really, but I couldn't help it: what if Wayne and her had been out somewhere kissing like Darla wanted to do with me that day up on Sand Mountain? That got me even madder, and so I kept yelling at Wayne, and at David, too, but they kept ignoring me until I went crazy the way I sometimes do. I cussed at them, and grabbed up the bucket of fence paint, and said I was going to dump it on them if they didn't shut up. David laughed at that and so did Wayne. Wayne said he dared me to, and David said, "Yeah, we both dare you," and they laughed some more until I ran over with paint sloshing all over the place and threw it on them.

I should have been the one to get in all the trouble, but instead Dad made Wayne and David Tremblay paint the rest of the fence, including the bamboo section. He said if I dumped all that paint on them, they must have done something to me to deserve it. Wayne tried to argue with him: "Honest, Dad, honest. We didn't do a thing. He just attacked us with the paint. We were standing there minding our own business—"

Dad told him that was enough and it was time to get back to work. Then Dad said for me to come on with him; we were taking the station wagon out to Panther Creek Sod Farm to buy a couple of squares of sod to replace the grass with the paint. It took us a while to get there; the sod farm was out east of Sand Mountain on the other side of the Peace River, way past The Springs.

We brought our own flat-head shovel, and once we got there, Dad had me do the digging—not too deep or you'd get more dirt than you needed, not too shallow or you'd damage the root system. We laid the sod squares on an old canvas tarp Dad spread out in the back of the car. They had a colored man there, who stood around leaning on his own shovel, but I think Dad meant to teach me a lesson by making me do the work instead.

On the way home, Dad cleared his throat a couple of times

like he'd swallowed a bug. I kind of knew what was coming. "Son, your mother and I are concerned about how you've been behaving since school started up."

"Yes, sir," I said. I knew he was looking at me but I kept staring the other way, out the window at the sod farm with its sprinkler system set up over top of the field like a giant daddy longlegs, then once we were past that, there were some groves, then cow pastures, then nothing, just that ugly land they had a lot of around Sand Mountain with some stumps and ditches but mostly just acres of flat nothing with what looked like somebody's sorry old worn-down dirty-green carpet that was grass that didn't grow any higher than algae.

Dad said, "We don't feel that you have been acting very responsibly with what happened the first day of school, and now today this episode with the paint—even if the boys did do something to provoke you. Do you think it would be all right at the mine if I threw the survey equipment out of the truck just because I was mad about something, or even hit somebody with it? What do you think would happen if I behaved that way?"

I still didn't look at him. "You'd get fired?"

"You're darn right I would get fired, and do you know what? I would deserve to get fired."

"But what if it was the other guy's fault?" I knew better than to say that but I couldn't help it. I wouldn't have thrown that paint on Wayne and David Tremblay if they hadn't been whispering about stuff and laughing at me.

"I don't think you're seeing the big picture," Dad said. "If you're the one that reacts in the wrong way, and if you're the one that keeps running off and not doing your job, then it's your fault, not the other guy's. We're talking about self-control, Dewey. Self-control."

"I thought we were talking about responsibility."

"We're talking about self-control *and* responsibility," Dad said, but this time he wasn't so nice, so I said I was sorry, I understood. And then I said I was sorry again. In the middle of one of those ugly flat fields there was a burnt tree and it had a buzzard on one of the limbs, and that was how I felt right then.

"Well," Dad said, "here's what we're going to do. You're getting too old for the belt, and I'm not putting you on restrictions. There's not going to be a punishment. We'll put down this sod where you dumped the paint, and it's going to be your responsibility to water it every day until the roots take hold. We'll consider that your special chore for this week."

"OK, Dad," I said. "I promise I'll take care of it." I asked if he wanted me to be the one to dig up the other grass, with the paint, so we could put in the sod.

Dad said we would do that together when we got home. Then he thought for a second, and just about the time I figured he was letting me off the hook, he said he guessed there was something else, too, that he wanted me to do—not something that should be considered a punishment, but rather a duty.

He said, "Tomorrow afternoon there's a funeral at the Peace

River Cemetery, and they need you to play 'Taps' on your bugle when they lower the casket. I told Mr. Juddy, the dragline operator at the mine—I told him you would be able to do that, and that you've done it before. It's a friend of Mr. Juddy's, a man he served with in World War II, and they're having it be a military funeral. You'll need to wear your Scout uniform and get there early."

By the time we got back to the house, I had slumped so far down that I was practically lying on my back on the front seat, that's how depressed I was. I hated being around dead people or people who were sad that people were dead. I hated riding my bike by the cemetery, especially if it was dark, and if for some reason I did have to, I stuck so far to the other side of the road that a couple of times I crashed into the ditch and got all muddy. Also I tried not to even look at the cemetery whenever I rode by, which made it even harder to steer straight, since my head was turned the other way and I was pedaling so fast.

I was supposed to have a dance lesson that afternoon but didn't want to see Darla, since I had decided I was mad at her for running off with Wayne from the Skeleton Hotel, and I had also decided I wouldn't tell her or Wayne about seeing that ghost lady when I went back to look for them, and hearing the Howler. The only person I talked to for the rest of the day was Tink, who got me to help set up a tent under the dining room table with a blanket over the top and down the sides, and a bunch of pillows underneath. She also got me to stay under there with a bunch of her dolls while she went for a snack. I lined up the dolls from the biggest to the littlest while she was gone and then lay down next to them on all those pillows. I kind of liked that, hiding under there, and when Tink came back with marshmallows and pickle juice, I told her about what happened at the Skeleton Hotel, although I left out the part about sneaking out of the house, plus I made it sound like the whole thing happened a long time ago.

Tink stared at me the whole time with her eyes open real wide, but when I asked her if she was scared, she said no. I knew she was, though, because when I had to climb out to go to the bathroom later, she said she thought she would just go with me and wait outside the door, and if I left the bathroom door open a little bit that would be OK, too.

"Don't tell Mom and Dad," I said, and she said she wouldn't.

"And don't tell Wayne, either," I said, and she said she wouldn't do that but could she tell Scooty, who was this one friend of hers that was always coming around. I told her no, not even Scooty, and she said I was mean and I couldn't come back in her tent with her. I said fine, but then she was going to be all by herself under there and was she sure that's what she wanted, because it was pretty dark and pretty scary. We were having this conversation while I was peeing and she was standing in the hall, and when I finished, she said she guessed I could come back under the tent after all, and she promised she wouldn't tell anybody about the

Skeleton Hotel but I had to let her sock me on the arm. She was always wanting to sock people on the arm, and it never hurt or anything so I said sure. She wound up and socked me as hard as she could and I said, "Ow," and pretended it hurt, and that made her happy.

Chapter Fifteen

AFTER CHURCH THE NEXT DAY, Mom said it was too hot to cook, so we drove down to this colored lady's house named Miss Deas on a dirt street in the Boogerbottom to pick up a Sunday chicken dinner, which she cooked from her house and sold to people like us. Usually you had to tell her in advance so Miss Deas knew how many dinners to fix, but she sometimes had extras of fried chicken, mashed potatoes, etc. I hated going down to the Boogerbottom as bad as I hated the cemetery. All those houses looked alike to me, with their dirt yards in front and their screen doors and their cement block steps and hardly any of them painted, and their chicken coops on the side or in the back, and sometimes chickens with their heads cut off hanging upside down from a clothesline, tied by their feet so the blood splashed from their necks out on the ground where a dog could lick it up.

Two little colored boys sat in Miss Deas's yard playing with cars, and one of them didn't have any pants on, which Tink just had to point out to everybody in a voice so loud even the little children heard her. If it had been me, I would have run away, but they just sat there and looked at us with their big white eyes, and their runny noses, and their gnats that they hardly noticed except to brush away every once in a while. I thought about how me and Wayne were going to have to come back down here to pass out Dad's campaign flyers in a couple of weeks, and not just on Miss Deas's street but all of them. I kind of got a sick feeling about it all over.

Tink wanted to know how come the lady was called *Miss* Deas instead of *Mrs.* Deas, since she must be married, because she had those two boys sitting there, the one with pants and the one without pants who had his you-know-what showing. Mom said it was just something people said sometimes when they were talking about colored people, but that Tink had a very good point.

Tink said, "I do?" She started to say something else—she even had her mouth open—but then closed her mouth again, at least for a minute, and then she said, "How come that boy doesn't have any pants on, anyways?"

Before Mom could answer, I said so he wouldn't poop in them, so he could just poop in the yard instead. Mom said, "Dewey Markham Turner!" then asked me if I wanted her to wash my mouth out with soap. I said, "No, ma'am."

Wayne had gone inside with Dad and they came back with a couple of big brown paper bags that were already soaked in grease on the bottom. Wayne handed me one through the window and made me hold it. I wasn't very hungry when we got home, thinking about the funeral and playing "Taps" on the bugle that afternoon and having to pass out those darn flyers in a couple of weeks in the Boogerbottom, and only ate two wings, a drumstick, and a neck.

Mr. Rhodes, the guy who died who was the friend of Mr. Juddy's, was a Moose or an Elk or a VFW, I forget. Maybe he was all of them. They had already had the Christian service at his church, so the graveside service later that afternoon was a combination of the military and the Elks and all. First they had the honor guard that came over from a base near Tampa, and the seven-gun salute. Then they had the Elks part, which involved about nine old men in funny hats that looked like something you might see on Jughead in Archie comic books. One of the old men held open a big book and yelled out Mr. Rhodes's name four times: "Carlton Rhodes, Carlton Rhodes, Carlton Rhodes, Carlton Rhodes." Every time he shouted, he faced another direction, north, south, east, west. Then he turned to the other eight guys and saluted the one that was the commander, then said, "I have called his name, but he does not answer." I didn't see the point of that whatsoever but didn't have time to think about it too much because the funeral director, Mr. Lauper, gave me the signal, and I wet my lips to play.

> *Day is done.*
> *Gone the sun,*
> *From the lakes, from the hills, from the sky.*
> *All is well.*
> *Safely rest.*
> *God is nigh.*

You could hear the widow, Mrs. Carlton Rhodes, crying, really sobbing, before I finished. That was the closest I came to missing a note but I held on OK until they got the casket lowered into the grave. You would think when people got that old, they wouldn't be so upset when their husband died, since they'd had all those years to get used to the idea of it happening, but that's not how it was for Mrs. Rhodes.

When I finished, I held the bugle down at my side and stood at attention, and for about a second didn't mind where I was or what I was doing or what was going on, because I figured everybody was watching me and probably thought I looked brave standing over there all by myself after playing the saddest song ever but not showing it on the outside no matter how much I might be feeling on the inside. I wondered if they had a merit badge in Scouts for playing your bugle at funerals.

The last thing they did was the folding of the flag, which they handed to Mrs. Rhodes, who sat under a tent that covered her and the rest of the family and the casket and the grave, and shortly after that the hearse left, and the family behind it, and all the cars drove in a big snake line in the winding road, which kept anybody from going too fast through the cemetery. Mr. Lauper came over and shook my hand and offered me an envelope that he said was from the family. I said I wasn't allowed to accept any money, my dad told me not to, and he nodded real serious, like a doctor on TV, and stuck the envelope in his pocket.

About a second after he did that, a guy walked up in an army uniform, who I didn't recognize at first was Walter Wratchford. I don't know where he came from—I guess he must have been there the whole time watching the funeral and then watching Mr. Lauper with the envelope—but he grabbed Mr. Lauper's arm and said, "Give it to the boy."

Mr. Lauper tried to pull away but couldn't break loose from the grip. He said, "Now, look here, you let go right now. This isn't right."

But Walter Wratchford wouldn't let go. He told Mr. Lauper again to give it to the boy, which meant me, and which meant the envelope. He jabbed at Mr. Lauper's pocket. "You were gonna keep it, weren't you?" he said.

Mr. Lauper said, "Certainly not. The boy wouldn't accept it, so I was going to return it to the family."

Walter Wratchford said, "Yeah, I bet you were. Just give it to him."

Mr. Lauper looked at me like he wanted me to explain everything to Walter Wratchford about how my dad wouldn't let me accept any money from playing "Taps," but my mouth wouldn't work. Also I guess I really did want the money, and I figured if somebody made Mr. Lauper give it to me and made me take it, then it wouldn't be the same thing as disobeying Dad. "Tell him," Mr. Lauper said, but I still couldn't say anything, and he got disgusted with me and pulled the envelope out of his pocket and said, "Here," and when I didn't reach for it right away, he dropped it on the ground and jerked his arm away from Walter Wratchford and spun around on his heel and stomped off.

Walter Wratchford picked it up, looked inside, and handed it to me. "It's five dollars," he said.

I didn't move and he said, "Well, go on and take it," but all of a sudden I couldn't do that, either, so I said, "You keep it. I don't want it."

Walter Wratchford said a cuss word, then he told me again to just take the dang money. I shook my head and said I wasn't allowed to. He said, "How come?" And I said my dad wouldn't let me because it was a patriotic duty to play the bugle for the funeral since it was a soldier's funeral. That made Walter Wratchford laugh, and then he pulled a pack of cigarettes out of his uniform pocket and stuck one in his mouth. He lit a match, then held the match to the envelope with the five dollars stuck back in it, until that started to burn, and once it was shooting up in a big flame and you could see the five-dollar bill inside on fire, too, he lit his cigarette from that and he held it while it burned down closer and closer to his fingers. Finally he dropped it on the ground, where it burned out by itself. "I'll tell you something about patriotic," he said. "There isn't nothing more patriotic than taking money for something. Especially if you might of earned it. Otherwise you're just a sucker." The way he said it, though, I kind of thought he didn't really mean it.

He saluted me but not like he really meant that, either, and then he left, just like that. From behind I could see he had all his long hair bunched under his hat. Down on the ground, there was still a corner of the five-dollar bill that hadn't quite burned all the way up. I figured it was probably worth about a nickel, so I stuck it in my pocket. Walter Wratchford's old Ford Fairlane chugged past on the road and he waved to me, still holding his cigarette, and I waved back. I put my bugle back in the case and tied it on to my bicycle basket so it wouldn't bounce out when I was riding home, and I hoped Mr. Lauper wouldn't call my dad and tell him about the thing with Walter Wratchford, because I wouldn't ever be able to explain what happened since I wasn't too sure myself.

Chapter Sixteen

I WENT BACK OVER TO DARLA'S HOUSE for a dance lesson
Monday after school, and I decided to quit being mad at her when
she didn't seem to even notice. Her mom got on to me about staring at my feet. She said it was like typing: you looked at the document, not at your fingers, which was why they called it *touch*
typing, for goodness sake, except that in dancing, it was your
partner instead of a document that you were supposed to look at,
but not ever your feet.

Darla sat in a chair in the corner and folded a piece of paper
smaller and smaller until it looked like an ant could use it for toilet paper, and then when I had to go, she gave it to me and told
me to give it to Wayne. I asked her what it said but she wouldn't
tell me, and just to make sure, she wound Scotch tape around it

about fifty times before shoving it back in my hand and then me out the door, as if I had done something wrong or tried to read it already even though it wasn't meant for me.

She did the same thing the next time I saw her at her house, on Wednesday, and I couldn't imagine what she might have to say to Wayne in a letter, or in an ant-toilet-paper-size Scotch-taped-up paper wad, either. I told myself I didn't care, although I really did, but there was no way to get inside what she gave me without tearing something or folding it back the wrong way. It was very frustrating. I asked if she wanted to go riding bikes to Bowlegs Creek, or even Sand Mountain, but she said she couldn't, she had too much to do, her and Darwin had to rehearse with their mom for a talent show in Tampa. Her mom had just left to go to work at Dr. Rexroat's, though, so I swore I wasn't coming back, dance lesson or no dance lesson. But then after another couple of days, there I was, knocking on her door again.

Darwin came down sometimes, and sometimes he didn't. Sometimes he sat at the top of the stairs and I could barely see him up there just sitting in the dark, not moving, not doing anything, like he was watching me but not speaking, since I wouldn't ever go up to his room with him after that one time.

I heard their grandfather every once in a while—coughing up stuff and spitting really loud upstairs somewhere. His footsteps and the floorboards creaking when he went from his room to the bathroom. The toilet flushing. More coughing and spitting. Calling for Darwin.

Me and Darla still didn't talk much at school, I don't know why. Maybe it had something to do with how I especially noticed then that she didn't look like the other girls, mostly because of her Shirley Temple hair. All the other girls had straight hair, or curled on the sides, or bangs. They wore blue button shirts or yellow button shirts with Peter Pan collars, and plaid skirts, and long socks, and penny loafers, like it was their uniform. Sometimes Darla wore that, too, but it never looked the same on her as it did on them. Once, I saw her at Wayne's locker, standing by herself like she was waiting for him, but he didn't show up. I don't think Wayne talked to her at school, either.

One night when we were lying in bed I asked Wayne what the heck was going on with all the notes from Darla, plus how come he never told me what happened to him and her that night at the Skeleton Hotel?

"Will you shut up?" he said. "I'm trying to sleep."

"So that means you're afraid to tell me."

"Why would I be afraid to tell you? Why would I be afraid of anything from you?"

"OK, then, tell me."

"We were looking for you."

"Yeah. Right. And how come she keeps writing you notes?"

"I don't know. She's a weirdo."

"No, she's not."

"OK, she's not. It's all part of a secret spy ring. I can't tell you any more about it or you'll be in danger. The whole family will be in danger. They'll kill Mom and Dad and Tink. They'll kill you first."

"You are such a liar."

"Believe it or don't believe it. I don't care. You're such a baby, anyway."

"Oh, yeah? Well, would a baby do this?" I swung my pillow down at him hard and knew I scored a direct hit to the face, because he yelled that I scratched his eye, which might or might not have been true. You never knew with Wayne when he was faking. He yelled some other things that I also couldn't repeat, and he kept it up, trying to make me feel bad for mutilating him, for actually blinding him, until Dad came in and threatened us both with the belt if we didn't pipe down.

It should have been that Wayne was mad at me since I hurt his eye, but for some reason he wasn't. Instead I was the one who stayed mad, so that the next time Darla gave me one of her notes, I didn't hand it over to him. I opened it right up once I left her house. There was nothing about a spy ring, and there was nothing about what I was really worried about, which was them maybe kissing. There was nothing about anything, really. All it said was, "Why don't you ever write me back?" I couldn't see the point of a whole entire note with all that careful folding and taping just to say that to Wayne. I could have told her he never wrote to anybody, not even Santa Claus at Christmas when we were little. Mom said he owed all our relatives thank-you notes for presents from three years ago, and whenever he bought Mom or Dad a birthday card or a Mother's Day or a Father's Day card, he always forgot to sign it, much less write a note or something. So what chance did Darla Turkel have of getting a letter of her own from a guy like that?

I threw her note in the trash.

At school meanwhile, everything was about the same. The Mighty Mighty Miners had won all their games so far, even against Zephyrhills, their archrival. Those seniors Moe and Head kept taking my rolls at lunchtime off my lunch tray, and nobody looked at me or said anything except that sorry kid Connolly Voss, who wouldn't shut up about it ("What are you—a man or a mouse?"). I tried one more time to go to the boys' restroom, but Moe saw me and said he was going to conk my head against a locker if I ever did that again, so I kept peeing outside, behind the cafeteria, killing a bigger and bigger circle of grass even though I tried to aim in exactly the same spot every time.

I didn't ever get my red belly, and I asked around about it and found out that I wasn't the only one. Actually there was a bunch of seventh-graders that didn't get the red belly, either—like Darwin Turkel and people like that—which got me thinking that when they said the seniors gave *everybody* a red belly who was in seventh grade, they didn't mean it. The truth was they only chased you down and gave you a red belly if you counted for something, so in a way, not getting a red belly was worse than getting a red belly. Maybe not for the Darwins of Sand Mountain, who had probably already given up on getting people to like them and fitting in and all, but I hadn't given up on those things yet. I was still pretty sure I could eventually figure out what I needed to do, like grow some more, and get faster, and not try to be so smart in class—stuff like that.

I wasn't so sure anymore that being the Chattanooga Shoe-Shine Boy in the minstrel show would make people like me, but since Boopie Larent seemed to be doing OK in school, a lot better than me, and since he got his red belly the first week, I wasn't so sure that being the Chattanooga Shoe-Shine Boy in the minstrel show next year *wouldn't* help, either, as long as I kept the shoe polish off and nobody thought I was trying to be colored for real. So I figured I would keep going to lessons even though Darla seemed sad and didn't talk to me much unless her mom made her dance with me, and I even practiced sometimes when I didn't think anybody was looking.

One day I had a hall pass to take the absent and tardy slips to the principal's office during homeroom and I went by the auditorium on the way there. The doors were open and Chollie the janitor was just finishing mopping the stage, leaning back on his mop and I guess admiring his work. I looked in again on my way back to homeroom and he was gone. The auditorium was dark except for the stage lights, like there was about to be a performance or something, only nobody was there, only me, so for some reason I went in. I was pretty nervous, so I closed the doors behind me, held my breath, and listened for about a minute. Then I went up onstage.

I pretended everybody applauded for a long time, but I breathed deep to get my concentration. Darla's mom said you should never hurry. She said you can't rush greatness. I waved to the crowd, took my time shoving the hall pass into my jeans pocket. Then, when I was good and ready, I did a sort of tap dance like I'd seen Darla do, though her mom hadn't taught me any of that stuff yet. The people loved it, anyway, and I took a big bow when I finished.

Chollie hadn't just mopped up there, he had also waxed, so I took my shoes off and just kept on my socks, then took a running start offstage and into a long slide through the lights. I twirled and glided through a bunch of silky moves I made up, like Fred Astaire. I tried to spin around like a ballet dancer, but that made me dizzy, so I flashed my arms out to my sides and dropped to one knee and did the "Swanee, how I love you, how I love you," like I'd seen in the minstrel show. I did everything I could think of up there, even the lean-way-forward-and-pretend-to-run-but-not-really while I was singing: "Chattanooga Shoe-Shine Boy."

Then Chollie walked back in. I stopped cold, or tried to stop, only I fell down instead. He had come back for his bucket and mop, but I hadn't heard a thing until he was right there. He took hold of his mop handle, with the mop in the bucket, and looked it over like he was inspecting for damage, although he was chuckling, too, I guess about me falling on the floor like that. Then he looked down at me.

"Why you in here messing up my floor?" he said. I didn't know what to answer at first, so I just stared at him. He was tall and mostly bald but not old or anything. He wore his janitor's uniform of khaki pants and shirt with his name stenciled over the pocket. His voice was low and didn't sound mean like you might expect.

"I have a hall pass," I said finally. I got to my feet and stuck it out toward him.

He kept looking from me to his mop, then back to me. He didn't take the hall pass. "I don't think you have a hall pass to the auditorium to mess up my floor," he said.

"No." I looked down at my feet.

"Why you trying to dance like that, anyways?" he said.

I shrugged my shoulders. "For the minstrel show. To be the Chattanooga Shoe-Shine Boy."

"Is that right."

"Uh-huh."

He tapped his foot. I still didn't look at him. I hadn't ever really talked to anyone who was colored before, and I remembered the time when Dad and Wayne and me saw Chollie after the minstrel show in August, and Mr. Hollis Wratchford asked Chollie how he thought the Rotary Club did that night and said

Chollie was the expert, but I wasn't sure what he might be the expert of except how colored people were supposed to dance.

Chollie said, "Practicing, huh?" and I nodded my head. Then he said, "Well, you better keep practicing. You better practice a lot."

I nodded again and said I had to go, the bell was about to ring. As soon as I said it, the bell did ring and I knew I was going to get in trouble for not making it back to homeroom before first period.

I grabbed my shoes and ran off the stage, down the steps to the auditorium, up the aisle to the double doors in the back.

"Wait," Chollie said, and I stopped just before the doors and turned around. He could have been an actor in a play, standing there all alone in the middle of the stage in the lights with his mop and his bucket. "One more thing, there," he said. "Don't you be doing your business outside on my grass anymore, either. I know your daddy, and I know you don't want me to have to talk to him about a thing like that."

That made me nervous even though Chollie still didn't sound mad the way grown-ups usually do when they get on you about something. I wanted to explain it to him, that they wouldn't let me into the WHITES ONLY, but I couldn't say that to a real colored person—at least I guessed I couldn't—especially since I didn't look colored anymore myself. It was all too confusing. I didn't even know where Chollie went to the bathroom, either, I realized, and he was still standing there, waiting, so I said, "No, sir," about doing my business in his grass anymore, even though I had never said "sir" to anybody colored before, either.

"That's a good man," Chollie said, and I was happy to hear him say it, although later I didn't know if he meant me, for minding what he was saying, or if he meant my dad.

Chapter Seventeen

ALL THAT STUFF WITH CHOLLIE happened on a Friday, so I had the weekend to think about where else I could pee from then on at school. I didn't want him mad at me or telling on me to Dad, but I also didn't want Head and Moe to get me for going to any of the whites only bathrooms inside the school, either. It was also the weekend for the Scouts camping trip that would be the first one for guys moving up from Cub Scouts. I might not have had a red belly yet, but I knew everybody was going to get the initiation into Boy Scouts.

Wayne had gone through it the year before, so that afternoon after school, I begged and begged and promised to do about a hundred weeks of chores from the job jar if he told me what was going to happen. David Tremblay was there at our house—he'd probably had all his Scout stuff packed since July because he was so desperate to get away from his own house and his sorry step-dad. He grabbed Wayne and got him in a full nelson and yelled, "Don't tell him! Don't tell him!" The way David saw it was if they made *him* suffer last year, then everybody else ought to have to suffer this year, too.

Wayne said, "OK, OK," and David let him go, but I bribed it out of Wayne later on, anyway: all about the snipe hunt, and them blindfolding us and tying us to trees in the woods at midnight, plus other stuff that was even meaner.

We set up camp that night near Lake Kissimmee, on a dry hammock mostly surrounded by swamp. One of the Scoutmasters was Mr. Ferber, a chemical engineer Dad knew from the phosphate mine. He didn't have any kids of his own, so I don't know why he was there exactly. He had a metal plate in his head from where somebody accidentally threw a shot put into his skull when he was in high school, and sometimes he let us knock on it with our knuckles, which kind of hurt. Mr. Ferber told us where to raise our tents, and how to do our trenching and stuff, then he set off a couple of DDT bombs around the edges of our campsite to kill all the mosquitoes.

The other Scoutmaster—he was this kid Ronnie Dick's dad— broke out a camp stove and a deep fryer and poured amber-colored goop in it, which was creosote that they used for treating the cut ends of fence posts and telephone poles to keep the wood from rotting. Once the creosote heated up in the fryer, Mr. Dick dropped whole potatoes in, and when they sort of bobbed their way back to the top after about a minute, they were done: creosote potatoes. You couldn't eat the skins or you might die. That's what Mr. Dick told us, anyway.

The snipe hunt started at dusk, when they stuck us new guys out in the woods with sacks and said to wait there and don't move and don't say anything, they were going to go bang on pots and stuff and drive the snipes our way so we could catch them. Somebody asked what snipes were and they said, "Oh, good grief, what are you guys—retarded or something?" So we waited and waited like they told us to until it was really, really dark. I brought my Scout knife and worked on my whittling, since I knew there wasn't any such thing as a snipe and they were just tricking us to make us look stupid. I even told a couple of the other new guys that, but they didn't believe me. One guy, Telmo Lewis, told me to be quiet because he had to concentrate.

Finally they came and got us and laughed at what morons we were, while the senior Scouts tied us up and blindfolded us and hauled us into the back of a truck, just like Wayne had told me they would. They drove somewhere that seemed like a long ways away but that Wayne had also told me wasn't very far from camp, it was just that they were going in circles. Once they figured we were confused enough, they tied us to a tree and told us there was another one of those half man–half gators near there in Lake Kissimmee that was always crawling up onto land and eating kids.

The truck drove away and the black, black night got so still you could hear every mosquito and cricket and frog and owl, and then what sounded like a bear or a half man–half gator. Telmo Lewis started crying and saying he wanted to go home. I didn't know it was allowed for anybody to act like such a baby, but decided I would be nice to him, anyway.

"It's all fake, Telmo," I whispered, since I didn't want to get in trouble for already knowing that. "They're just trying to scare us on purpose. It's all fake." He didn't stop crying, though.

We kept hearing bears and footsteps, and hands kept grabbing at us and poking us, kind of like that Turn Out the Lights game with Darwin, and that kept happening for a long time, maybe about an hour. Telmo started screaming, and kept it up until the kid tied up on the other side of him must have jabbed him hard in the ribs, because he suddenly crunched up against me. I had to elbow Telmo back on his other side to make him get off.

Eventually the truck came back and they threw us in again with our feet still tied together and our hands tied behind our backs and our blindfolds still on tight. Telmo was sobbing by then, but nobody seemed to care much, except one voice said, "It will all be over soon." For some reason that made Telmo cry even harder. I guess maybe he thought they were going to kill us. What they did instead was drive us a ways, drag us out onto the ground, and tie another rope to our feet. They explained what they were doing after that, since we couldn't see: throwing the rope over a tree branch, tying the other end to the back of the truck, driving the truck a little ways, about ten or twenty feet, to hoist us off the ground until we were hanging upside down.

Meanwhile Telmo had turned hoarse, but he hadn't wet his pants yet. That came a little later when they lifted our blindfolds one by one to show us the branding iron. I saw a fire a little ways off.

"This is the Scout brand," one of the senior Scouts whispered, holding the iron close enough that I could feel the heat on my face. It glowed red and looked like blood or something. "We're gonna brand you right between your shoulder blades, where nobody will see it while it heals up, because you have to swear to keep a shirt on at all times. But you'll know it's there, and we'll know it's there. Now, what's the Scout motto?"

Hanging upside down was starting to make me feel sick, and my head felt too heavy for me to speak very well, but I somehow managed to get it out: "On my honor I will do my best to do my duty to God and my country and to obey the Scout Law—"

"No, you dummy. I said the Scout *motto*."

"Oh." My head was spinning. The blindfold was back down and tied tight. There was too much blood rushing to my brain. "Be prepared."

"Right," he said. "So are you prepared for this?"

"Yes, sir."

When they did it to me, I played along—grunted like it hurt a lot—and the shock of it did almost fool me. What they did was switch the branding iron with a chunk of ice at the last minute, and with freezing and burning, the idea is you can't tell the difference. Everybody else screamed when they did it to them, and that was when Telmo must have peed his pants. Those older Scouts backed up the truck slow and laid all of us down on the ground like big fish. Most of us stayed there when they untied us, but Telmo took off running into the woods, barking, which I guess was the only noise left he could make.

I saw Wayne and David Tremblay about then. A couple of the senior Scouts sent David off to go catch Telmo, which he did, although it took him about half an hour. I think maybe part of that time he was just sitting with Telmo out in the woods and talking to him to calm him down and make him feel better.

When they finally came back, we all went to bed. I felt bad for Telmo, of course, but was also glad it was him and not me that fell apart. Wayne and David got in an argument once we were in our tent about whether Wayne had told me about the initiation. David said he knew Wayne did because I would have been just as pee-pants scared as Telmo otherwise. I didn't say anything and I was so tired that I didn't care, either. Even though I'd had to bribe him and all, Wayne had sort of looked out for me that night, and so I got to just be one of the guys and for once not who everybody was laughing at, which was OK by me.

There were more DDT bombs and creosote potatoes the next day—and dumb nature hikes, and merit-badge crafts and stuff—but no more initiations. That next night, they cooked a rattlesnake Mr. Ferber said he killed even though nobody saw him do it. Mr. Dick accused him of buying it off of a colored man they had seen fishing, but Mr. Ferber knocked on his metal plate and said, "Scout's honor." Everybody had to try some. It was fried, of course, but not in the creosote. I thought I'd be scared to eat my bite, but somebody said it tasted like chicken and they were right: it did.

Ronnie Dick, the son of Mr. Dick the Scoutmaster, said rattlesnake was colored-people food, and that started a conversation about what all else was colored-people food. Somebody said any kind of snake, and somebody else said raccoon and squirrel. The list went on for a while: rabbit, fried chicken, grits, watermelon, swamp cabbage, poke salad, collards.

The colored-people-food list got longer and longer—bugs and dirt and stuff like that. David Tremblay said dogs, he knew for a fact colored people ate dogs, and everybody laughed at that one. Finally I couldn't help myself and I told a story about when Hurricane Donna knocked down a tree in our front yard and left a nest of possums on the ground. A colored man knocked on our door, who must have thought it was all right to come up out of the Boogerbottom because of all the damage left behind that somebody would have to clean up. He asked Dad if he could buy those possums off of us. Dad said, "You catch them, you can keep them." The possums hissed, but the colored man was too quick for them to bite him. He grabbed their wiry tails and slung them into a croaker sack, even the babies. We asked Dad what he wanted them for and Dad said he figured the man and his family planned on eating them. I asked if Dad thought they would keep the babies for pets but Dad said he guessed not.

Nobody said anything when I finished. Wayne and David Tremblay looked kind of embarrassed and I guessed I hadn't told it right. But that silence only lasted a minute, and then there was some more colored-people talk, the way it always was when guys didn't know what else to say. I didn't stay for it, but instead went and climbed in the tent and zipped myself up in my sleeping bag. I hadn't spent the night away from home much before that weekend, and telling that story made me kind of homesick. I missed Mom and Dad and our dog, Suzy, and even Tink. Plus, it was funny: I missed Darla, too, and I wondered what she was doing right then, and realized I didn't have any idea how she spent her nights at her house—if they watched TV like regular people, or if she and her mom danced or something, or if she hid away all alone in her room, which was kind of what I thought, and which made me sad if it was true.

We packed up and went home the next day, which was

Sunday. Telmo Lewis stuttered for the rest of the camping trip and mostly stayed in his tent, and he never did come back to Scouts once the camping trip was over. I didn't particularly like Scouts after that, either, but Dad said me and Wayne needed to keep going because it helped build character. I don't think he ever knew about the initiation. They made us swear not to tell.

Chapter Eighteen

THAT NEXT WEEK WAS STILL SEPTEMBER, but Dad decided
it was time to start his campaign, so Wayne and me and David
Tremblay went to work delivering flyers all over town. I should
have felt pretty good about things since at school that day I figured out a new place to pee: a kind of blind corner behind the
gym, where there was a hedge but no grass that I might kill, just
dirt and ants. On the way home from school I started feeling low,
though, and as soon as we started with the flyers, I felt even
lower. First we went out to the houses in our neighborhood, then
down Orange Avenue, south toward Bowlegs Creek, to some
crummier streets where people had houses that looked like the
ones the colored people lived in down at the Boogerbottom. We
decided to save the Boogerbottom for last, and hoped if we put it
off long enough, Dad would forget he wanted us to go there.

As usual I picked the houses where nobody looked like they were home, so I could ring the doorbell, stuff the flyer in the mailbox, and run back to my bike. Wayne and David Tremblay made fun of me, but at least I hardly had to talk to anybody that way, and the only thing I had to worry about was dogs.

Most people who were home just took the flyer and thanked us. Usually they were ladies and said they would give it to their husbands. Wayne and David got some things to eat at a couple of houses where the people were friendly or knew my dad and I guess liked his platform—a piece of chocolate cake one time, which made me jealous since I didn't get one because I was busy hiding behind a tree while they went in. Twice, though, the men were home and took one look at the flyer and crumpled it up with a sour look on their faces. One of them didn't have a shirt on and he said some things to Wayne that I couldn't hear from where I was hiding but I could tell from the man's face that he was mad. Wayne looked nervous when he came back after the guy shut the door—actually slammed it.

"What'd he say?" I asked Wayne. He looked like he was about to cry but I knew he wouldn't.

"Nothing," Wayne said. "I think I woke him up."

I didn't believe him and neither did David Tremblay. "He was mad because you woke him up?" David asked him. "What else?"

Wayne grabbed his bike. "He said Negroes ought to pave their own dang streets."

David and me hopped on our bikes, too. "He said 'Negroes'?" I said.

Even pedaling behind him I knew Wayne was rolling his eyes. "No. But he did say he thought Dad was a great leader for the twentieth century and we ought to be proud of him for standing up for his communist beliefs."

"Really?" I said.

"No."

"Let's dump the rest of these flyers," David Tremblay said, already tired of the whole business. "We have football practice. Give them to Dewey." Next thing I knew, all the flyers were piled in the basket on my bike and Wayne and David were out of there. I rode back to the house and told Mom I had a lot of homework and couldn't pass out any more flyers. We were back at it the next day, though.

David Tremblay's mom, who we hardly ever saw, took a flyer that next afternoon and read it in their living room, though I didn't know how she could even see since it was so dark in there. We had only stopped by for David to get his greasy comb to Elvis up his hair in case he saw any girls. His mom said, "Well, isn't that something"—about the flyers, not about the comb—then she asked me and Wayne to please tell Mom she would love for her to come over for a visit sometime again; it had been so long since the last visit; she would make sweet iced tea. The one lamp she had on was cracked at the base, and the two pictures on the walls both looked crooked. We got out of there as fast as we could, and nobody faster than David.

The next day at school David said his stepdad had got hold of the flyer we'd given his mom and he'd torn it into little pieces and said Hank Turner was a great damn disgrace to the white population of Sand Mountain.

It didn't seem like too many people liked Dad's platform. Walter Wratchford drove by us and stopped in the middle of the road and asked for a bunch of them flyers. I handed over about a dozen and he didn't even look at them, just shoved them in his glove box and said, "All my parking tickets was getting lonely in there." Then he asked didn't our daddy know that you could annex the whole dang world to make it dry and there'd still be somebody opening a new bar somewheres else, like on the moon?

David was with us and said he wished there was a bar on the dang moon—they could just send his stepdad up there from now on. Walter Wratchford just sort of nodded at David and said, "Maybe not a bad idea."

When Tink stepped on a nail later in the week, Mom took all of us to Dr. Rexroat's for tetanus shots even though me and Wayne didn't think that was fair. Darla's mom was at her reception desk and said, "Hey there, sweetie pie," to me, which made me nervous, but pretty quick she started goo-gooing over poor Tink's bloody foot. Wayne handed her a campaign flyer. He gave one to Dr. Rexroat, too, when we went in the examination room for the shots. Dr. Rexroat must have already read it because he only just laughed and said, "Ah yes, the crusading Turner family." Mom smiled but you could tell she didn't mean it.

Darla's mom must have read her flyer while we were in with Dr. Rexroat, because she wasn't so nice when we came out. She seemed kind of upset and asked Mom about a hundred questions about Dad wanting to tear down the Skeleton Hotel. She wanted to know why he wanted to do such a thing as that, and wasn't it a matter of private property, and didn't Dad ever consider that it was a famous landmark for Sand Mountain, or maybe not famous, but a landmark, anyway? Mom just said it was an idea that would be good for the town council to discuss, even if they didn't end up doing anything about it. That got Darla's mom calmed down, and she said, "Well, of course," and that she guessed that made sense, and also it was nice that Dad wanted to help the colored people, and maybe it wouldn't be such a bad idea to annex the city limits over on the other side of the Peace River and shut down The Springs.

Nobody else said anything mean about Dad and his campaign, but I guess that was mostly because nobody much was home. It took us forever, almost a whole week, to get the flyers delivered to everybody—except for the Boogerbottom.

One afternoon after Wayne and David Tremblay took off for JV practice, I went back over to Darla's and she invited me to ride bikes with her out to Moon's Stable, where she kept Bojangles. I don't know what made her change to want to do stuff with me again, but I was glad about it. You get tired after a while of just hanging around hoping somebody notices you're there.

Bojangles wasn't anything like I expected, which was a beautiful pony like My Friend Flicka. Instead he was old and had a sway back, but I guess Darla didn't see him that way because she hugged his head the minute she saw him and gave him a carrot and a sugar cube and brushed him for about an hour like a maniac, then braided his tail and his mane, even though he seemed to be missing clumps of his hair. His eyes leaked some kind of stuff that Darla kept wiping off and not mentioning anything about, and when it was time to ride him, she got on bareback from the top of a fence.

"Come get on behind me," she said.

I wasn't so sure. "Don't you have a saddle?" I said. It didn't look safe to me, plus I wasn't sure how I could sit behind her without us being squashed together at the lowest point of Bojangles's swayed back.

"Sometimes I do," she said. "But today I don't." I asked her what that was supposed to mean, and she said she didn't exactly own a saddle but had to rent one from the stable, which usually she couldn't afford on top of the boarding fee. When I asked her how much was the boarding fee, she said they paid in kind, and when I asked her what "paid in kind" meant, she said her mom took care of that and I should stop asking so many dumb questions.

We hadn't seen anybody since we'd been there, just some other horses that looked a lot nicer and happier than Bojangles, running around in a pasture they had, and a few more in their stalls in the big barn. The barn had a new paint job of green with a red roof, but you could tell it was kind of run down, since there were boards missing or half-hanging, and weeds—a lot of weeds. Somebody was in the office, or what Darla called the office, which was just a shed off the side of the barn. I smelled cigarette smoke. "Come on and get on," Darla said again, so I finally climbed on Bojangles and immediately slid right down his back until I was pressed up against her, which made me nervous, but which I liked, too. Darla took us for a walk around the ring, which was all mud and horse poop, then she kicked and let out the reins some, which got Bojangles to trot even though I thought he might die from the effort and I might die from how bad it hurt my butt. It was all I could do to keep from getting bounced off, so I held on to Darla, since there was nowhere to grab the horse.

After we'd been trotting for a couple of circles, she tried to make Bojangles gallop, even though he was obviously too old and too tired to gallop. He refused and I guess as punishment for Darla even having such an idea, he slowed back down to a walk.

The office door slammed open about then, which was easy to hear because it was a tin door hitting the tin wall of the barn. I had thought who walked out would be Mr. Moon, who owned the stable. I had seen him once, at Honey's Drugstore, drinking a big vanilla Coke one Saturday, a bandy-legged old man with a chewing-tobacco stain down his chin. It wasn't him, though. Instead the guy that walked out of the office was none other than Walter

Wratchford. I nearly fell off Bojangles when I saw him. His hair was wild and matted to one side like he'd slept on it that way and forgot to comb it or take a shower, and he had on his army jacket even though it was a hot day and no shade outside where we were.

Darla waved and he sort of waved back with his cigarette. He fumbled in various pockets on his jacket and finally came up with a pair of sunglasses like pilots wear, which he jammed on his face, then he took a big drag off his cigarette and blew out the smoke through his teeth.

"Do you know him?" I asked Darla.

"Of course," she said. "He manages the stable."

"What about Mr. Moon?"

"What about him?"

"I thought it was his stable."

"It is. He just hires somebody to manage it, that's all. What did you think?"

"I don't know what I thought. I didn't think Walter Wratchford worked here, I guess."

"Well, it's not like he does hardly anything, I can tell you that. He sits in his office and listens to the radio and smokes cigarettes all day."

Walter Wratchford came over to the ring and leaned on the fence. He smelled kind of like old beer, but he wasn't drunk or anything. "I see you got you a little copilot," he said to Darla. "You better be nice to him. He's a big patriot of the U.S. of America." He nodded toward me. "Isn't that right?"

I said, "I guess so," and he said, "You're darn right I'm right." Then he asked Darla what her mom was doing. Darla said she was at work at Dr. Rexroat's, of course. Walter Wratchford said for Darla to tell her mom he said hi, and Darla said why should she? I couldn't imagine ever talking that way to a grown-up but nothing happened except Walter Wratchford just winked.

"Did you know her mom was a mermaid one time?" he said to me.

I said, "Yes, sir." Everybody in town already knew that about Darla's mom.

He said, "Did you know her mom could hold her breath longer than anybody in Florida?"

I said, "Yes, sir," again, since everybody in town also already knew that, too.

He said, "Do I look like an officer to you?"

I said, "No, sir," because I thought that was the right answer on account of the way he asked the question, and he said, "Then you quit calling me 'sir,' then." I said, "OK," and he must have thought that was funny, because he laughed to himself the whole way back to the office.

Once he was gone, Darla asked me why Walter Wratchford said I was a big patriot and I told her about the funeral and "Taps" and Mr. Lauper and the five-dollar bill. Then I asked if Walter Wratchford was her mom's boyfriend.

"He certainly is not," Darla said. "Why did you ask me that?"

"Just because he said to say hi to your mom," I said.

"That doesn't mean anything," she said. "My mom is nice to everybody, but that doesn't mean they ought to get any big ideas. Also my grandpa won't allow him."

"Won't allow him what?"

"Won't allow him anything. My grandpa said if he ever came to the house again, he would have him arrested."

"Have Walter Wratchford arrested?"

"Or anybody else."

"Why?"

"Because my grandpa doesn't want any strangers. He said my mom met enough strangers at Weeki Wachee Springs."

"How come I get to come over?"

"Well, I guess I know you so you're not a stranger, obviously."

"When was your mom a mermaid?"

"When she finished up high school. She ran away with her girlfriend named Luanne to Weeki Wachee Springs. They had jobs as dancers somewhere until somebody found out my mom could swim and hold her breath so long. Then they made her a mermaid. She could have been in show business but she decided to have her children instead. That's why she came back to Sand Mountain."

"You mean you and Darwin?"

"Well, we *are* her children." She said that in a very sarcastic way, but I decided to ignore it the same way Walter Wratchford did.

I asked her where her dad was, and she said he was over in

Weeki Wachee Springs, in fact he *owned* Weeki Wachee Springs, didn't I know that? She said he was rich and sent them a big fat check for five hundred dollars every month that her grandpa put in his bank account. She said pretty soon they were going back to Weeki Wachee to live, but right now they had to stay in Sand Mountain to take care of her grandpa, which I guess they must have been doing ever since I could remember, because Darla and Darwin were always in the same grade as me at school even if we hadn't ever been friends before now.

"What's wrong with your grandpa?"

"He's sick."

"Is he going to die?"

"Of course not."

"Is he going to get better?"

"No. I doubt it."

"How come I never see him?"

"Because I already told you. He's sick."

"Is he a general?"

"A general what?"

"Of the army. Of World War II."

She thought about that for a minute, then said, "Well, yeah."

I asked when was the last time she saw her dad—I guess I was being pretty nosy—and she said, "Oh, all the time," but I didn't really believe her. I didn't believe they were ever going to go live in Weeki Wachee Springs, either, or that her grandpa was a general, or much of the rest of the story. Usually I believed whatever anybody told me, but you could just tell that Darla was making a lot of that stuff up.

"Are you scared of your grandpa?" I asked her.

She turned around on the horse and stared at me for a second like she might yell or something. "Of course not," she said. "Don't be ridiculous." She kicked Bojangles in the side, I guess to make him go fast, but he just twisted his neck real slow to look back at us with the stuff still leaking out of his eyes, and then he turned his head back just as slow and kept walking around the ring.

"Let's go out on the road," Darla said. "I'm bored of this." I wasn't sure if she meant riding around in circles, or the conversation about her family, or both, but I didn't ask. She steered us over to the fence, where she leaned down like a real cowboy and unlatched the gate. The next thing I knew, she had Bojangles trotting again, this time down the stable driveway out to the Old Bartow Highway. Once we got there, she turned him north and we rode for a long time right there on the road, which was really more like the memory of a road, since big sections of the asphalt were missing or worn away or grown over with not grass exactly but what passed for grass in places like that around Sand Mountain. We didn't talk for about ten minutes because I was worried about cars, anyway, and the ditch next to the road, and the train tracks on the other side of the ditch, but we only saw one car the whole time, and it slowed way down, and we never did see a train.

It didn't take long before we were out of sight of Moon's. At first there were some oak trees that marked the back side of the Pits for about a quarter of a mile, almost like a fence. After that there was nothing because they had mined everything out for miles in every direction back in the old days before reclamation, so everything along Old Bartow Highway looked like pictures of the surface of the moon. There were craters and dirt piles and rocks and old dams and slime pits. There were rusted truck beds and dead tractors nose-down in the sand like something praying for something. There was the wreck of an old dragline, a small one, fallen off of its track with the boom buckled in half and the bucket and cables missing, probably stuff somebody took for another machine years and years ago or for scrap metal. There was pipe everywhere, hundreds of feet of pipe along the road that looked like it was shedding metal flakes just while you looked at it, and then nothing but the shell of a booster pump that could have been a space satellite that crashed from outer space. And there was hardly a tree or a bush or a palmetto stand that wasn't twisted and crippled and looking so desperate for water it made your mouth dry just to see them.

Whenever I was on top of Sand Mountain, I didn't like to look in that direction because it was so sad and lonely and *desolate*—a word Mom taught me. You couldn't ever say anything about it to my dad, though, because he would just tell you, "Don't complain with your mouth full because that's what's putting food on this table, young man," even though I think it bothered him, too, that the mines had left the land looking like that, and you could tell he was proud of the reclamation projects they had him in charge of, almost like he'd had the idea himself, even though it was the state law now.

But Darla didn't seem to mind or notice, just the same way she didn't seem to mind or notice what an old nag her poor horse was, or how phony her whole story about her dad owning Weeki Wachee Springs was, or anything like that. After riding awhile, and probably forgetting I was even squeezed in behind her, sweating like a little pig, Darla started singing, and once she got going, she didn't stop—it was just song after song after song. I joined in on some of them and she didn't seem to mind.

Eventually we turned around, I guess when Darla was half out of songs, because she sang all the way back, too, and only got quiet for about the last ten minutes, so I figured she had used them all up. I took the opportunity to ask her something that had been bothering me and that as usual I had been so slow figuring out that it worried me I might be retarded.

"Is Wayne your boyfriend?"

She turned partway around but didn't quite look at me before she snapped her head back forward and said, "I wouldn't have him for a boyfriend if you paid me a million dollars."

"Oh," I said, feeling stupid now just for asking, and for ever thinking I'd figured this thing out that obviously I hadn't.

"Your brother," she said, not through yet. "Somebody ought to tell him he thinks he's really something but he's not anything but a I-don't-know-what—"

"How about a maggot?" I wanted to help her if I could.

"Yes, a maggot. You brother is a big maggot."

I liked this a lot and wanted to keep helping. "How about a tapeworm?"

Darla nodded. "I don't know why I even bothered to be nice to him, anyway." Her shoulders shook and I knew it wasn't because of the horse because of how slow we were going, so I figured she was laughing. I laughed with her for about a second, really more of a chuckle, until I realized she wasn't laughing after all, so I stopped and said I was sorry. I meant I was sorry for laughing when she wasn't, but I had the idea that she might have thought I was sorry for something else. Either way, I guess it was the right thing because she said, "That's OK," and wiped her eyes, and by that time we were all the way back at Moon's.

Chapter Nineteen

DAD DIDN'T FORGET ABOUT THE BOOGERBOTTOM, not at all, so me and Wayne went on Friday, even though David Tremblay tried to talk us out of it. He brought up that business from the Scout trip again about colored people eating their dogs.

"I ain't kidding, either," he said. "I knew a guy one time his dog ran away down to the Boogerbottom and the guy went looking for him and finally found him in a bag down by the Peace River, or what was left of him, just his bones picked clean."

I asked how the guy knew it was his dog, and David nodded like he was waiting for the question. "Collar," he said. "Found that, too."

Wayne said it was all baloney and for me to just come on and let's get this thing over with. David kicked at Suzy, our little dog, and said we should bring her with us, see what would happen.

Tink, who had been listening to us talk but not saying anything, screamed and picked up Suzy, or tried to, though Suzy was too long and heavy for her, but Tink somehow managed to stagger like that to the house still screaming the whole time.

"Way to go," Wayne said.

David just pulled out his comb. "There's other stuff goes on down there you don't even want to know about. Don't say I didn't warn you."

The worst thing was Mom caught us before we left and said we ought to look presentable and for Wayne to put on a button shirt and for me to put on a new orange Ban-Lon shirt she had bought to take the place of the other one I burned up with the magnifying glass that day at Bowlegs Creek.

One of the things you notice first off about the Boogerbottom is there isn't any grass. They have weeds there, but no grass. Just dirt. Dirt yards, dirt streets. Dirt. And where there isn't dirt there's sand, which was why we ended up pushing our bikes whenever we tried to ride down the middle of the streets, because the tires sunk down too low and we couldn't pedal. It wasn't as soft on the sides, but there was about a foot or two-foot ridge at the edge of the road, where it was sunk down from I guess years of people driving on it but no pavement, and there were no sidewalks, either—just the road, the ridge, and the start of people's yards. Wayne said he bet when it rained here they couldn't hardly even drive cars because of all the mud they must have in the streets, and I said I bet that wasn't a problem because I didn't see too many cars, anyway.

The first person we met was an old lady with a rag on her head raking her yard in long careful lines, and she was the first we gave a flyer to. She blinked at us like she'd never seen white boys down there before, then she blinked at the flyer. Then she said, "Is this for the insurance? Are you with that Mr. Cowans?"

Wayne said, "We don't know a Mr. Cowans. This is for the city council election, for Mr. Turner, who's running for the city council, and he would appreciate your vote. He wants to pave your streets here." Wayne nodded toward the street. "That's his campaign promise. It's all written right here."

She blinked at Wayne, blinked again at the flyer, blinked at Wayne again. "Not for the insurance?"

"Nuh-uh," Wayne said. "For the election."

"All right, then," she said. She folded the flyer without reading it. Folded it some more, the way Darla had done those notes to Wayne only without all the Scotch tape, then tucked it down the front of her dress somewhere and went back to raking.

The next couple of houses were easier. Nobody was home, so we tucked the flyers in the screen-door handles. I was careful not to scrape my hand, because they were so rusty.

We kept going deeper into the Boogerbottom and it didn't take long before a gang of little kids was following us—staring and whispering and every now and then yelling something like,

"Hey, hey you!" and then laughing when we turned to look at them. "Hey, hey you! Hey, hey you!" They stayed a couple of people's yards behind but inched closer when we left our bikes and went up to one house together, so after that one of us stayed with the bikes. We didn't want them to get stolen. Hardly anybody was home at any of the houses, and if they were, it was usually an old woman like that first old woman, raking the yard, or hanging clothes out on a clothesline, or sitting in a chair under a shade tree, fanning herself, or holding a dirty baby, or swatting at flies and gnats.

The kids started chanting after a while: "Hey, hey you! Hey, hey you!" There had been just a couple at first, then more, finally a dozen, all about six or seven years old except for a littler one, who they made come closer to us, who didn't have pants on, like the boy we saw that Sunday in front of Miss Deas's. His eyes got wider and wider, but whenever he turned around to go back, the other kids shouted at him, "Go on. Go on or I'll hurt you, boy."

So he kept coming. He got to about ten feet away from us and I smiled at him. I wished I had some candy or some bubble gum to give him, he looked so scared, and I wished they wouldn't keep doing that to him, making him come closer even though he didn't want to. His eyes were so wide I thought his head might explode if they got any bigger, and I was just about to tell him it was all right, we wouldn't hurt him, when he lifted his arm up and threw a rock at us that hit Wayne on his ear.

He ran back to the other kids, and when Wayne picked up the rock and took a step toward them, they scattered like a leaf pile in a hurricane.

"Let's just go home," I said. "They don't want us here."

Wayne ran his fingers over the rock and stuck it in his pocket. His ear was red, but that could have just been from the sun. "No, we have to finish up. Dad told us to."

"We can tell him we did. We can just say it. We can leave the flyers right here and let people pick them up."

Wayne said he wasn't going to lie to Dad and I said it wasn't lying, we already passed out a bunch of them, and we couldn't help it if they didn't want us down here, and I bet colored people didn't even vote, anyway. Wayne said of course they don't vote.

I said, "They don't?"

"Heck no."

"Then what are we doing down here?"

"Because," Wayne said, "Dad thinks they might want to vote if there's something in it for them."

I looked at the street with all that loose sand you couldn't ride a bike through, and the ridge up to people's yards, and the place where there wasn't a sidewalk. I looked at those unpainted houses with their screen doors without screens and their raked yards. Why didn't they just grow some grass? Why couldn't they have a nice lawn like everybody else? Why couldn't they all wear pants like normal people? Why did everything smell like smoke and dust and burning rubber tires?

184 •

Wayne said, "Uh-oh," then, and I said, "What?" but saw what he was talking about before he had to answer: those kids that had been following us were back, only this time they had their big brothers with them. A couple of the big kids threw rocks. Wayne threw one back. I threw some pebbles, and they threw some more rocks, and Wayne threw some more, too, and for some crazy reason, I pulled off my Ban-Lon shirt and threw *that,* and then the kids came after us, and we jumped on our bikes and tore out of there as fast as we could go.

The problem with getting away from the colored boys and their rocks was we had to go deeper into the Boogerbottom to do it, and we didn't know where we were going, and we had to ride through people's yards because it was too slow pedaling through sand. I recognized that lady Miss Deas's house because of the chickens hanging from the line and the dogs circling underneath that stopped every now and then to lick at the blood puddling up in the dirt. If colored people really did eat dogs like David Tremblay said, then they hadn't gotten around to eating *those* dogs. We kept going, but after that there weren't any landmarks to navigate. The streets got narrower and darker where the fat oak trees grew together in a canopy that made it seem like we were riding down a tunnel to somewhere underground. There were houses with front doors three feet off the ground and only a stack of concrete blocks to get up that high because the porches had fallen off and been dragged to the side in a heap of broken boards and rusted nails. There were the bodies of cars or rather parts of different cars welded together and made to stand up on other concrete blocks like somebody might someday come back and reattach them to an engine and some tires to see if they could run, maybe one of those gunk-coated engines we saw at a couple of houses hanging by thick rope from fat tree limbs. There were more chickens than dogs running around, and hardly any cats, and a goat that we saw tied to a tree, and a girl hitting him with a stick. I felt kind of naked without a shirt on. We saw a bunch of other colored girls in one yard, playing double jump rope, three of them jumping all at once and going so fast that it made me dizzy and I nearly wrecked my bike swerving around them. A couple of the girls joined the chase then, too, and grabbed their own rocks like the boys and threw at us but missed by a mile.

At the Peace River the oak trees were so big and covered with so much gray Spanish moss that it looked like clouds. We couldn't go any farther in that direction unless we planned to ride straight through black mud and cattails and then swim, and since bikes don't float, we turned north instead. The street there was in better condition, baked hard I guess because there was more clay that near to water, so we picked up speed, and when I looked back, I could still see the colored kids a couple of blocks behind us but fading, and by the time we reached the Tire Tower after another few blocks, they were nowhere in sight.

"Jeezum Crow," Wayne said. "Look at all those tires." A short colored man with gray hair and a gray beard waved a rag at us from inside his fence, and behind him about a hundred feet high and covering about an acre of land was tires like you'd never seen before: hundreds of them, thousands, ten thousands of tires—car tires, truck tires, tractor tires, tires from some mine vehicle so big with treads so wide you could almost fit somebody to hide in one, and retreads, tire scraps, inner tubes. I said, "It's like the colored people's Sand Mountain. You think anybody gets to climb the Tire Tower?"

Wayne said he doubted it. We rode on a little slower after that until our hearts stopped pumping ninety miles an hour from the chase. Eventually we came to a one-lane paved road in the middle of some orange groves that we hoped would take us to somewhere we knew, so we went that way. I asked Wayne if those colored boys were the same ones that we got in the mud war with that time at Bowlegs Creek. Wayne said he couldn't tell, it all happened so fast, and everybody said they all looked alike, anyway. "Yeah," I said. "I know."

All the flyers had got bounced out of our baskets during the chase through the Boogerbottom, but neither me or Wayne got hit by any of the rocks except that one that the first little boy threw and that Wayne still had in his pocket for a souvenir. It turned out that it hadn't really hit Wayne in the ear like I thought; it just plinked him.

"Well, you must have done something to antagonize them." That's what Dad said when we told him the story that night. It was during dinner and I immediately lost my appetite the way I always did when he yelled.

"We didn't, Dad," I said. "Wayne, show him the rock."

Wayne just sat there looking down at his plate. I could tell he was mad, because he wasn't saying anything. Tink said she wanted to see the rock but Wayne still didn't budge. Dad said never mind about a rock; he wanted to know exactly what happened.

"They just followed us," I said. "They got the little one to throw the rock. Wayne picked it up and they ran away. They came back with the big kids and started chasing us." I didn't mention the Ban-Lon shirt. I had told Mom that part when we first got home, and she said there was no need to bring it up with Dad, because it would make him too mad.

Not that he wasn't mad enough as it was. "And nobody said anything to anybody? You didn't call them any names?"

"No, sir."

Mom was rubbing her temples. She said, "Hank, I think the boys have told you all there is to tell. Isn't it possible that you miscalculated the attitudes down there? Those people have plenty to be resentful about." Mom knew a lot about this stuff because she had been reading a book, I believe it was called *The Killer Mockingbird,* that sounded like a horror story but she said it was about Negroes.

I asked if I could be excused. Tink asked if she could *please* see the darn rock already? The whole house felt like it was made out of glass or something. I didn't even know why everybody was so upset. I couldn't wait to tell Darla, and to tell people at school, too—that me and Wayne got attacked by colored kids. It would probably make me pretty popular for them to know that happened. In fact, if I wasn't nervous about using the phone, I would have started telling people that very night. If there was one thing I had figured out, it was that people like you better when something bad happens to you that wasn't your fault. I learned that lesson in the fourth grade from a kid named Bobby, who had leukemia. Everybody was always giving him things, saying prayers about him, asking him if he wanted to do stuff. I was pretty jealous of him. He was very popular until he died.

I thought maybe if I finished my homework fast I might be allowed to go outside even though it was dark and a school night. Then I could go up the block and tell David Tremblay, at least, before Wayne got the chance to, and maybe zoom over to Darla's and tell her, too. "Can I please be excused, please?" I asked again, but all I got for an answer was somebody knocking at the back door.

"Good garden peas," Dad said. Mom said I could be excused to go see who it was, so I did. I expected it to be David Tremblay, or that girl Scooty who was Tink's friend, but when I got to the door, it was none of them. It was Chollie the janitor, and he was standing on the carport in his work uniform and holding a cap in his hands that he was wringing out even though it didn't look wet to me. Chollie looked startled when I turned on the back porch light—so startled I almost turned it off again, but then I figured that would be rude, so I just said, "Are you here to see my dad? Hold on, I'll go get him. Just a second. I'll be right back." I had never in my life seen anybody colored come to our house at night—I didn't think it was even allowed—and hardly ever in the day except every now and then looking for yard work, or maybe to buy a possum after a hurricane.

"Well, who is it?" Dad said.

"It's Chollie." That's when it hit me: he must have come to tell Dad about me still peeing outside at the high school. He must have found my new spot behind the gym!

Dad looked surprised. "Mr. Ellis is here at the house?"

I said, "Who's Mr. Ellis?"

Dad was already getting up from the table. "Mr. Ellis is Chollie Ellis. *You* call him Mr. Ellis."

"Yes, sir," I said. Mom was kind of nervous, you could tell, though probably not about the same things I was nervous about. We heard Dad open and close the back door, and he also turned off the back porch light, which I bet Chollie—Mr. Ellis—appreciated. But we didn't hear anything else for a few minutes except the low mumble of them talking until even that got drowned out by the racket of the dishes that Mom started stacking right there at the table, even though whenever me or Wayne or Tink did that, she got on us about it and said we should be more careful, we might chip a plate, and we should always take them one at a time to the kitchen, and also it wasn't ever polite to scrape food at the table, but there she was doing that, too.

Dad sat us down in the living room after Mr. Ellis left and Mom took Tink off to put her to bed. "I don't want you to tell anybody about what happened down at the Boogerbottom," he said. "Mr. Ellis has been helping me with the election and he's looking into it and says those boys will be punished for throwing the rocks. I believe it was all a big misunderstanding, and I don't want this to affect the campaign." He clapped his hand on Wayne's knee and said he knew he could count on us, but Wayne pulled his leg away and stood up.

"It wasn't a misunderstanding, Dad. Those kids hate us. You can tell. And I don't see why we have to go down there, anyway. Everybody knows they don't vote or anything, and they're not gonna vote no matter what you promise them. And everybody else isn't going to vote for you, either, because of what you promised. And I don't see why we have to do all this work when it's you that's running for the election and not us. It's not fair—"

I was just happy neither Dad or Mr. Ellis had mentioned my peeing, but it was obvious from the way Dad was frowning that Wayne had gone too far. Even Wayne must have realized it, because he stopped talking suddenly. Dad just said, "Are you through?"

Wayne stuck his hands in his pockets. "Yes, sir."

"You sure there's nothing else you need to say?"

Wayne hung his head. "I'm sorry."

"Sorry for what?" Dad's voice was calm, the way he got sometimes just when you were sure he'd start yelling instead. It was pretty effective at making you feel bad for whatever it was you did—a lot more effective than the yelling, actually.

"Sorry for being disrespectful," Wayne said.

Dad nodded. "All right, then. I think it's time you boys did your homework and got ready for bed."

"Yes, sir," Wayne said.

"Yes, sir," I said. Wayne left but I stayed behind. There was something I had to ask. "Dad, did Mr. Ellis say anything else about anything else, or was it just about what happened to me and Wayne?"

"What do you mean? Did he say anything else about what?"

"I don't know, just anything."

Dad made the church roof and steeple and open the doors and see all the people with his fingers. "No, I don't believe so."

"OK. Thanks, Dad." I headed for the bedroom, relieved, but then Dad said, "Oh," and to wait a minute, he guessed there was this one other thing Mr. Ellis told him.

"What was it?" My voice sounded about like a mouse squeaking.

"He just said he thought you were quite the dancer," Dad said. "Now, where do you suppose he got an idea like that?"

I said I didn't know. I looked over at Dad to see if I was in trouble or something but he was smiling, which was a big relief.

Something woke me up in the night. It was voices from the other part of the house. It was Mom and Dad having an argument. Dad said, "I thought you wanted me to," and Mom said, "I did but maybe you're trying to do too much," and, "Maybe you started something that's gotten out of control," and, "Maybe the children shouldn't be involved," and Dad said, "I'm not alone. A lot of people agree with this," and Mom said, "And a lot of people don't. You might pave some of the Negro streets—they would let you do that to keep things peaceful—but you shouldn't have gone after annexation, too," and Dad's voice got louder, and Mom said, "Don't be so loud; you'll wake up the children," and Dad said, "I'm not loud," and Mom said, "Yes, you are," and I heard footsteps and a door close and I fell back asleep but I dreamed about those colored kids chasing us, and then it was those guys Moe and Head laughing and laughing and laughing at me because I wet my pants and everybody could see the dark stain spreading wider and wider no matter how I tried to cover myself up.

Chapter Twenty

ON SUNDAY THE TIRE TOWER CAUGHT FIRE, down in the Boogerbottom. The whole sky over Sand Mountain turned black and stayed that way. You couldn't go outside without choking on the smoke, and it stunk worse than a skunk or a polecat or a pulp mill. A black film got all over everything and everybody, and if you stayed outside too long, you started to look like you were colored. People said they put the owner of the Tire Tower in jail for letting it happen, and not having a permit, either. Me and Wayne had seen him when we were on our bikes running from the colored kids. He didn't seem like somebody who belonged in jail, but I guess you never know what makes a criminal.

There was a story going around that somebody set the Tire Tower on fire on purpose, but nobody seemed to know why they might have done it. I also heard that all those tires in the Tire

Tower were worth a million dollars and that the Firestone Company would pay that much so they could melt them back down into rubber and make new tires, but I doubted that was true or else why was it just the one colored man collecting them all those years?

There was nothing the Sand Mountain volunteer fire department could do about a tire fire except make sure it didn't spread onto trees or houses or anything, and it wasn't until a couple of days later when the fire finally burned itself down to where it just smoldered that we learned what was really going on. That's when Dad got a note saying, "Now you see what happens." It was written on the back of one of Dad's campaign flyers that somebody mailed back to us. There was also a picture somebody drew of two people kissing—one white, one colored—and they wrote underneath it that Dad must love colored people, only they didn't say it quite that way. I saw it on Dad's dresser and showed it to Wayne.

"Oh, man," Wayne said. "They must mean the tire fire."

"Yeah," I said. "I know." Except that I didn't really know. Why would they burn down the Tire Tower? Dad just said he was going to get the streets paved in the Boogerbottom, not anything else, and he didn't have anything to do with the Tire Tower, anyway.

A police officer came to our house and his name was O. O. Odom. I wondered if he was the same one from the night me and Wayne and Darla went down to the Skeleton Hotel and he chased me from the Sinclair station. Officer Odom looked over the flyer pretty carefully. Him and Dad were in the front room but we could see them from the family room, where we were pretending to watch TV, only we turned it down really low so we could hear what they were saying, too.

"Now, what makes you think this here is connected to the tire fire?" Officer Odom said. He pronounced it "tar far."

"What else would it be referring to?" Dad said.

Officer Odom scratched his head. "Well, I guess it could just mean they expect people are going to be mailing you back your papers like this fella did. 'So now you see what happens.' They don't want it, so they send it back to you." He paused. "Maybe they think you're being too keen on the colored people."

Dad stabbed his finger in the middle of the flyer. "Exactly," he said. "Which was why they set fire to the Tire Tower and wrote 'Now you see what happens.'"

Officer Odom shook his head. "But it doesn't *say* anything here about the tar far."

Dad threw up his hands and said, "Fine, fine. Maybe you're right. Thank you so much for coming by and looking in to all this. We'll rest easier knowing you're on the job."

Officer Odom looked like Dad hurt his feelings, and I had to admit Dad did sound kind of sarcastic. "You don't have to be that way," Officer Odom said, and picked up his hat from the coffee table.

Mom came out of the kitchen and went past us into the front room. She must have heard what Dad said and how he said it, because she was really nice to Officer Odom. She shook his hand and thanked him for coming over, in a way that sounded like she meant it. After he left, she gave Dad a look and then he left, too. Mom said he was going to the shed to work on something, but I snuck out later and peeked in the door and saw he was in there smoking a cigarette even though he was supposed to have quit a long time before.

On Wednesday I went over to Darla's for a dance lesson. Her mom said it was time I learned the tango, which was fine with me because I was sick of worrying about the election and the threats and the tire fire and was happy to think about something else for a while. At first Darla's mom did it with me, but my head only came up to her boobs and they kept knocking me around, which was very embarrassing. You have to be really close for the tango, and any time I leaned my head away from getting hit, she pulled me back in. I couldn't say anything about the boob-knocking, of course, but Mrs. Turkel must have finally noticed because she said for Darla to come over and practice with me instead.

Darla had obviously done the tango before, because she grabbed my one hand and pulled our arms out straight in front of us, and she pressed her cheek against my cheek, and she held my other hand down by our sides. Mrs. Turkel put on the record and away we went, following our arms to one end of the room, then dipping, then changing arms and cheeks and following our other arms back to where we started. The only problem was our knees bumping into one another when we did our turns, which must have been my fault because Darla told me it was.

"Watch out, dummy. That hurt," she said, but I didn't have to say anything back because her mom told her if she was going to speak to a partner on the dance floor, she should always make sure she was a lady about it. After that when our knees bumped, Darla smiled really big and said, "Pardon me, sir, but I think you might have injured me and could you please not?" It was very phony, but I guess better than being called Dummy.

Anyway, I liked the tango a lot and thought I was getting pretty good at it until Mrs. Turkel said OK, now Darla was going to demonstrate with Darwin, who I hadn't even noticed was hanging around at the door. Darla said she didn't want to dance with Darwin, he always squeezed her too tight. Darwin told her not to be a baby—it was beginning to sound like me and Wayne—but once they got started, I could see that it was true. Darwin squeezed so close to Darla that you would have thought he was her boyfriend instead of her brother.

Darla said, "Mom!" but Mrs. Turkel just said, "If you're going to learn proper technique, you have to practice proper technique." Then she turned to me and said she hoped I was taking note, and I said, "Yes, ma'am."

I was happy it was just me and Darla again and Wayne was out of the picture, and I even sat by her at lunch the next day, which I was pretty nervous about. It surprised her, I could tell, and it surprised Darwin even more, because when he saw us at a table together as he came out of the lunch line, he stopped and stared for a minute.

"Do you want my roll?" I said, hoping Darla would say yes and take it before those guys Head and Moe came along, but they showed up before she could say anything and before we could have a conversation at all. Moe grabbed my roll and popped it in his mouth. Head looked hard at Darla, like he was trying to figure something out. His two eyebrows crawled together in the middle of his forehead, then he asked Moe, wasn't this the girl they caught at the cemetery with the colored boy? He said it like Darla wasn't sitting right there.

Moe was still chewing but didn't mind talking with his mouth full. He said, "Back last summer?"

Head nodded his head. "You think maybe it was Little Sambo here she was with?" He was talking about me and I wished I could slide under the table and crawl right out of there, or I wished they would both die of a heart attack. But mostly I wished I hadn't ever sat there by Darla in the lunchroom. Moe said, "Could be, could be," then he said there was no way to know for sure; they all looked alike.

Eventually they wandered off toward the lunch line but I could still hear them, sounding like Laurel and Hardy or Abbott and Costello or funny guys like that.

Darla didn't look up from her tray the whole time, and I

stared down at my tray for a while, too, but I could tell people around us had heard everything. I guess I should have said something to make Darla feel better, but then she should have said something to make me feel better, too.

She mashed her peas with her fork, every single one of them, and then mashed them together, and then drew some patterns in the green muck, and then swirled in some powdered mashed potatoes we had that day, and then poured some of her milk in there to make a kind of a lake around everything. She acted like nothing had happened and started talking about Moon Pies— how come nobody ever ate Moon Pies anymore? Sometimes when she brought up a new subject all of a sudden, it gave me a headache and this was one of those times. It was like looking down to see if your shoe was tied and walking into something, or stepping on a rake and the handle coming up and hitting you in the head. My stomach growled from still being hungry.

The next day after school, I went over to Darla's house because I told her I would, even though I kind of didn't want to. She didn't mention what happened with Moe and Head, and I didn't mention it, either, so after a while I managed to feel better about being there. The only way anybody might know there was anything wrong was that we were a lot quieter between us than usual, which was what got me to finally tell her about seeing the lady that night of the Skeleton Hotel, since I couldn't think of anything else to say. Also I was starting to doubt what I had seen with my own eyes, and I didn't want that to happen. Telling it to somebody else would make it real again.

We were sitting under her dining-room table, hiding from Darwin, only without the blanket and pillows and dolls like that time with Tink. Darla wanted to know if I saw the Howler, too.

"No," I said. "But I heard him after the lady disappeared."

Darla wanted to know why I never told her, and I said I was kind of mad about her and Wayne not looking for me that night, plus I didn't want her to be too scared. She said she wasn't scared, and then she said we should go back to the Skeleton Hotel and we should do it Saturday night. It all happened so fast I didn't even have a chance to argue with her about anything or make up any excuses why not.

"You meet me at the corner down from your house," she said. "Saturday night. Midnight. And don't bring Wayne."

I had almost forgotten that nobody knew about me going over to the Turkels for dance lessons and to hang out with Darla, until I left that day and as soon as I got out in their yard along came Tink on her little bicycle.

"What are you doing here?" she said.

"Nothing. I was just checking the air in my tires." I had my bike there, too.

"Why are you doing that here?"

"Because I thought they might be low, but I guess they're not."

Tink blinked a couple of times. "How come you came out of their house?"

"I didn't," I said. "I just thought I'd see if they had a pump, but they weren't home. I don't even know who lives here."

"Why'd you need a pump if your tires weren't low?" she said. "And how come they're not here if their car is here?"

I got on my bike. "How come you ask so many nosy questions?"

Tink followed me up the street. "I'm not nosy," she said.

"Yes, you are."

"No, *you* are," she said, then she started crying. I wanted to just get the heck out of there and away from Tink, but I couldn't stand it when she cried, either—I couldn't stand it when *anybody* cried—so I stopped and asked her what was the matter. Then, of course, she had to pout and tell me, *"Nothing,"* until I was nice to her for a while and said she could ride with me.

She wiped her eyes. "Where are we going?" Wayne and me never let her go anywhere with us, so I guess she thought it was a very big deal that day. I said how about we ride down to Bowlegs Creek, and she said, "OK," but she wasn't allowed to cross the highway. I said she was with me so it would be all right, though I wasn't actually sure about that. Tink was very excited.

Once we got there, we just sat on the bridge the way I usually did with Darla when we went. Tink collected a bunch of sticks and threw them in two at a time so they could race under the bridge while we watched, and she made me bet which one would win. I tried to pick the one I was pretty sure would lose, so Tink's would be the winner and she could say, "Ha!" Little kids like it when they get to win, no matter what they're playing.

After a while Tink said she wanted to show me something. She had a bunch of stuff in her bike basket, including the notebook she used for taking messages when anybody called for Dad's campaign, which from the looks of it wasn't very often. She flipped through to the back where she had drawn a picture of a dog. Underneath it she had written, "Suzy Your Pet," and underneath that she had written, "Do Not Run For The Election Or We Will Steal This Dog. Now You See What Happens."

"What is this?" I asked Tink.

She threw two more sticks in Bowlegs Creek but didn't make me pick one to win. She said she was going to put her picture with the note in our mailbox so Dad would quit the election and then nobody would be mad about anything anymore, and what did I think?

"I think you better not," I said. "Dad'll know you did it and *he'll* get mad."

Tink dumped all her sticks in the creek. "How will he know, if I don't put my name on it?"

"He'll know because it looks like a little kid wrote it and he knows what your writing looks like." I thought Tink would argue with me, but she didn't. "It'll be OK," I said. "Will you let me keep this? I like the picture of Suzy, and I can cut it out and put it on my wall."

Tink studied the picture for a while and said no, I couldn't have it. She liked it, too, and she wanted to keep it for herself.

We rode home slow, back up Orange Avenue. Tink wanted to know if they had those cards on the walls when you were in high school that showed you how to write all the letters of the alphabet in cursive, only she didn't call it "cursive"; she called it "real writing." She told me unless she looked at the cards they had on the wall in elementary school, she could never remember how to do the capital X and especially not the capital Q. I had to be honest with her and tell her that no, they didn't have the cards in high school, but she shouldn't worry about it because you hardly ever used the capital X and Q, anyway. Some people might have thought Tink asking me that was stupid, but I used to worry about the same thing when I was her age, so I understood. I hoped that was all she worried about, besides the election. I didn't like to think that she also worried about everything else the way I did.

"It's all going to be OK," I told her again, and this time she smiled like she might even believe me.

When we got home, there was a car I had seen before, a blue Ford Fairlane with red doors, parked in front of our house. The passenger side looked like it had sideswiped a tree, only not too recently, and the door was tied shut with a rope, and when I saw that, I knew for sure whose car it was: Walter Wratchford's.

Chapter Twenty-one

WALTER WRATCHFORD WAS SITTING in the front room, on the couch, wearing his army uniform like the time I saw him at Mr. Rhodes's funeral.

Mom stood up when we walked in, and Walter Wratchford did, too, after a second. Then Mom said, "Corporal Wratchford, I'd like to introduce my children. This is my son Dewey Turner. Dewey, you can shake Corporal Wratchford's hand. And this is my daughter, Patricia."

I don't know which surprised me more—Walter Wratchford being there in the first place, or Mom introducing him as *Corporal*. I shook Walter Wratchford's hand like she told me, and Tink did, too. He said, "Pleased to meet you," to Tink and just kind of smiled at me. He settled back on the couch after Mom sat down, but his eyes jumped around like he had to check out everything all at once—the front door, the windows, Tink, me, Mom, the pictures of Mom and Dad getting married, the pictures of me and Tink and Wayne when we were babies, the Readers Digest Condensed Books that came every month lined up on the bookshelf built into the wall.

Mom turned to me. "Dewey, Corporal Wratchford has come by to ask a favor of you."

"For what?" I said.

"For you to play your bugle this afternoon."

They talk about in stories how somebody's heart sinks when they find out something lousy happens, like their star pitcher is missing and it's the day of the championship game and it looks like he's not going to show up. That's what it felt like to me when Mom said that, like my heart sank down about to my stomach, and then when Walter Wratchford said, "It's for a colored soldier shot and killed in Vietnam. I believe he's the first from here we've given up to that particular war," it sank about all the way to my shoes.

Mom told me to go run and put my Scout uniform on, but Walter Wratchford said to wait; he only wanted me to do it if I wanted to. "It's at a colored church, too," he said. His voice sounded froggy. Then he said, "There's just going to be colored people there."

I looked at him pretty good right before I answered. His eyes were red, I guess from smoking his cigarettes and maybe not sleeping much. If he'd been drinking liquor, Mom would have smelled it on him and she wouldn't have even let him come in the house.

I didn't really have to think about it, anyway. I just said the only thing I figured you were ever allowed to say to a grown-up: "Yes, sir." That wasn't quite good enough for him, because he said, "Yes, sir, you don't mind if it's at a colored church?" and I just said, "Yes, sir," again, with my heart so low now it was about six feet underground with the dead bodies they buried in the cemeteries, white or colored.

Actually Walter Wratchford *was* drinking liquor. He had a bottle in his car that said VODKA on the label, but you couldn't smell it. He handed it to me along with a little half-empty carton of milk once I'd changed into my Scout uniform and we were driving, and he said, "Pour some of that into there, would you?" I started to pour the milk into the top of the liquor bottle, but he grabbed my hand and almost made me spill some and said no, he meant the other way around, so I poured as much of the liquor into the milk as would go. He took the carton back and told me to put the bottle under the seat, which I also did. From the way it looked, if somebody like a police officer or sheriff saw Walter Wratchford driving along, they'd just think he was having some milk.

The whole thing still made me nervous, as if I wasn't already nervous enough going to a colored church to play "Taps," but at least he didn't try to get me to drink any of it, too. I asked him if he knew the colored soldier whose funeral we were going to, if they were in Vietnam together. Walter Wratchford shook his head. "Nah. I never met him. I saw one of his buddies that told me." He said the colored guy used to play football at the colored high school out in the county and used to be pretty good, too, and must have played at a colored college but he got drafted for the war. I didn't know what to say back. I hadn't even known there *was* a colored high school out in the county.

Walter Wratchford didn't say anything after that, but just drove us out of town, across the Peace River bridge, and past The Springs, where I had heard he went on the weekends and brought his big carved bird finger he got in the war. There was a dirt road off to the right that I must have seen a million times but never went down, but we went down it that day and bounced along in Walter Wratchford's old Ford Fairlane at the edge of a field on our left and some woods to the right. Occasionally you could look through and see the Peace River even though it was narrow there and the bank was steep. Everywhere around us there were black cypress knees and cattails, and it smelled like mud and rotting leaves and alligator breath.

It took me a while, but finally I got up enough nerve to ask him about being in the war and what was it like in Vietnam and was he ever in any of the Vietcong tunnels. That made him laugh a little bit, and he said, "Heck, no, I wasn't inside any of those tunnels—are you crazy? They got all kinds of booby traps down there. They take a snake, one of those poison vipers, and tie him to a piece of string hanging from the ceiling of a cave, and if you come crawling along not knowing where you're going, you bump right into him and he bites you in the face."

I said, "Right in the face?"

He grunted. "Right smack-dab in the face. I saw a guy one time, his face was the size of a watermelon it swole up so big."

"From a viper?" I said.

"You're dang right from a viper," he said, and then he said again, "You couldn't pay me to go down those tunnels. And I don't want to hear about you going down there, neither. OK?"

"Yes, sir," I said.

He took a drink from his milk carton. "I know I told you not to call me sir, since I'm not an officer."

I said but I thought he was a corporal and he said he *was* a corporal, but a corporal wasn't an officer, it was a noncom. I nodded like I knew what that was supposed to mean, and I didn't call him sir anymore. Not that I had much of a chance to, anyway, because Walter Wratchford finally stopped his car at the place where the road ended. It was a clearing of a couple of acres, and other cars were everywhere, mostly old cars that looked like they should have been in a junkyard, but a couple of shiny almost-new ones, too, including a big black Cadillac with fins that looked like the Batmobile from a certain angle. There were five or six gray-board shacks with porches and raked dirt yards like they had down in the Boogerbottom, and across the clearing was the church, which was wood painted white and a steeple also wood painted white with a cross on top painted gold. Most of the colored people must have already been inside the church, because we could hear singing and clapping and somebody banging on a piano a lot louder than they ever did in our church, where they played the organ for hymns instead. But there were still a few colored people, some men, standing outside next to a low black hearse at the side of the church. They all wore suits, black suits, with the coats buttoned up, and they all smoked cigarettes.

Walter Wratchford lit a cigarette, too, and when he wasn't taking a puff, he was flicking it, tapping it, fidgeting it around, sort of worrying it until it looked so wrung out and limp that it was hard to believe he could still be smoking. I felt stupid in my Scout uniform, when he got out of the Fairlane and motioned for me to get out, and seeing the colored men in their suits, I was embarrassed by how Walter Wratchford looked, too, with his uniform and long greasy hair. I was afraid he was going to make me go inside the church, but he didn't. He walked over to the colored men by the hearse, with me a little ways behind him, and he told them we were there to pay respects to the fallen soldier. That's what he called the colored man who died—the fallen soldier. The men just nodded, but I could tell they thought Walter Wratchford was strange, and when they looked at me, I could tell they thought I was strange, too, and they didn't want us there any more than those colored kids had wanted me and Wayne delivering flyers down to the Boogerbottom. I wished we could just get the heck out of there before people came out of the church.

About that time, somebody did leave the church. It was a boy about my age. The door banged open and he stumbled outside, crying really hard and yelling. He fell down on the concrete-block steps and started hitting his face with his fists, and then hit his head on the steps one time before the colored men next to the hearse could get to him to grab him and make him stop. Some colored women came out of the church and rushed over to him, too, but he pulled away from everybody and ran away, yelling and crying, and saying, "Jesus, Jesus, Jesus, Jesus."

I wondered if the boy was related to the colored soldier that got killed—maybe his little brother—and that made me wonder how I would be if Wayne ever died or got killed in the war. I doubted I would hit my own head or run off like that boy did, but I knew I'd be sadder than just about anything. Just thinking about it made me want to go home and crawl in my bed.

Walter Wratchford dragged me back a ways while the colored men chased after the boy and caught him, which wasn't hard, because he seemed like he was blind, running into cars, throwing himself on the ground even though he had his Sunday suit on, then getting back up and running again. They took hold of his arms and had to hold him up, because once they got to him, his legs crumpled and he couldn't stand anymore. Other people came out of the church, and one must have been his mom, because they brought him over to her and she took him in her arms and sat on the steps and just held him. She called him "baby-baby" and said that over and over like it was one word or one name. I felt like crying from seeing all this, but the service inside never stopped the whole time, except they weren't singing now. But the preacher was shouting instead. I couldn't understand what he was saying, partly because of the way he talked, or shouted, and partly because the people in the congregation said things back, not like the readings from the back of the hymnal we had at the Methodist Church, where the minister read one sentence and all of us down in the pews read the next sentence together.

The boy on the steps with his mom wasn't yelling anymore, but just shaking, his face buried in his mom's lap while she rubbed his back until the colored men and some other ladies helped them both up and they went back inside the church. Walter Wratchford lit another cigarette from the butt of the first one, and I just stood there with him, not wanting to move unless somebody might notice us again. I looked down at my uniform and was glad at least I was wearing the long khaki pants instead of the shorts with the high green socks and red garter belts.

I asked Walter Wratchford if we were going in, too. He said no, they didn't want us in there, and he didn't like churches besides, so we waited in the sticky afternoon and there wasn't any talking after that. I hoped if I was just silent this might all end without me having to do anything except eventually just get back in Walter Wratchford's car and him drive me back home.

The wind shifted and the sky got darker, but I couldn't tell if it was storm clouds or smoke from the tire fire.

Walter Wratchford reached in his car for his milk and drank the rest of it, and the doors opened from the colored church and out came everybody, starting with the preacher, a tall, crooked old man with a big Bible, followed by six colored men in black suits carrying the wood coffin. At Mr. Rhodes's funeral there was an American flag spread out on top of the coffin, but there wasn't one this time. It was a nice box, though—some kind of dark polished wood with shiny brass handles. The six men carried it up on their shoulders and didn't seem to have any trouble getting it down the steps. They headed off not to the hearse but around the side of the church, where everybody followed. I didn't know most of the colored people except for a few: Chollie Ellis, and the fried-chicken lady Miss Deas, and the boy that had run outside the church before, and his mom holding on to him like she was afraid if she didn't he might run off again.

"Come on," Walter Wratchford said. "Get your trumpet."

I started to tell him it wasn't a trumpet, it was a bugle—a trumpet had keys to change the notes, and a bugle was just about how you positioned your lips and how you blew in it—but he probably didn't want to hear all that, so I didn't say anything. We didn't follow the crowd of colored people directly, but went the opposite way around the back of the church instead, where it turned out they had a little cemetery. They didn't have any grass there, either, just like in their yards, but they took good care of it, anyway, and there was one big tree right in the middle, an oak tree that spread out pretty wide so it shaded most of the graves.

Where they brought the coffin wasn't in the shade, though, but just outside it, in the sun. The wind must have shifted and blown away the smoke from the tire fire. It was actually a pretty nice day except for the funeral.

Walter Wratchford and me stayed a ways away from where the colored people gathered together with the coffin, but I could still see the ropes they had laid across the open grave they had dug. The men from the hearse took hold of the ends of the ropes while the pallbearers set the coffin down, and then they lowered the coffin into the ground.

The old preacher raised up one of his hands and read the "dust to dust," and then "I go before you to prepare a table at the house of my Father," which is what they read at Mr. Rhodes's funeral, too. Everybody was crying, even Walter Wratchford a little bit, but I wasn't for some reason, and I didn't know why. The preacher finished and they all bowed their heads in the sunshine, but now it seemed cold to me, and when Walter Wratchford told me, "All right, you can play," my bugle felt like it weighed about fifty pounds. I got through it all right, though—"Day is done, gone the sun"—but kept my eyes closed the whole time. When I opened them, I expected all the colored people to be looking at me, but most of them were already heading back to the front of the church and their cars.

Chollie Ellis nodded, and I appreciated that, but the colored boy who was the little brother looked kind of mad and kept glaring back at me and Walter Wratchford while his mom and some other people led him away. He looked like he wanted to spit on us or at least at us, but he was too far away and probably his mouth was too dry. I don't know if he was one of the boys that chased me and Wayne out of the Boogerbottom, but I bet if he had a rock right then, he would have thrown it at me.

Me and Walter Wratchford waited until all the colored people's cars were gone. You could see a big cloud of dust from where they had all been parked, and pretty soon we were the only ones still there except for the few cars at the houses. I didn't say a word to Walter Wratchford most of the way home, and he didn't say anything to me, either, except to lay a five-dollar bill on the seat between us. I knew I wasn't supposed to, of course, but I took it, anyway, and stuck it in my pocket. I felt bad, but not too bad, because Dad hadn't ever said anything about me not taking money for playing at a colored person's funeral. Plus, I didn't want Walter Wratchford to set fire to that five-dollar bill and burn it up, too.

Finally, when we got to the Peace River bridge, I said something. I asked Walter Wratchford about when he told Mom that the colored soldier was the *first killed*—did he mean first *soldier*, or first *colored* soldier?

He looked at me hard for about a minute. I thought he was going to crash the car. Then he said, "You think we ought to distinguish between the two?"

"No, sir," I said, even though he'd told me about a million times not to call him sir. "I didn't mean that. Not anything like that." I wasn't sure what I had said wrong, but I didn't want him mad at me so I said I was sorry.

He asked what-hell I was sorry for, but I knew he didn't expect an answer. We bounced across the bridge past the Sand Mountain city limits sign, and I leaned against the car door until I felt the rope give and the door sway open a little so I had to sit back up.

Walter Wratchford turned and spit out his window. After that he stared straight ahead as we drove through town and back to my house. Without looking at me this time, he said, "I knew what you meant."

Then he said there was this thing he had figured out in the war and he guessed I didn't understand it just yet—a lot of people didn't understand it—that there might be hundreds of categories for the living, but there wasn't but one category for dead.

Dad still wasn't home from work when I got back, and I changed right away and didn't say anything about it at dinner, and neither did Mom and neither did Tink. Wayne just wanted to know where I got all the money, and when I told him, he said he didn't believe me. We were in bed and I was too tired to get in an argument with him.

I kept thinking about what Walter Wratchford had said about only one category for dead. I didn't understand it but wanted to. I thought about that colored boy I saw, too, and could almost still hear him crying, "Jesus, Jesus, Jesus, Jesus." I thought about the way the colored people looked at me like they didn't know what the heck I was doing there with Walter Wratchford and my bugle, playing "Taps," and I wondered if us being white to them was like them being colored to us—sort of the only thing they saw: not me exactly, or Walter Wratchford exactly, just the white—and I figured probably so.

Chapter Twenty-two

THE NEXT NIGHT WAS SATURDAY, which was when I was supposed to be meeting Darla and going to the Skeleton Hotel. I didn't ever go to sleep so didn't have to wake myself up when it got to be midnight. I didn't even get undressed before I went to bed.

Wayne snored like a train, so I could barely hear myself climb down from the top bunk, or open the bedroom door, or walk down the hall. I decided that instead of climbing out the window, I would just go out the front door and leave it unlocked, which was what I did, and there wasn't a single soul awake anywhere on Orange Avenue when I walked down to the corner by David Tremblay's. I thought about peeking in some windows but didn't want to be late for Darla, and besides, I didn't know what there was to see, anyway, since nobody had any lights on.

I was scared to be sneaking out again and maybe get caught by Mom and Dad and put on restrictions, and scared to be going back to the Skeleton Hotel, too, with the ghost lady and the Howler, but I also was kind of looking forward to it being me and Darla squeezed together between two of the Sinclair gas pumps to watch the hotel, and I was kind of thinking she might even want to do some kissing. I had been thinking about that a lot lately, actually, and once I even had a dream about it.

As for that story about Darla and the colored boy and the fireworks—I decided it was probably a big fat lie, and even if it wasn't, maybe I didn't care.

I saw Darla coming down Second Street from the direction of her house, right in the middle of the street, partly walking and partly tap-dancing until she saw me, and then she looked around and said, "Wayne didn't come?"

It hurt my feelings that she asked me that. "No, you told me to make sure he didn't—remember?"

She nodded but didn't smile. "Good," she said. "So let's get going," and we did, but she kept looking behind us, I guess checking or maybe even hoping we were being followed by my stupid brother, not that you could see too far back, as dark as it was. After a while, though, when we got to the churches near downtown, she grabbed my hand and swung it and then pulled me and said, "Let's run the rest of the way," which we did, all the way to the Sinclair station.

It was quiet as anything once we got there, just like the time before. In fact, just about everything was like the time before, except no Wayne. And just like I hoped, Darla and I sat together between the two pumps. I felt the bones of her—shoulder and elbow and hip—so it wasn't soft at all the way it had been when we rode Bojangles. She still held my hand, which was nice except my palm was sweaty and I wanted to wipe it off on my pants, but I was afraid if I did she might not hold my hand again and I knew I would be too nervous to reach over for hers. It was all very complicated in my head, so I figured the best thing to do was just nothing, so that's what I did except for making a hoot-owl noise until Darla told me to hush and don't be so silly. I said I wasn't being silly; that's what you do in Scouts to signal to somebody where you are. She said she guessed it was OK then, but who was I trying to signal? Of course I wasn't trying to signal anybody really but I wasn't about to tell Darla that, so I said you also did it just in case there was another Scout anywhere around you didn't know about.

She said, "Well, I don't hear another hoot owl."

"No," I said. "So that's good; now we know there's nobody else here."

Darla said, "Your hand is sweaty."

I said, "How do you know it's not your hand that's sweaty?"

She said, "Girls don't sweat; they expire."

That made me laugh. I told Darla she meant "*per*spire" not "*ex*pire." She didn't think it was so funny, though, and she pulled her hand away and told me I could hold my own sweaty hand

220 ·

next time, and anyway, she didn't think anything was going to happen here tonight, and she didn't believe I ever saw anything that other time, and she bet I made the whole thing up.

I didn't even have to defend myself because right then we heard the elevator at the Skeleton Hotel kick on with the loud hum of the gearbox and the grinding of the pulleys and the creaking of the steel girders. Darla grabbed my hand again and squeezed so hard I thought she was going to break my fingers, and when the elevator hit bottom and somebody walked out from the tarp at the edge of the farmers' market, she squeezed even harder to where I heard my knuckles pop.

It was a lady again, the same lady in the same coat but she didn't have a hood over her head like before, so when she got in the middle of the intersection under the stoplight, we sort of saw her face, and when she got under the streetlight on the corner nearest to where we were hiding, we saw her face real good and there was no doubt about it—it was Darla's mom.

Darla's mouth was open for a second while she stared, and I could tell she was holding her breath. *Mrs. Turkel.* What the heck was she doing there? She kept walking, right near us, and she opened a purse she was carrying and pulled out a hairbrush and brushed her hair a couple of times, hard like she was mad at it, and then she threw the brush back in her purse and snapped it shut.

She was past us by then and we only saw the back of her for another second, and then she was gone, just like the time before, when it was just me, except we could hear her hard shoes on the sidewalk—they cracked and echoed, cracked and echoed with every step, fainter and fainter until I wasn't sure if I still heard them or not.

I said, "Darla, that was your mom."

She didn't say anything back.

"What was she doing here?" I said.

Darla still didn't say anything.

"Darla?" I said. She was still holding her breath.

"Darla?" I was afraid she might faint if she didn't start breathing pretty soon.

I shook my hand loose and grabbed her shoulder. She was starting to scare me. "Darla?"

She turned and looked at me and her face was blank like she forgot I was even there. "What?" she said.

I said again, "That was your mom."

She said, "No, it wasn't. Don't be ridiculous."

I said, "It was. You saw her. She walked right by us."

Darla said, "That wasn't my mom. You probably need glasses. I saw that lady before. She works at the A&W Root Beer."

I knew who she was talking about, and the lady that worked at the A&W didn't look anything like who we just saw, but at the same time, Darla was so sure the way she talked, it made me wonder a little bit if I was going blind or something and maybe she was right, maybe I did need glasses. But I could have sworn that was Darla's mom, I really could.

I was just about to ask Darla what the heck the lady from the A&W *or whoever it was* was doing at the Skeleton Hotel, anyway, but I didn't have the chance because the elevator started up again and we heard it going to the top and then it stuck there for a minute and then came back down.

"It's the Howler," I said, but Darla said it couldn't be the Howler—he wasn't howling, for goodness sake. It was just somebody leaving that was up there, too, and she was right, because pretty soon a car started up from behind the Skeleton Hotel and we saw it when it came around the building to the stoplight—that old blue Ford Fairlane of Walter Wratchford's with the red doors. He didn't even bother to stop at the light; he just motored right through the intersection going real slow, the engine chugging and smoke pouring out of the exhaust. I saw Walter Wratchford; he had one arm hanging out the window, and the other holding a cigarette, and one finger all alone on top of the steering wheel, and he headed east down First Street toward the Peace River bridge. It must have taken about five minutes after he was gone for that big cloud of exhaust to settle.

As soon as it did, though, Darla was halfway across the road before I even quite realized where she was going, and I took off after her.

"Wait," I said. "You can't go there. What about the Howler?" She didn't look back at me.

I said, "Where are you going?"

"Up there," she said. She meant the top of the Skeleton Hotel.

I didn't want to follow her, but I didn't want her to leave me, either, so I kept going, too: under the traffic light, under the streetlight, all the way over to the Skeleton Hotel. My head hurt from everything happening so fast. Plus I didn't get how Darla could be scared one minute—as scared as me—waiting for the Howler, and then the next minute see her mom and Walter Wratchford and have everything change. Now she didn't seem scared, just mad and upset and a bunch of other things I didn't understand because my mind wasn't hardly working at all except to tell me to stay with her, even when she pulled back the tarp of the farmers' market and ducked in, and even when she fumbled with the cage to the elevator to pull it back, and even when we got in on a wood pallet that was the elevator floor, and even when she pulled on some levers, trying to make something work until the elevator jerked to a start and I lost my balance and grabbed on to her as it went up and she grabbed me back and we both held on like that all the way to the top.

We got there pretty fast and the elevator jerked again when it stopped, and this time I did fall down. Darla didn't grab me, though, but just walked out on the roof, which was flat, and I crawled out behind her. There was nothing around the edge up there, just like the elevator, but Darla went right over to it and looked down at the intersection and the Sinclair station and the City Hall and the 7-Eleven while I stayed crouched in the middle at a little shed next to the elevator. I was shaking even though it wasn't cold, and my teeth were chattering and everything, and all

I could think about was what if Walter Wratchford came back and caught us. I pulled my knees up and wrapped my arms around them to try to get warm and couldn't believe I was where I was, and so scared I thought I might wet my pants.

I whispered, "Let's go back down now," but I don't think Darla heard me. She was staring off in the direction of her house, even though you couldn't see that far—not that I was about to stand up and go over there and check about that myself. She walked all the way around the edge of the roof like she was look-ing for something, and then she came back to the shed next to me and looked in. There was a bottle of something and she didn't even wait or anything, she just unscrewed the cap and took a drink from it and handed it to me.

"What is it?" I said, still whispering.

She said, "Booze."

I hadn't ever held a bottle like that, except for that one time with Walter Wratchford, since we didn't have it in our house and Mom and Dad didn't drink or anything, and just holding it scared me, too, but Darla said, "Drink some."

I said I didn't want to; I just wanted to go home. Darla said I was a baby and grabbed the bottle back and took another drink and then stepped inside the shed to where I couldn't see her, so I crawled over and looked inside, too. It was just an old tin shed with tin walls and a tin roof and an open front. There was a crate inside with a candle on it and Darla found some matches and tried to light it, but there was a breeze that kept blowing out her match. She said, "Cup your hands around this," and I did, and that time she got it lit. She slid the crate over a little ways out of the wind so the candle would stay lit and then she sat down on a kind of a bed that was just a long wood pallet with a thin mattress and a couple of blankets on it. She took another drink from the booze bottle and I thought she was crying.

She said, "That wasn't my mom," and I said, "OK, it wasn't," I didn't care, I just wanted to go, and couldn't we go, please, now?

She said, "In a minute," and she told me to sit by her, which I did, on that pallet, even though there was also an old stuffed chair up there without any legs, and a pile of cigarette butts in a pot next to it. Darla asked me why was I shaking like that and was I cold? I said I wasn't cold, but my teeth were still chattering and I guess I was still shivering and she took one of those blankets and put it around me, and her, too. She had put the bottle down, but she picked it back up again and stuck it under my nose. "Drink it," she said, and this time I took a tiny swig, which I thought was going to burn up my whole insides when I swallowed it. My eyes watered up so I couldn't see for about a minute, and I dropped the bottle. Darla just left it lying there on the roof near our feet. There wasn't enough in it to spill or anything.

Then Darla finally did kiss me—right on the lips. She did it so hard it hurt my teeth. That swig I took still burned in my throat and my stomach, and I kind of wanted to throw up but I couldn't say anything because Darla kissed me softer after that and even licked me with her tongue on my lips, and that scared me, too, but not as much as what she did next with her hand on my pants, or rather in my pants. She pulled on me down there for a minute and I forgot all about wanting to throw up or anything else, just how it felt the way she was pulling, except I could tell she was crying, and she said, "That wasn't my mom," and she pulled and I couldn't even move, I just sat there like I was a frozen zombie, and she said, "Say it," but all I could say was nothing except I didn't want her to stop pulling like that, and she didn't until there was an earthquake and stuff came out, I could feel it, and when Darla stopped and wiped her hand on the blanket, I still couldn't move, I just sat there leaning against her with my eyes closed because I didn't want to see what the world looked like after something like that.

There wasn't any moon that night, but the streetlights made shadows from us while we were walking home. Darla couldn't stand up too well, I guess from the booze, so I put my arm around her shoulder so she could lean on me, and I helped her like that all the way to her house. On the one hand I liked holding her, but on the other hand I wished I was away from her already and back in my own house and in my own bed. I also wanted to change my pants, since it looked like I had had an accident in them, and I didn't know what I was going to do with them so my mom wouldn't see when she did the laundry and asked me about them, but I couldn't exactly bury my jeans the way I did that Ban-Lon shirt. I only had two pair and I wore one or the other of them all the time.

Darla didn't even thank me when I got her home and boosted her up to a window in their living room that she had left open to sneak out of and then sneak back in. She didn't say anything and hadn't since the last time she told me that wasn't her mom we saw. I said, "Bye," and then I ran the whole way back to Orange Avenue, to my yard and my house and my bedroom and my bunk bed. Everything looked different to me, even though it also looked exactly the same.

Chapter Twenty-three

I GOT UP BEFORE EVERYBODY ELSE the next morning. I don't
know how, since I hadn't hardly slept at all, but my mind was
wide awake as soon as it was light outside. I leaned over the edge
of the bunk bed and looked down on Wayne. His pajamas were
all twisted around him like he'd been wrestling somebody and
lost the fight. His blanket was on the floor, where he must have
kicked it off, and his pillow was crammed up against the head-
board. His head was barely on it. You'd have thought it was him
out the night before, having the wild adventures instead of me.
I wanted to wake him up and tell him about what happened with
me and Darla, and the other stuff with Darla's mom and Walter
Wratchford. But as soon as I thought that, I thought I didn't
actually want to tell him or anybody. I wanted to keep it a secret
to myself. Plus, what if I told him about the whole thing with

Darla and he said, "Oh yeah, me, too"? So I decided I would keep the secret. Maybe I wouldn't even say anything about it to Darla, in case she changed her mind and decided it didn't really happen, which was just the sort of thing she might do.

I was starting to feel really lonely, which I guess is what secrets do to you, but then remembered I had to get up and do something I had never done before.

Laundry.

I had hid my jeans from the night before under the bottom bunk, so now I had to get on my belly and reach way in to fish them out of there along with my underwear. I scoured the room and got all the rest of the clothes I could find that were dirty: more underwear, and socks and T-shirts, plus Wayne's football gear, and I carried it all out of the bedroom, through the living room and the kitchen, out to the back porch. The jalousie windows were open and it was cool back there but not too dark, so I didn't have to turn on the light to see the washing machine. I dragged out a kitchen chair to stand on, then threw the stuff in and turned on the washer, which I had thought would be hard but wasn't once I figured out that you didn't just twist the knob around to "Normal," but you also had to pull it out toward you, until you heard a click, to make the water rush in. Since I didn't know how much soap to use, I went with three scoops, which seemed like a good number. After that was when I realized Mom was standing behind me, in the doorway to the kitchen.

She had on bedroom slippers and a light blue bathrobe, and

hadn't brushed her hair. Her face was kind of puffy, I guess from sleep, which was a way I had never seen her before. She still looked like Mom, only not the usual Mom. She said, "Don't forget to close the lid or it won't rinse and spin after the wash cycle."

I said, "Yes, ma'am," nervous about what she would say next, or what lie I could tell her about why I was doing what I was doing.

She asked if that was my sheets in there, and I realized she thought I must have peed the bed, which would have been a great lie if only I'd thought of it. Unfortunately my sheets were still on the bed, so I had to tell her no, I just thought I would help with the laundry today, that's all.

Mom lifted some hair off her forehead with the back of her hand, sort of brushed at it, then let it drop down in the same place. She crossed her arms. "You decided to get up early on a Saturday morning and help with the laundry?"

I said, "Yes, ma'am," again, and then asked could I help fix breakfast with her—would she like for me to do that, or set the table or something? When she didn't say anything back, I said also I was all ready for the job jar, wasn't it time for the job jar, shouldn't we get going on the Saturday chores?

Mom said she didn't know what on earth was going on with me today, but she guessed if it had me eager to do work, she wasn't going to worry about it. Then she changed her mind and got out the thermometer and checked my temperature. "It's a little high, but you don't have a fever," she said. She felt my face with her hand, then hugged me, then let me go and said I could help with breakfast if I wanted—I could get out the orange juice and everything to go on the table—and if I wanted to go ahead and pick first out of the job jar, I could do that, too.

I was hoping I'd get lucky, but instead picked out the worst jobs there were: CLEAN THE BATHROOM and TAKE OUT THE TRASH.

On Monday at school I stabbed Moe in the hand with my fork. I'm not sure why. He took my roll the way him or his big fat twin, Head, always did off my lunch tray, but that had been going on since school started—so long that I was almost used to it. Maybe part of the reason was Connolly Voss, who had been bothering me more than usual for letting Moe or Head take my rolls: How come I never did anything about it? What was I, a man or mouse? He had started calling me Darwin Turkel, which was worse than being called a girl, as everybody knew, and the other guys at the table actually thought that was funny and laughed when he said it. Once he was doing that and I was telling him to shut up or else, and the real Darwin walked by. I don't know if he heard or not, but he gave me a look like he was sad but at the same time used to that sort of thing, and I felt bad.

Probably all of those things were good enough reasons for what I did, but I guess the other one was that I was very hungry that day because I was almost late for school so missed breakfast, and all they had for lunch was canned peas and carrots, canned meat with canned gravy, canned banana pudding, and those homemade rolls they baked in giant trays that were fluffy and warm and brown on top from where they painted the margarine with big paint brushes and you could smell them cooking all over the school for about an hour before lunchtime. It was clear that the only good thing I would have to eat all day until I got home from school was my one single solitary roll.

But Moe showed up at the exact minute I got out of the lunch line and put down my tray. It happened so fast I didn't even have time to think about it. He was reaching for the roll and saying, "Thanks, Sambo," and I stabbed his hand with my fork.

Moe said, "What the heck." He had the roll in his fist. The fork hung there for a second and then fell on the floor. He said, "What the heck," again, but that was all for the first minute. There was hardly any blood, just a few drops was all. Moe shifted the roll to his other hand—I guess so he could examine the place where I stabbed him better—and the longer he stood there, the more you could see it was bleeding. I don't think anybody else at the table breathed. They didn't say anything, and my eyes got so big watching Moe and waiting for what would happen next that I thought I might go blind.

What he did was slap me so hard that tears squirted out of my eyes. I think they might have even landed on his shirt. My ear felt like it must have gotten knocked off, and there was a screaming noise inside my head that made me dizzy. Then, I guess because I really was the biggest idiot on the planet and also because I was in so much pain I didn't know what I was doing, I slapped him back, although it barely grazed his cheek because he was a lot taller than me. He reached back to smack me again but Wayne pushed his chair away from the table and pulled me out of the way and said why didn't Moe pick on somebody his own size?

Moe started after Wayne but that other guy Head appeared from out of nowhere and grabbed Moe's arm. My face stung like anything and my ear was still ringing, but I touched it and it was still there, at least. Moe's face looked like a big cloud of thunder about to break open and cause a flood of forty days and forty nights, but after Head whispered in his ear for a minute, he calmed down and got one of those evil grins on his face that you're always reading about.

"How tall are you?" he asked Wayne. Wayne said he was five foot six inches. David Tremblay stood sort of next to Wayne and sort of behind him, I guess so Wayne wouldn't feel all alone.

Moe, who must have been six feet tall, said he guessed Wayne and him were about the same size, then, so he guessed Wayne would do. Then he looked at his bloody hand and then he looked at his buddy Head and said, "Don't you guess he'll do?" Head said, "Yeah, I guess he'll do." Moe said he guessed he'd see Wayne in the parking lot after school, then, and Head nodded along and said yeah, he guessed the two of them ought to be able to get things all taken care of in the parking lot after school. I looked around, wondering where the lunchroom ladies were. Usually they came out of the kitchen and caught you if you so much as leaned back in your chair, but today they were nowhere around, nor any teachers, either.

The rest of the day was terrible. I wanted to turn all the clocks back and hold them back to keep them from getting to the end of school. Every time a bell rang for the finish of one period and then five minutes later for the start of the next period, my face hurt like Moe was right there slapping me again. I saw Wayne in the hall a couple of times, but he wouldn't look at me or say anything, and that made me feel even worse.

Moe didn't even say anything when Wayne showed up in the parking lot, he just hit him in the face and kept hitting him. We were all standing there—me and David Tremblay and the others over on one side, Moe's friends on the other side, plus a bunch of other people who just wanted to see a fight. But it wasn't a fight. It was just Moe beating up Wayne, and me doing nothing but watch, until one of the coaches, Coach Lundy, the baseball coach, came running out of the gym and yelled at them to break it up.

Moe didn't look at Coach Lundy and didn't say anything. He just walked off with his friends, even when Coach Lundy said, "Hey, you. Come back here when I'm talking to you. I want to know who started this." I couldn't believe he didn't know who Moe was. Everybody knew who Moe was.

Wayne hadn't ever fallen down the whole time he was getting beat up, which was a miracle, but you could see how shaky his legs were. Me and David Tremblay went over to hold him up, and I wanted to cry because of all the blood. David Tremblay actually took his shirt off and used it to hold against Wayne's bloody nose. I said I was sorry, but Wayne spit out some blood and I figured that meant he didn't want to hear it. David said, "Way to go, Wayne. I saw you get him one time. I think you got him in the kidney."

Coach Lundy stuck his big meaty face down to look at Wayne's. The bill of his baseball cap nearly jabbed into Wayne's forehead. "Think you're going to make it, there?" Wayne grunted something but I couldn't tell what. Coach Lundy looked at me and David Tremblay. "Y'all know where he lives?"

"Yes, sir," I said. "He's my brother."

Wayne spit more blood.

David Tremblay said we could get Wayne home OK. Coach Lundy said, "That's good. That's good." He straightened back up. "Now, I don't want to see any more fighting around here, y'all understand?" I nodded but he wasn't looking at me. "That goes for all of y'all," he said to anybody who was still around, which wasn't too many since most had run off when Coach Lundy first came out of the gym.

"All right, then," he said. "Can you walk OK there?" Wayne nodded and the coach slapped him on the shoulder. I thought it was going to knock Wayne down, but he just swayed a little.

"All right, then," the coach said again.

"Yes, sir," David Tremblay said. "Come on, Wayne." And he

pulled Wayne over in the direction of our bikes. I took Wayne's other arm, but he pulled away from me, so I said I would walk Wayne's and my bikes home. David left his bike, so he could hold on to Wayne, and said he'd come back for it later.

"I'm sorry," I said one more time to Wayne, but he didn't even bother to spit.

The official story was Wayne's helmet came off during JV football practice and he got mushed in a pileup. Mom was the first to see him and she made him lie down with an ice pack on his face so big I thought if it melted he might drown. She wanted him to quit the team, but Dad said the kind of thing he was always saying: if a horse throws you off, you have to climb back on right away and ride him again.

"I think it's stupid," Tink said. "They ought to put them all in the jail."

"All who?" Dad said. We were sitting down to dinner, all except Wayne, who got to have his on a TV tray in the living room and watch television while he ate, which ordinarily I wouldn't think was fair but I felt so lousy about getting him beat up that I even helped set up the TV tray, which wasn't easy. Wayne's lip was swollen and he said his teeth hurt, so Mom had made him soup.

"All the football players that did that to Wayne," Tink said. "I think they did that on purpose."

"Accidents happen," Dad said. "It's all part of the game."

Mom said something under her breath that I think he might have heard because he said, "Now, Rennie," which was my mom's name.

He seemed so relaxed about everything that I started to worry maybe he knew what had really happened and was just playing along for some reason, to catch us in more stories and bigger lies. But I didn't worry too much about that, either, because of the silent treatment Wayne was still giving me—not so much as a word or a look, even though I tried everything.

"Hey, Wayne, you want me to do your chores from the job jar?"

Nothing.

"Hey, Wayne, you want me to make you a peanut-butter-and-banana sandwich?"

Nothing.

I sat alone at lunch the next day, at a table in the corner of the cafeteria, but it didn't matter. Moe still found me and took my roll, plus he took my carton of milk, too. I hardly noticed, though, because I was too busy watching Wayne and David Tremblay and Boopie Larent and all those guys talking and laughing and messing around, making fun of Connolly Voss, over where I used to sit with them. The worse I felt, the better the time they had, and it didn't seem like anybody missed me, either. I kept waiting for them to look over my way, especially Wayne, and then I'd at least know that they knew I was gone and they cared *some,* but nobody did.

I guess I could have gone over and sat with Darla, or even Darwin. He was at another corner table, across the cafeteria from me, with one other boy from the tenth grade everybody called Hoot, who was supposed to be a math genius, although to be a genius in Sand Mountain didn't take too much of an IQ, and anyway, he never looked anywhere but at his shoes when he was around people. They didn't seem to talk hardly at all, and didn't sit in any of the seats right next to each other.

I guess I could have gone over and sat with Dottie Larent, too. She didn't have regular friends, and one day I saw her at the end of a table by herself with a couple of chairs between her and anybody else. People said she had a BO problem and didn't take a bath or a shower except once every now and then like colored people, but I didn't believe it. I'd been around Dottie some and never smelled her once.

But I guess I still thought it was better to be miserable and alone than embarrassed for people to see me hanging out with somebody that was supposed to be smelly like Dottie Larent, or worse than a girl like Darwin Turkel, or a retarded genius like Hoot, or even Darla, who dressed so funny and had the Shirley Temple hair and set off firecrackers with a colored boy in the cemetery, and you never knew when she might suddenly start singing or dancing, and you also never knew when she might take you up to the top of the Skeleton Hotel and do things that you didn't know what to think about later so you tried not to think about them at all and you tried to not have to look at her anymore or talk to her or anything, even though that was probably mean—

So I sat alone.

Mom finally noticed something was wrong with me, I guess, because after school I went in my bedroom and shut the door and crawled up on the top bunk and stayed there until dinnertime. I might have fallen asleep, because she was just there next to the bunk bed with her hand on my head. When she saw I was awake, she said, "Do you not feel well, Dewey? You're all hot and sweaty."

I said I was OK. She said she thought she would get the thermometer and I said I wasn't a baby. She said, "Well, you're my baby."

I said, "Oh, Mom."

She laid her hand on my forehead and it felt cool, and for some reason I just about started crying. She asked if Wayne and I weren't getting along, and I said, "Sort of." She said it would get better. I said what if it didn't? What if it got worse and worse? That could happen, too.

She seemed surprised by what I said. "Your brother loves you very much. That doesn't mean you always have to get along. But he does love you, and he has always watched out for you."

I said I doubted he would anymore, and she asked me why I said that. I said I didn't know. Mom didn't say anything for a little while. Her back was to the window and the blinds were closed and it was dark in the room, so I couldn't see her face very well. There was an orange light coming through the blinds that made a kind of outline around her. She had taken her hand away from my forehead when I said that about Wayne maybe not watching out for me and stuff, but she put it back. She asked me if I remembered the song she used to sing to me when I was little.

"You mean 'Mack the Knife'?" I said.

"No, the other one, when you were a very little boy." I said no but I really did. It was "Dewey Was an Admiral on Manila Bay."

She started to sing and I said, "Oh, Mom," again like it was embarrassing, but she kept singing, really soft, her cool hand still on my head.

> Dewey was an admiral on Manila Bay.
> Dewey was a morning in the month of May.
> Dewey were her eyes as she pledged her love so true.
> Oh, do we love each other? Yes, indeed we do.
> Oh, do we love each other? Yes, indeed we do.

Chapter Twenty-four

EVERYTHING CHANGED TWO DAYS AFTER the fork stabbing. It was the first week of October and the first cool day we'd had, not quite cold enough for a jacket but not warm enough for just a T-shirt, either, so what I did was wear two T-shirts. Some leaves danced around in the street when I rode my bike to school, and I didn't pay much attention to what I was doing because of watching them and so bumped into the side of a car that was parked on Second Street. I didn't get hurt except that two girls saw me and laughed, but they were in elementary school so I didn't care.

All that morning, I kept looking out the windows of my classes and watching the leaves falling and dancing. Always in the past I had just woken up in October and realized it was autumn and had been for a while, but that particular day was different— I was actually seeing it happen, actually seeing the end of the summer and the beginning of the fall. The problem was I kept getting called on in class, because even though I didn't raise my hand, the teachers were so used to it that they called on me, anyway, only this time I not only didn't know the answers, I didn't know the questions, either. That Americanism vs. Communism teacher, Mr. Cheeley, got mad at me and told me I had to write a letter to General Westmoreland on "Why I Should Be Fighting in Vietnam." I said, "You mean why *America* should be fighting?" but he shook his head and said, "No, I mean why *you*, Mr. Turner."

I couldn't wait until lunch, partly so I wouldn't get called on anymore, and partly because I had to scoot outside and pee, which I went and did as soon as the bell rang. I had just come in and got my food tray—I hadn't even sat down yet—when David Tremblay came up and said, "Hey, Dewey." I was pretty happy at first that at least somebody wasn't giving me the silent treatment anymore, and thought maybe he was even going to invite me to sit with him and Wayne and them. He had something in his hand that he was hiding, but at the same time trying to look like he wasn't hiding, and he put it on my tray. It was his roll. "I'm switching," he said. "But don't eat it." Then he grabbed mine and left before I could say anything.

About a minute later, after I sat down by myself, Moe and Head came in the cafeteria and swung by my table the way they usually did on their way to the lunch line. Moe said, "Snack time," and snatched up the roll and my milk. He popped the roll in his big mouth and practically swallowed it whole and then opened the milk carton. Then he stopped. He had a funny look on his face and he said, "Bleah," and stuck out his tongue the way you do when you eat something rotten or sour. He sniffed the milk and drank it straight down, swishing the last gulp around his mouth before swallowing. Head said, "Well?" and looked back at me like I might have done something.

Moe said, "Bad roll."

David Tremblay and Wayne were watching the whole thing, their eyes as wide as mine the day I stabbed Moe and he slapped me. David's mouth hung open even though he had food in it that he'd been chewing, and all I could think was, *Oh no, what now?* I put my head down on the table because it felt too heavy, but when I closed my eyes I saw Wayne again in the parking lot, and Moe hitting him, and the blood, and the way Wayne could barely stand up afterward and people thought that was a great thing because nobody had ever been able to stand up after a fight with Moe, even if Coach Lundy did break it up. Only this time it was me getting beat up in the picture I had in my mind, and there was no way I would still be standing afterward, or probably even live.

I didn't see what happened next, but I heard about it between fifth and sixth periods. Somebody said Moe went to the bathroom with a hall pass and he felt something was wrong while he was peeing, and when he looked down he saw he was peeing blood. A teacher heard him hollering, and by the time the teacher got to the bathroom Moe had a nose bleed, too, and it was so bad it wouldn't stop even when they put ice on it in the nurse's station. Moe bled so much that they finally called Dr. Rexroat, even though it was during Dr. Rexroat's lunch, which took up about three hours in the middle of the day, and everybody knew what that meant. He came after half an hour and didn't look too steady when he got to the school. Everybody heard him yelling, "Call the ambulance. Get this boy to Bartow Hospital *stat*"— which I learned later meant *right away*.

Everybody was hanging out in the halls by then, not even going to class because the teachers were buzzing around talking to one another and going down to the office, and nobody could believe it, and there was a rumor that Moe was bleeding not only from his nose and in his pee but also out of his butt, and also a rumor that he had drunk a cleaning solution from the janitor's closet. We all saw the ambulance finally pull up in front of the school, which was actually the hearse from the Kingdom Come Funeral Home since there wasn't an ambulance in Sand Mountain, and that got the rumor started that Moe was dead. But when they wheeled him out of the nurse's station on the stretcher, we could see he was alive, though he was still bleeding from his nose. His eyes looked worse than Wayne's with all the bruising around them, and so that started the rumor that a gang of colored boys had snuck up to the school and attacked him—I don't know why colored boys, except that any time there was any kind of rumor going around like that, people always blamed it on colored boys.

Head ran alongside the stretcher while they wheeled it down the hall to the front of the school to load it on the hearse and then, I guess, drive Moe up to Bartow, and Head was crying and yelling, "Hang on, buddy. Hang on, buddy. They'll save you."

At one point I saw Wayne and David Tremblay, but they wouldn't look at me and I knew the reason was something to do with that roll from lunch, the one David had switched. When I tried to get through the crowd to find out what was going on, they had already snuck off somewhere and I couldn't find them.

Wayne caught up to me that afternoon after school. We were riding our bikes down Second Street. He didn't even say hi, or he was sorry for giving me the silent treatment, or anything. He just said, "You can't tell anybody what happened."

I told him I didn't know what happened, and what did he care, anyway? Also I said maybe I was giving *him* the silent treatment now, so he should stop talking to me.

"If you're giving me the silent treatment, you can't tell me that you're giving me the silent treatment, or else it's not really the silent treatment," he said.

"I'm not talking to you," I said.

"You just did again," he said.

I swerved my bike over at his and he had to jerk his handlebars to swerve out of the way so I wouldn't hit him. Then he rode back next to me and grabbed my handlebars and made me stop, even though I punched him on the arm really hard.

I could tell by the look on his face that he wanted to punch me back, but he didn't. "Just listen for a minute," he said. "You can give me the silent treatment after that."

"What?" I said. "What the heck happened? Did David Tremblay poison Moe? Is that what happened? He poisoned him?"

"Yes," Wayne said.

"What?" I couldn't believe this. I expected him to deny it, to tell me it was all a big coincidence, a big joke, a big *something*, but not *this*.

"How?"

"With d-Con. It was just supposed to make him sick. David must have put too much in."

"What's d-Con?"

Wayne told me not to talk so loud. "Come on," he said. "Let's walk our bikes. Nobody can hear any of this." So we walked our bikes, although the more he told me, the more I forgot to keep walking and he had to pull me along. D-Con was rat poison, and David Tremblay had brought some to school and hollowed out his roll with his finger and poured a bunch of the rat poison in to get back at Moe for what he did to Wayne.

"I told him not to," Wayne said. "I kept telling him I wasn't hurt, it was no big deal, but David said he was going to get him. He said he read the directions, and it was just supposed to make the guy sick."

"The directions on rat poison tell you how much to give to a human?"

"Well, no. David just estimated or something."

"Is Moe going to die?"

"No," Wayne said. "No. It was just supposed to make him sick."

"What if he dies?"

"He's not going to die. Quit saying that. He'll be fine."

"If he was fine, they wouldn't of taken him to the hospital. And now they're going to think I did it. They're going to blame it on me."

"No, they're not. Just don't say anything. Just say you don't know what happened. They'll think it was something else that did it. Food poisoning."

"They're going to blame it on me. Why can't David Tremblay tell them he did it?"

"He's afraid they'll send him away to reform school like they did Ricky. He says he has to protect his mom from his step-dad. You never got in trouble before, so they won't do anything to you."

"You said nobody would even know."

"Well, if they did figure it out or something. Just tell them it was an accident."

"No."

"You have to."

"No."

"Please."

I couldn't believe any of this was really happening.

"Please?"

"Leave me alone."

"Promise me, Dewey."

"Leave me alone." I got back on my bike, and when Wayne grabbed my handlebars again, I socked his hand and he let go. I took off.

He yelled after me. "Dewey!"

I yelled back. "Leave me alone!" I yelled some other stuff, too: that I hated him and David Tremblay, and I told him to go to hell.

I had thought the first day of school, the day I skipped because I looked colored, was the worst day of my life. Then I thought the night me and Wayne and Darla snuck out to the Skeleton Hotel was the worst day of my life. Then I thought the day Dad made me and Wayne pass out the campaign flyers in the Boogerbottom and the colored kids chased us was the worst day of my life. The thing now was that even though *this* should have really been the worst day of my life, I was pretty sure that there were going to be still more worst days, maybe every day setting a new record for the worst, and it would go on like that for the rest of my life.

I turned my bike around when I was almost home and rode in the other direction, and didn't even care if I ran into Wayne trying to catch up to me again. That didn't happen, though. He must have turned around himself to go to JV practice, so I kept riding back up Second Street, over past the high school, past the Skeleton Hotel and the 7-Eleven and City Hall, past downtown and the railroad tracks, past the turnoff to Sand Mountain. I kept riding out to the Old Bartow Highway and Moon's Stable, and by the time I got there, I was out of breath and stopped. Probably I hoped Darla would be there, but she wasn't—at least not so I could tell from the road, since I didn't want to go any closer. Nobody was there that I could see, except Walter Wratchford's car and no sign of him. A couple of the horses in the field were playing between where I was and the barn. They were running around, chasing each other.

The sweat on me cooled off pretty quick. I didn't even get off my bicycle; I just had my foot on the fence holding me up. I folded my arms and closed my eyes for a minute and felt like a cowboy or something, out in the West, all on my own, nobody in a hundred miles or a thousand miles in any direction. I thought about the Painted Desert, which was a place where I had always wanted to go since I saw a picture of it one time. I liked the sound of it, and thought it must be the prettiest place in the world, and there wouldn't be anybody there. Just me.

When I opened my eyes again, there was somebody at Moon's, though, and it was Walter Wratchford. I hadn't seen him since that night at the Skeleton Hotel. He had come out of his shed, I guess to check on the horses and look around, maybe breathe some air that wasn't all cigarette smoke. He had on his usual army jacket and had his usual hair over his collar. He walked over to an old horse standing under a tree next to the fence but didn't notice me on the other side of the field next to the road, and then he did a strange thing, or strange for Walter Wratchford, anyway—he gave the horse something out of his pocket, probably a sugar cube, and when the horse leaned his head down to nibble it, Walter Wratchford leaned his own head against the horse's like it was a pillow. The horse didn't try to get away; he just let Walter Wratchford keep leaning against him for a long time. They both might have even fallen asleep standing up or something, because they stayed that way for about five minutes, and then all of a sudden they both started and jerked away from each other, like they didn't know where they were and had woken up confused. Walter Wratchford punched the horse in the head, but not hard or anything, more like the way a guy might punch another guy sometime who was his friend.

Walter Wratchford stuck his hands in the pockets of his army jacket and hunched up his shoulders like he'd gotten cold standing there, and I realized I was getting kind of cold, too, even though I had on the two T-shirts. Next thing I knew, he was walking across the field in my direction because I guess he must have seen me sitting there on my bike. He yelled something at me and I thought about taking off but was kind of scared to because what if he got in his car and came after me or something? There was no telling what he would do. So I waited, and in a second he was there at the fence offering me a cigarette like he did that time he picked me up at Bowlegs Creek.

I said, "No, thank you, I'm not allowed." He had shaken some up out of the pack, and then when I said no thank you, he tapped the pack on his hand and they went back down again. I thought about asking him if he knew about lung cancer and all, but decided not to. Anyway, he wasn't my dad, so if he died from it, I guessed I wouldn't miss him too much.

Walter Wratchford blinked through his cigarette smoke and blew out a big kitchen match he had lit up with his thumbnail. I could smell the sulfur.

He asked me was I looking for Darla and I said I kind of was. He said, "Well, she's kind of not here."

He squinted at me, and I realized the sun was behind me low in the sky so it was in his eyes. Usually he wore sunglasses but he didn't have them today. There was a scar by his right eye that I'd never noticed before and I wondered if he got that from the war.

He said, "You know I'm a friend of her family don't you? A friend of her mother's."

I said, "Yes, sir," even though I knew Darla's grandfather wouldn't let Walter Wratchford in their house, and of course I also knew about him at the Skeleton Hotel with Darla's mom, and the bottle, and the little shed up there.

He said, "I want to ask you a question."

I said, "Yes, sir?"

He said, "You haven't been fooling around with her, have you?"

That made me nervous. I said, "You mean like kissing?"

He made a snorting sound like one of those horses. "Yeah. Like kissing."

I shook my head. "No, sir."

"You promise? Because I like to see she does OK and I hate to see somebody move in on her, take advantage or something."

I said, "No, sir, I wouldn't ever move in on her," even though I wasn't too sure what he meant by that except it wasn't just about kissing and it probably was something like what happened at the Skeleton Hotel, only me doing it instead of Darla.

He said, "All right, then," and he said, "She's a good girl. People say things sometimes but she's a good girl. You remember that, you got it?"

I said, "Yes, sir."

He said, "People think they know things about people but usually they don't, not really. They think they know all kinds of things *about* all kinds of things, but mostly they don't know their head from their A-double-S, pardon my French." He looked at me hard. "You know what I'm talking about?"

I said I thought I did—like gossip and stuff, and how people make up stories about you like that you're colored when you're really not, or that you gave a guy at your school rat poison when it was somebody else, or that your dad loves colored people because of his election flyers.

He nodded and I thought he was agreeing with me, but then he said, "Rat poison?"

I made myself kind of laugh but probably it just made me sound guilty, and then I said, "Not really. I was just talking about stuff people might say about somebody that wasn't true or something." He kept looking at me hard the way he had been before and I got more nervous that he could see I was lying, even though I wasn't lying but it still felt like I was. I said, "I think I have to go home. It's probably dinnertime. We're probably about to have dinner. I probably have to set the table or something."

Walter Wratchford grabbed my handlebars but not in a mean way. He said, "The reason I wanted to talk to you about all this is I just want you to be nice to Darla. I'm just saying she needs a friend and maybe you might be her friend; just don't take advantage is all. That's what I wanted to tell you. That's all. Just be nice to her. You think you can do that?"

I said, "Yes sir," and he said didn't he already tell me once that he wasn't a sir and not to call him sir—that that was for his *father,* or for *officers*? I nodded, but I still wasn't about to call him anything else because, even if he didn't mind, I knew my mom and dad sure did.

Dear General Westmoreland,

My teacher Mr. Cheeley said for me to write this letter to explain to you Why I Should Be Fighting in Vietnam. The problem is I am not old enough to volunteer for the army since I am

twelve, but I read in the newspaper about all the tunnels the
Vietcong dug everywhere to hide in and live in and make sneak
attacks on the American soldiers from. The Vietcong are a lot
smaller than the Americans and so they need littler holes to
crawl down and littler caves to live in. But what I could do is,
since I am smaller, too, I could crawl down in those tunnels and
since the Vietcong wouldn't be expecting it, I could catch them by
surprise. I have also dug some of my own caves and lived in
them before, so I have a lot of experience, a lot more than you
would expect from someone my age. I also have a lot of practice
at the commando crawl and patrolling the perimeters. I know it's
not the same to just practice, and that war is real, not pretend.
But my mom told me that Alexander the Great got started when
he was my age and he conquered the whole world with his horse
Bucephalus. I should also mention that I am a very good horse-
back rider in case you need that for the jungles, since tanks and
armored cars can't go a lot of places where the Vietcong are. Also
I have a friend of mine who was a soldier in Vietnam and he told
me everything about it. We talk about it all the time, so I can be
prepared. In conclusion, this is Why I Should Be Fighting in
Vietnam. Thank you. Your friend (I hope) and fellow American,

    Dewey Turner

    That was what I wrote that night while I was waiting for them
to come and get me for poisoning Moe. I thought it was pretty
good, although the part about being a "fellow American" was

from LBJ, and of course I wasn't exactly a very good horseback rider and I made up the whole thing about talking to Walter Wratchford about Vietnam all the time, but it wasn't exactly a lie because of when he told me about the Bouncing Betties and when we went to the colored soldier's funeral. As usual I got the idea in my head for a while, while I was writing, that I could actually convince General Westmoreland to let me come to Vietnam, and so I wouldn't have to worry about anything after that, the same as when I had the idea of going to military school over in Tampa. But as soon as I finished and remembered that I wasn't going to mail my letter but just hand it in to Mr. Cheeley, I started worrying all over again about what was going to happen.

Wayne had left me alone when he got home from JV practice, and during dinner, and after dinner, until Mom said it was bedtime. The phone rang once and I got very nervous, but it was only David Tremblay calling to talk to Wayne. You never heard so much whispering like Wayne was doing during *that* conversation. The phone cord wasn't very long, but he tried to stretch it all the way from the kitchen down the hall to the bathroom so nobody could hear him.

When we were in bed, he started up again about me not saying anything. He had all these arguments he was making, trying to get me to feel sorry for David Tremblay and his mom, and what happened to Ricky Tremblay having to go to reform school, and it was all an accident, and Moe was going to be OK, and if Moe ever tried to do anything, they would protect me.

"They who?" I asked him. It was the first and only thing I had said to Wayne since that afternoon.

"Everybody in the neighborhood—me, David Tremblay, everybody."

"You didn't say anybody else's name."

"Well, that's because they don't know what happened. Nobody knows except you and me and David."

"And Moe." I don't know why I was giving Wayne a hard time. I felt so guilty about everything that I had already decided I wouldn't tell on David Tremblay and would just let everybody believe I had been the one to poison Moe, even though I could just hear Dad now, how he was going to yell at me, and Mom, too, which was worse because she wouldn't yell; she would just come in my room the way she had the day before, when she sang "Dewey Was an Admiral on Manila Bay," only instead of making me feel better, she would make me feel worse than anything when she said what I knew she would say:

"Dewey, your father and I are very disappointed in you."

I worried for a long time into the night, long after Wayne started snoring because of his hay fever, long after probably everybody else in town was asleep except the police and maybe Darla's mom and Walter Wratchford with their secret meeting on top of the Skeleton Hotel. Thinking about them got me thinking that probably everybody had some kind of a secret, like Darla and the colored boy in the cemetery, and me and Darla also on top of the Skeleton Hotel, and Darwin and his Turn Out the Lights game. That made me feel a little bit better. Plus, I hadn't told anybody about Darla's mom, or ever asked Darla about her and the colored boy, or said a word about Darwin. And I wasn't going to say a word, either, about David Tremblay and the rat poison.

Keeping all those secrets, or just letting people's secrets be—I figured that had to count for something.

Chapter Twenty-five

MOE DIDN'T DIE, but he didn't come home from the hospital right away, either. Even though nobody came to the house to arrest me, I still worried about it anyway, and that Friday night, I dreamed the whole town of Sand Mountain was lined up to give me a red belly. Somebody drove onto our front yard in real life and peeled a wheel that night, really late, and tore up some grass, but Dad said it must have just been teenagers, and he went by himself out to Panther Creek Sod Farm. On Saturday, after we did chores from the job jar, Dad made me and Wayne pass out more campaign flyers, even though we had already put one on every house and business in Sand Mountain before, but at least we didn't have to go down to the Boogerbottom again.

David Tremblay came with us, of course—he showed up at breakfast and kept trying to do my chores, but I knew what he was up to and didn't let him. He wasn't going to get off the hook that easy. He didn't say anything about the rat poison. Wayne and him kept being nice to me all day, anyway, like not making me have to talk to any of the people in the neighborhoods where we went. "You just carry the flyers in your basket," Wayne said. "Me and David will run them up to people's doors." They also bought me a chocolate milk shake at Honey's Drugstore downtown when we were done, and a Batman comic book, and when there was a big football game with everybody from the neighborhood that afternoon at the field by our house, they kept giving me the ball. It was enough to make you sick, and I thought about just leaving because I knew how phony they were being, but this dumb part of my brain still wanted to believe that everything had changed, just like that, and for no reason other than that Wayne and David Tremblay and maybe everybody else had just woken up that day and suddenly noticed what a great guy I was. I guess it was pretty sad. But at the same time, maybe you're an idiot if you don't take what they're giving you, no matter why it is they're doing it and no matter what they want in return.

So I sat on the bike and was happy I didn't have to talk to people about the flyers, and I sat in the booth at Honey's and drank that milk shake until the straw collapsed from nothing left, and I lay on the cool concrete of our carport back home and read Batman, and I scored two touchdowns with my amazing speed and guys mysteriously falling down trying to tackle me, and when it was all over, I wished I could live the day again and this time go ahead and let David Tremblay do my chores from the job jar, too, what the heck.

I didn't actually forget about Moe in the hospital, and about waiting to get blamed for him being rat-poisoned, but it was like the atom-bomb drills we used to have in elementary school where they had you run home and get in the bathroom with your whole family unless you had a fallout shelter. I worried all the time about the atom bombs and radiation, but there was also a part of me that didn't believe it could ever really happen.

At church on Sunday, Reverend Dunn said a prayer for Moe even though Moe was a Baptist, but nobody knew who the prayer was about, at first, because Reverend Dunn kept calling him "Charles": "And Lord we ask you to extend your mercies to one of our young high schoolers in the community, Charles Borgerding. We pray for the safe deliverance of Charles, and for the safety of all our young people in the congregation and the community." Reverend Dunn could hardly even say the last name, Borgerding, and me and Boopie Larent, sitting in the vesper choir, both started laughing and had to hide behind our hymn books. It was Ronnie Dick, that Scoutmaster's son, who was also in the vesper choir, who whispered to us that Reverend Dunn was talking about Moe.

"I heard he got attacked by colored boys that snuck up to the school," Ronnie Dick whispered.

I whispered back that that was just a stupid rumor, and Moe probably just had food poisoning. I was pretty nervous lying like that, but figured it was good practice.

Mr. Rupert, the choir director who was so mean, hissed at us and told us to zip it, which was actually what he said: "Zip it." We almost started laughing at that, too, but you never knew if Mr. Rupert might throw something at you, or even give you the Horse Eats Corn right there during church, so we didn't. Then the prayer was over and we had to sing, "Holy, holy, holy, Lord God Almighty," only Ronnie Dick, who was always messing around, sang, "Holy, holy, holy, Lord *Godamighty*," and me and Boopie just about choked.

Later on that day, I went to find Darla—not because I really wanted to but on account of what Walter Wratchford had said about being her friend and all, and not moving in on her, and not believing what you hear. Her mom came to the door when I knocked, and she said, "Hey, stranger," in this funny way like in the movies, but I couldn't look at her without thinking about the way she brushed her hair that night when we saw her coming out of the Skeleton Hotel. I don't know why that was the thing I remembered the most—the way she brushed her hair like she was mad at it and all—but I did.

Darla and me hardly talked when we got on our bikes, and I don't know how we ended up going back out to Sand Mountain, since neither one of us said anything about it. It must have been like the force of gravity that pulled us there, and just like the time before, we were the only ones. On the climb up, when she wasn't breathing too hard, Darla told me about this book she had just finished reading, called *Ethan Frome,* about a guy who must have been about the most miserable guy in the world. He was in love with a girl named Mattie Silver, and he hated his wife, old Mrs. Frome, who kept having her organs taken out because she didn't like them, and Ethan and Mattie at the end of the book rode on a sled in the snow down a giant hill and crashed into a giant elm tree on purpose. I think that was the part Darla liked so much— them doing that because they were in love but couldn't get married or anything, like Romeo and Juliet. But what happened instead was they didn't die; they just got hurt real bad and turned into cripples, and old Mrs. Frome ended up having to take care of them, even though she probably didn't have any organs left, and they were trapped with her all in the same house, forever.

Once we got to the top, Darla wanted to pretend we were Ethan Frome and Mattie Silver, which I thought was kind of a dumb thing, but that's how it was with Darla. We couldn't just ride down Sand Mountain on a piece of cardboard; we had to pretend we were trying to kill ourselves crashing into a tree. Only there weren't any trees anywhere near Sand Mountain, but I suppose if there had been, Darla would have wanted to crash into them just so we'd be able to do things right, the way they did them in the book. I asked Darla if there was any kissing in the story and she said I had a dirty mind, which made me mad, especially after what happened at the Skeleton Hotel. But I was too embarrassed to say anything about that, so I didn't say anything at all.

Darla started singing, "You Don't Have to Say You Love Me," which was playing a lot on the radio, and which surprised me because usually she just sang old songs that I didn't know or that I had heard because my mom sang them around our house.

I knew I should interrupt her, make her hop on the cardboard so we could ride back down and get the whole Ethan Frome business over with and so I wouldn't be too late getting home, but there was something about being up there on the top of Sand Mountain with Darla right then that kept me from saying anything—the way it was just her and me, and her singing like there was nothing else in the world, nothing to worry about, nothing at all. Even though the song was about being blue and missing someone, it didn't seem like that; it was just pretty.

When she finished, I still lay there on the cardboard and looked at her. She didn't look at anything, just curtsied at her pretend audience and then closed her eyes and breathed. The sun was starting to go down, a big red ball turning orange through all the phosphate dust where the mines and the processing plants had messed up everything west of Sand Mountain. The wind picked up and it turned cool. Darla seemed to be waiting for something, but I didn't know what.

"I did something really bad," I said all of a sudden.

Darla turned around and stared at me for a minute like she'd forgotten I was there and it surprised her to hear my voice, or anybody's voice. I wanted to tell her about the rat poison and I figured she would ask what I had done, but when she finally spoke, she just said, "No, you didn't."

"I did," I said. "I did something bad. I mean it."

"No, you didn't."

"I want to tell you about it."

"No, you don't."

"I do."

"No, you don't."

I couldn't believe this conversation. "Well, why don't I?"

"Because you didn't do anything."

"I didn't?"

"No."

"Are you sure?"

"Yes. I'm sure."

"Oh."

"'Oh' is right," Darla said, not that I knew what that was supposed to mean. But I didn't have time to think about it too much because she said we needed to get back down from the mountain. She said she was probably going to get in trouble with her mom, and it was mean of me to keep her up there so long when I knew she had to be home already.

I said I was sorry, even though I could have pointed out that it was her idea to stay longer while I was the one who had wanted to go home already, but with Darla, what was the use of arguing? In her mind there was nothing to argue about, just like in her mind I must not have done anything bad because she didn't want to hear about anything bad and that was all there was to it.

She dragged the cardboard out from under me and over to the edge. "Sorry won't get us down the mountain," she said, and she took off before I could climb on behind her.

I stood up and yelled, "Hey!" really loud, but there wasn't anything I could do, it happened so fast. There went Darla.

It took her the usual five seconds to get to the bottom, but it took me forever because I didn't have my own cardboard and so had to jump my way little by little to the bottom and I kept falling down, and if I tried to run, I got going too fast and I fell down, and if I rolled, I couldn't control where the heck I was going or how fast, either, and finally I just sat down and scooted on my rear end like a big inchworm or something.

By the time I finally got to the bottom, Darla was long gone on her bike and I had to ride home by myself in the dark. Mom was waiting for me at the house and drove me to Sunday night church late, still wearing my sandy clothes. "Your father is going to want to have a talk with you," she said, and he did.

Chapter Twenty-six

THEY CALLED ME DOWN to the principal's office in the middle of fourth period on Monday.

They had the principal in there, of course—Mr. Straub. And Officer O. O. Odom, in his brown uniform, standing next to Mr. Straub's desk. And Dr. Rexroat, who looked like he'd had a pretty rough weekend. His suit was wrinkled and his white hair stood up in the back like he slept on it that way. He had missed some spots shaving, but his face was about as wrinkled as his suit, so I figured it was hard for him to smooth out his skin enough to do a close shave no matter what.

They had me sit down in a big chair right in front of Mr. Straub's desk. It was higher than the chairs we had in the classrooms and my feet didn't reach the floor unless I sat right on the front edge, which I didn't do. Instead I slid all the way to the back of the chair and wished I could keep sliding back until I disappeared.

"You know why you're here, don't you, young man?" Mr. Straub said.

I couldn't open my mouth or nod or move or anything. I just stared at him. He wore glasses with black frames and thick lenses that made his eyes a lot bigger from where I was sitting. He looked like a bug.

Officer Odom leaned over and grabbed the back of my chair. He smelled like an onion. "You need to answer the question. Your job right now is to answer all the questions."

I couldn't say anything to him, either. I could hardly even see anymore because of all the tears I was trying not to let go of, partly because I was so scared and partly because of his bad breath.

"This is a very serious matter," Mr. Straub said.

"That's right," Officer Odom said, still leaning over me. He was like a giant talking onion. "Very serious."

"He could have died," Mr. Straub said.

"Do you know what that means?" Officer Onion asked me.

I looked at my hands. They seemed too small and I wondered if I had always had hands that were too small, and if everybody else knew it already but me.

"We're going to need some answers, Dewey," Mr. Straub said.

Boy, my hands looked little.

"Have you heard of reform school, Dewey?" Officer Odom said.

I made my hands into fists so I wouldn't have to keep seeing how tiny my fingers were, but then my fists looked too little and I didn't want to see them, either.

Officer Odom shook my chair. "Are you paying attention here?" He turned to Mr. Straub. "Is there something wrong with him?"

Mr. Straub said no, he had my test scores right there on his desk.

"Then why won't he talk?" Officer Odom said. I opened my fists and slid my hands underneath me.

Dr. Rexroat burped, like somebody in a cartoon, and everybody looked at him. "Can't you see the little malefactor is scared?" he said. I didn't know what a malefactor was, but the way he said it, I knew it couldn't be good. Dr. Rexroat didn't move from his chair, where he seemed to almost be lying down more than sitting, but Officer Odom moved back over next to Mr. Straub's desk. Maybe him and Dr. Rexroat had a secret sign that told him to do that, I don't know.

Dr. Rexroat rolled his eyes toward the ceiling and I looked, too. A pencil stuck out of one of the soft panels up there and I wondered if Mr. Straub threw it one time or if it was a kid sitting right where I was, waiting for the principal to come in and expel him or something.

"Poison," Dr. Rexroat said, still not looking at anybody, "is a funny thing. Take penicillin. You wouldn't eat moldy bread because it would make you sick, or at least you think it would, but you would take an injection of penicillin, which comes from the culture of that very same mold, and it would fight off infection and save your life. Unless, of course, it killed you instead, which has been known to happen in some extreme cases of allergic reaction.

"Or say if we have a man with arterial blockage and thus a man who could stroke at any time. We can give that man medication to thin out his blood so it will trickle around arterial obstructions, even those obstructions that might otherwise cause him to stroke. But if we prescribe that same medication in excessive dosage, or in the same dosage to a smaller organism—for example, a rat—then the rat's blood will thin to the point that the walls of his arteries and capillaries cannot hold it all in, will actually collapse, and so he will bleed internally. Of course all that blood has to go somewhere, and so it does—out of his mouth, out of his eye sockets, out of his ears, out of his anus. His organs will become liquefied, and that will be that. In one situation, in one dosage, and with one organism, it can save a life, but in another situation, in another dosage, and with another organism, it can take a life. Or, to put it another way, one man's blood thinner is another man's rat poison."

Dr. Rexroat had crossed his legs and was tapping his knee with a little rubber hammer, making his top leg bounce. "Young man," he said, still not looking at anything but that pencil stuck in the ceiling. "Is it possible that we owe you a debt of gratitude? That you somehow detected the symptoms of potential stroke in this Mr. Borgerding, and through swift action—blood thinner, or should I say rat poison, in his lunch biscuit—saved his life? If that is the case, you are surely to be forgiven if your dosage was excessive, causing Mr. Borgerding to react as he did, with the bleeding and the bruising."

Boink. His leg jumped. *Boink.* His leg jumped again. "You see, despite what Officer Odom and Mr. Straub here told you, the situation for Mr. Borgerding was not life-threatening. But neither was it entirely comfortable for him, or his family, or apparently the entire school, or Poison Control, or the fine and dedicated doctors and nurses at Bartow Hospital.

"So, on to my question, then. Should we be thanking you, Mr. Turner? Or—and God forbid this should be the case—might there have been malice in your prescription for Mr. Borgerding?"

My hands had gotten so numb wedged under my legs that I couldn't feel them anymore. My feet had gone to sleep, too, I guess, because the front edge of the chair cut off the circulation. I wasn't sure what exactly it was he had said. *Malefactor* and *arterial blockage* and *organisms* and *anus.*

But I did understand what they were all getting at, of course, which was why did I poison Moe, which by now I had almost started to think I really had, and not David Tremblay. I wanted to tell them it was David. Or else I wanted to explain about what Moe and Head had been doing all that time, stealing my rolls and milk, and not letting me go to the bathroom because of their WHITES ONLY.

But I didn't say anything. What could I say? And I was too

· 271

scared, anyway, just like Dr. Rexroat said. I was a scared malefactor. Whatever it meant, I knew I must be one.

Officer Odom pulled out his handcuffs and said did they think he should put them on me. Mr. Straub said he doubted they were small enough, which got me thinking again about how little my hands were, but Dr. Rexroat said, "Don't be a damn ass, Odom," which probably hurt Officer Odom's feelings a lot worse than the way my dad talked to him that night he came to our house.

"I'm just trying to do my job here," Officer Odom said in kind of a whiny voice.

"You got no call to talk to him that way," Mr. Straub said to Dr. Rexroat.

Dr. Rexroat tapped his knee one last time real hard, which looked like it caused his whole body to sit up all at once. Standing was harder for him, though, and I bet he wished there was some place he could tap himself again to help with that, too. He was wheezing when he finally made it, and he just grunted at Officer Odom and Mr. Straub and walked out without saying another word. I was sorry to see him go. He was the only one there that I sort of liked, even if I didn't know what he was talking about.

After he left, Officer Odom and Mr. Straub mumbled between themselves for a while, and I just sat there with my numb hands and my numb feet that eventually went from being numb to aching, but I still didn't move. I heard a train whistle from very far away, off one of the phosphate trains. Those trains went so slow, I

272 •

don't know why they bothered. Anybody who wasn't blind could always see them coming at a railroad crossing, except a drunk guy I heard about one time who fell asleep on the tracks that ran through Mr. Juddy's property and probably no whistle loud enough in the world could have saved him, anyway.

In the end they didn't put handcuffs on me and they didn't take me to jail; instead they said I couldn't go to school for two weeks and they said I had to go to a psychiatrist all the way up past Bartow in Lakeland. It must have been my mom's idea.

When Dad got home that afternoon, he took off his belt, but Mom wouldn't let him use it on me. She said, "Dewey needs our help right now, Hank. I don't think we should handle it this way."

Dad said he at least wanted to know what I had to say for myself, and he held my arms and kind of shook me until Mom made him not do that, either, and anyway, it didn't matter because I couldn't seem to say anything back, and finally he just sent me to my room.

Reverend Dunn came and tried to talk to me, but I couldn't talk to him, either. I wanted to, but when I tried, nothing came out. It was like I had run out of words. Even when Mom came in once and put her arms around me and said, "Please, Dewey."

Reverend Dunn told me God had a plan for everybody and my job was to figure out how everything that happened fit into God's plan for me. The way to figure that out, he said, was to give myself up to God in prayer. I tried, but the only prayer that came into my head, besides the Lord's Prayer, was the one from when I was little, which always scared me: *Now I lay me down to sleep, I pray the Lord my soul to keep. If I should die before I wake, I pray the Lord my soul to take.*

God didn't say a word back, but Wayne did. He said he was sorry he got me into all this, and he bought me Batman comic books just about every day from Honey's Drugstore, until he ran out of money, even though I didn't read them but just kept sticking them under my pillow on the top bunk, where I spent most of my time for about a week.

They made me go to the hospital to apologize to Moe. I went but didn't say anything; I just looked at my shoes. So Mom said it for me: "Dewey wants to apologize for what he did. He showed very poor judgment but wants you to let him know if there is anything he can do to help out."

Moe didn't look sick or anything. In fact, he looked like he was having a pretty good time in the hospital, with all the flowers and candy and TV and food and attention. I wished it had been me in the hospital. His mom was there, and that surprised me. I guess I hadn't thought a guy like Moe would have a mom. When she thanked my mom, she didn't sound like she meant it, more like she just wanted us to leave. She pointed at me and said, "Ain't he going to say anything?" Mom looked at me and said, "Dewey?" but I couldn't think of a single word.

■　■　■

David Tremblay tried to give me all his Elvis and Beatles records the next day. He brought them in the bedroom and said, "Here," and left them on the desk, but I didn't touch them the same as with the Batman comic books, and after a couple of days, he took them back. He wouldn't look at me, either. I guess he felt pretty bad, too.

Tink drew me a picture of Suzy like the other one she had drawn that time.

Mom cooked macaroni and cheese one night. She cooked fried chicken another night. She even had doughnuts for breakfast one morning, which wasn't even a Saturday.

Darla Turkel came over one night and tapped on the window. I wouldn't get out of bed to talk to her, so Wayne did. She stood outside and they whispered through the screen for kind of a long time. I didn't even try to listen to what they were saying.

Mom said, "Dewey, do you think you're punishing everybody else? Well, you're not. You're only punishing yourself by behaving this way. This is not the way you show that you're sorry and that you take responsibility for what you've done."

Tink said, "Why won't you talk to me, Dewey? Are you mad at me?"

Wayne said, "You know, at school I heard some kids say they wished they were the ones to poison Moe. Everybody said nice things about him when he was in the hospital, but then they made fun of him ever since he came back."

Dad didn't say anything to me directly after that first day. He didn't say anything to me at the dinner table, or on the way to church—not anywhere. But I knew what he was thinking, that he was disappointed in me. I worried that I had probably messed up the election for him, too, which was in just three more weeks. I bet he worried about that, too. One night I saw out the window that there was a blue light coming from his shed and looked like it was moving. I got worried at first but then figured it was that Niagara Falls lamp he fixed that time I asked him about military school and tried to talk to him about what was going on with the red bellies and the bathroom and all.

Darla came another night and talked to Wayne again through the screen. She wanted to talk to me but I still wouldn't get up. She didn't leave, though, but just kept whispering to Wayne, and after a while he said he was going outside with her and don't tell Mom and Dad. It made me a little mad, him hanging out with Darla again like that first night all of us went to the Skeleton Hotel, but then I thought about how I didn't talk to her at school and what a sorry thing that was. Walter Wratchford had told me to be her friend but I knew I hadn't been her friend. I had been a pretend friend—only when nobody else could see—and I bet most people didn't even know I knew her or even knew her name.

Wayne came back after an hour and crawled in the window and crawled back in bed. He was pretty nice to me. "Hey, Dewey," he said, "why don't you come down and tell me one of your old stories. You can lie in bed with me." I wanted to but I didn't do it.

The psychiatrist up in Lakeland, Dr. Boughner, kept asking me how come I wanted to be colored. Somehow he knew about the shoe polish and the Chattanooga Shoe-Shine Boy. I didn't answer him, but he just kept talking about stuff.

He said that I must have an identity with the colored people and it was a sign of low self-esteem. He said a lot of times if you're angry at other people, it's because you're angry at yourself, and a lot of times when a boy is angry at himself, it's because he has desires and attachments to his mom and resentments of his dad, and did I think I had those? He said that he thought I had those and what did I think?

When I just lay there on the couch and couldn't say what I thought, he waited a long time, about half an hour, before he said anything else. He said, well, the thing I should know is that those feelings are natural ones and I shouldn't feel guilty about having them. It's not right to do what those feelings want you to do, he said, but it's OK to have them. He said what happens when a boy has those feelings and doesn't think he should is that he gets mad at himself and catches low self-esteem, and then gets mad at somebody else. Like Moe.

He said a fork is a symbol, and what did I think it was a symbol of? I guess somebody must have told him about me stabbing Moe, because I sure didn't. I wondered if the right answer was the devil's pitchfork and it meant sin, but I didn't tell Dr. Boughner that, and Dr. Boughner never told me the answer, either, but he did say the rat poison was a symbol, too, and it wasn't Moe I wanted to poison but somebody else, and who did I think the rat really was? He said could it be myself as a vermin for having the feelings I wasn't supposed to have, or could it be my dad keeping me away from what I wanted?

I got mad at him for saying that. Maybe I was the rat instead of Moe, but my dad wasn't the rat, and he shouldn't have said so. But I still didn't say anything.

Mom was waiting for me in the waiting room when we finished, and she stopped at a restaurant in Bartow called John's Restaurant, where they had hamburgers with hot cole slaw they put on them that I guess they were famous for. She must have thought I would want one, but I never did like hamburgers, and especially hamburgers with cole slaw. I would have eaten a hot dog but I couldn't quite make myself ask if I could order one instead.

She saw that I was getting sick on the ride home after that and stopped the car on the side of Bartow Highway so I could vomit. I kept my head out the window the rest of the way, and the wind in my face kept me from being sick again. I went straight to bed, and Mom brought a cool washcloth in to put on my forehead. I fell asleep and when I woke up, it was still there so I must not have moved at all but knew I had been asleep for a long time, because the washcloth was dry and it was dark outside.

There were voices in the living room and somebody was crying, but I could tell from the sound of it that it wasn't anybody in my family. The one crying in the living room was David

Tremblay, and I knew just in hearing it that him and Wayne must have told.

After a while somebody went out the back door to the carport, and after a little while more, Mom and Dad started talking, just the two of them. Dad said, "Well, we have to call the police; it's the only thing we can do at this point—try to get this thing straightened out." Mom said, "Are you sure, Hank? They've all been through so much with this and it's not all their fault. Why can't we just let it go for now?" Dad said, "You can't just let something like this go. Look what they did." Mom said, "And look why they did it. Give them chores, put them on restrictions, don't let them watch TV, make them read the Bible, I don't care, but enough is enough." Dad said, "What about Dewey?" Mom said, "You should go talk to him."

I was still in the bunk bed, numb to everything the way I'd been all week, when he came in. He didn't turn on the light but just stood next to my bed in the dark.

He said, "David Tremblay just came over here, Dewey, and he and Wayne told us what happened—that David was the one who poisoned the roll. They also told us about the incident with the fork and about what happened to Wayne and about the situation at school." He stopped for a minute. I didn't know what to say back, or if I even could say anything if I wanted to.

Then Dad started again. He said, "I wish you'd come to me about this before, Dewey. Will you promise me if anything like this happens again, you'll talk to me about it and let me help?"

I said, "Yes, sir."

Dad said, "I know it's not fair, but your mother and I are concerned about David Tremblay and his situation at home, and we think it's best if nothing is said about this any further. But it's going to mean some people will hold this against you when you're not the one responsible."

I said, "Yes, sir."

Dad was quiet for a while, then he said, "Dewey?"

I said, "Sir?"

He said, "I owe you an apology, son. I let you down on this one."

I said, "No, you didn't, Dad. You wouldn't ever let me down." Then I said I was sorry for making so much trouble for everybody.

Dad had his hand on my shoulder while we talked and he moved it to my head and rubbed my head a little bit. He stood there with me like that for a long time, until I fell asleep. He might have even stayed there all night.

Chapter Twenty-seven

DAD DIDN'T PUT ME ON RESTRICTIONS for what happened with Moe, but he did think there had to be some kind of punishment, even if I was taking the blame instead of David Tremblay. So on Saturday he ordered me and Wayne to pull up all the sandspurs in the backyard. It took forever. When Dad inspected, he found a few spots we had to do over again, but after that, he said he was proud of us both for a job well done. Only he wasn't through with us yet. "Next I want you boys to paint the shed out back," he said. "I've got some green paint already out there, and you know where the ladder is and the brushes, and be sure to use a drop cloth. And Dewey—no throwing paint on your brother."

We were at dinner when he told us that. Wayne asked if David Tremblay could help us, and Dad thought about it for a minute and then said yes, he thought that would be appropriate.

It had just about killed David Tremblay that he wasn't allowed to do any of the work on the sandspurs, and when we were out there, he climbed up in one of our trees and talked to us from a branch until Mom came out and told him he had to go home, that he wasn't allowed over for a while because of what happened with Moe. I never saw anybody as sad as David Tremblay then, or as happy when Wayne told him he could come back in the yard on Sunday and help us paint the shed.

I asked Dad why we weren't delivering more flyers for the election—wouldn't it be better for us to be doing that instead of all the chores?—but he said we'd done all the campaigning we were going to do, and it was time to sit back now and let the people decide. The way he said it sounded like he'd already lost, which made me sad, and one day, while I was still suspended from school, I got some of the leftover flyers and took them to houses up and down on our street, just me on my own.

Mom helped me with the work the teachers sent home that I was missing while I was on suspension, and when they decided to let me back in school, Dad talked to Mr. Straub to make sure I could use the bathroom without anybody bothering me. I saw Head and Moe that first day back, in Mr. Straub's office, and they left me alone in the lunchroom after that, too.

David Tremblay had started a rumor that Moe had actually gotten sick from eating the school lunch and not from rat poison, and I guess that rumor got around pretty good, because one of the lunchroom ladies stopped me on Tuesday, pulled her hairnet down tight on her forehead, and said, "Don't think we aren't keeping an eye on you."

People started calling Moe "Ratterding" instead of his real last name, Borgerding, which was pretty funny. Nobody ever said it to his face, but I guess he knew anyway, because somebody scratched it on his locker, and he always seemed to be a little nervous anytime I saw him. The strange thing was that nobody made fun of me too much. Wayne and David Tremblay and all the other guys from the neighborhood let me sit with them in the lunchroom again and sometimes they laughed when I told jokes.

The kids in my classes that didn't pay much attention to me before didn't pay much attention to me when I came back to school, either, so that was something that didn't change. I still said plenty of dumb things and I was still too short. And after a couple of days of thinking I wouldn't anymore, I started raising my hand again to answer all the questions in class. Mr. Cheeley in Americanism vs. Communism handed me back the letter I wrote to General Westmoreland one day, and in front of everybody, he said, "Perhaps you would like to add a postscript before you mail this off, and tell him about your skills as an assassin." I couldn't believe he said that and neither could anybody else, but that was about the worst thing that happened.

Wayne included me in stuff he did with David Tremblay for a while, so I couldn't be mad at him about that night he snuck out the window with Darla. And I wasn't mad at Darla, either. She kept inviting me to do stuff every afternoon that week—come over for a dance lesson again with her mom, or take our bikes to Bowlegs Creek, or ride Bojangles. Mostly I said sure, I'd like to do those things, and so we did do them, only we didn't talk as much as we used to. I guess there were just too many things that had happened that neither one of us wanted to have come up. I wished we could go back to when we didn't know so much. We always had plenty to talk about back then.

But it was still nice with Darla, for all that. We even sat together once at lunch and she tried to give me her roll.

On Thursday I went over to her house when nobody was around. Darla said her mom had to take her grandpa to the doctors up in Bartow. She asked if I wanted to see her room, and I realized I never had. In fact, I'd only been upstairs the one time back early in the fall, with Darwin. "You're not going to tie me up, are you?" I asked her.

Darla frowned at me hard and I said I was just kidding.

Her room was probably the same size as Darwin's but seemed a lot bigger because it wasn't full of junk like his, and because of all the yellow light coming in her giant window. It was a flood of light, with dust motes looping and swirling and falling, and so warm you'd have almost thought it wasn't autumn anymore.

She had a fancy brass bed with a pink cover by one wall, and a little table with her schoolbooks on it, and a chair. And a little dresser by another wall, with combs and brushes on top. And that was it.

"Where's all your stuff, Darla?" I said. It felt funny to say her name. I guess in all the time I'd known her, I'd hardly ever said it out loud to anybody except Wayne.

She'd been standing in the yellow light with her eyes closed, like she was in the shower or something, but stepped out when I asked her that. I followed her over to a closet door. She didn't open it, though. "In here are my clothes," she said. "And costumes. And my shoes, of course."

"But don't you have any toys, or dolls, or girl stuff?"

"We have Monopoly and Clue. They're downstairs somewhere. I got rid of all my dolls."

"How come?" I remembered seeing the piles of old stuff out on their back porch the first time I ever came over—the moldy board games and the headless Raggedy Ann and Andy.

"Oh, I don't know. They were just a lot of bother. I got rid of a lot of things so I could have more room."

"More room for what?"

Darla said she wasn't sure yet, but she was thinking about a fish tank. I asked if she liked fish and she said no, not really. She did one of her dance steps back under the shower of that afternoon light, and I could see then why she liked to have her room the way it was. With the sun coming through her big window, and her standing there inside, it was like she was on a stage.

"I have about a million pictures I drew of Bojangles, if you want to see them," Darla said, about when I figured the conversation was over. "They're in the bottom dresser drawer." She said she had all her school photos, too, from every grade since first, but she didn't let anybody ever see them and she wasn't sure why she kept them, and in fact, since I brought it up and reminded her, she thought maybe after I left she would throw them all away. Or probably burn them.

"You could give me one," I said. "And I could give you one of mine." Except for my mom and dad, I hadn't ever given anybody any of my school pictures, or had anybody ask me for any, either.

Darla thought about it for a minute, then said she guessed it was OK if I gave her one. But I couldn't have one of hers. She said it was her policy to not give any away or let anybody see them.

"Your 'policy'?" I said. She nodded. Her Shirley Temple curls bounced.

"My policy," she said.

I asked why she had a policy about something like that, and did she have other policies?

"Oh, yeah," Darla said. "I have a lot of policies. I have a policy about just about everything."

"Like what?" I said. "Or do you have a policy about not telling anybody the rest of your policies?"

Darla smiled. I could tell she liked that. "Maybe I do," she said. "And maybe I don't."

It was about the dumbest conversation I'd ever had in my whole life. It made me pretty happy.

When we went back downstairs Darla put on a record and said it was for slow dancing. She leaned her cheek on my shoulder and I felt her breath on my neck. Something like that would have been ticklish once, but it wasn't now. It wasn't kissing—we hadn't ever done that again, or the other thing, either—but it was kind of like kissing. I could feel her heart beating, too, and I tried to count the beats until the end of the song, but dancing so close like that, I kept getting mixed up on which ones were hers and which ones were mine.

There was a canoe trip with our Scout troop down the Peace River that weekend, which was the last weekend in October. I didn't want to go on account of all the torture and stuff that went on at the last Scout trip, but Dad said I had to. It had turned real cold by the time we started out Saturday morning, so our hands and fingers got numb right away from holding on to our paddles and getting them wet and getting our clothes wet from splashing. The whole day was pretty miserable, but Mr. Ferber and Mr. Dick wouldn't let us stop and build a fire or anything, except when we pulled the canoes over to eat lunch and have a couple of snack breaks.

About the only time I got warm all day was when we took one of those breaks, next to a cow pasture, and a bunch of us climbed the fence. I don't know where Wayne was, but I was walking next to David Tremblay and I said, "I bet you can't catch one of those cows," so of course he said, "I bet I can," and he took off running. We all ran after him and chased the cows around for a while, yelling at them and waving our arms and stuff. It was a lot of fun.

Mr. Ferber saw us and got mad, but we pretended we couldn't hear him yelling from across the field, and when he came to make us stop, he stepped in two cow patties, one with each boot. Somebody told him that me and David Tremblay started it, so he made us take his boots down to the river and wash them off, which got my hands even more freezing. I kind of liked it, though, that for once—even doing something disgusting like that—it was me and David together and not just him and Wayne.

The cold got even worse at night. Nobody brought enough clothes, and we slept wrapped up in our ponchos on the ground. At least we did until about midnight, when Mr. Ferber and Mr. Dick got everybody up yelling "Pee call! Pee call!" because they didn't want anybody peeing in their sleeping bags. We woke up shivering the next morning, expecting we'd have a fire, but nobody had covered the wood, so it was all wet from the dew. Mr. Dick hadn't even brought any gasoline. We ate beans out of cans and then got in the canoes.

A bunch of us just sat there, at first, and said we wanted to quit and go home, but Mr. Dick and Mr. Ferber said the only way out was to paddle, so we paddled and paddled all day Sunday, and didn't even care when we passed a meadow with about twenty alligators sunning on the bank. The sun was silver and just about as cold as the night, and probably colder because of the wind that blew where there weren't any trees. We would stop paddling and breathe on our hands every now and then until we felt our fingers, but that almost made it worse once they got wet again and cold again and numb again. Mr. Ferber started this song, which he made us sing over and over, that he said was what the Canadians or the Eskimos always sang when they paddled their canoes way up north. We were supposed to sing it and paddle at the same time, and it was supposed to help us, so we sang it for about ten hours:

> *Dip, dip, and swing them back,*
> *Flashing like silver,*
> *Swift as the wild goose flight,*
> *Dip, dip, and swing.*

Everybody hated it.

When it was over and we got to the place and dragged the canoes out and loaded them on the cars, everybody just sat there frozen until they yelled at us and poked us and threatened to not stop at the 7-Eleven on the way home. Then we dragged ourselves into the cars and sat *there* frozen instead — nobody talking, nobody moving, nobody doing anything but sitting, even the guys that fell asleep. They just slept sitting up, was all.

They dropped David Tremblay off at his house, and me and Wayne at our house. All I wanted to do was get in the hot shower.

Mom was waiting for us in the kitchen, where she was cooking dinner, and Dad was in there, too, drinking a cup of coffee, and Tink had a coloring book, even though she was too old for coloring books and even though she was good at drawing her own pictures, too, like that picture of Suzy.

I'm not sure how, but I could tell something was wrong as soon as we walked in. I wondered if there'd been another letter, like the tire-fire one, about the election or something. I said, "What's the matter?" Mom put down her wooden spoon on the counter and twisted her hands in her apron. Her face was red and puffy. Tink started to cry.

Dad said, "Just put your gear over there by the door, then I want you boys to come sit down."

Wayne said, "What is it, Dad?"

We sat next to each other on the old church pew we used for a bench at the kitchen table.

Dad squatted in front of us. "There's a girl in Dewey's grade, Darla Turkel." He said it like a question and I said, "Yes, sir," and Wayne nodded.

Dad looked over at Mom, then back. "I'm so sorry to have to tell you this, but there was an accident while you were gone."

All the air went out of me and I barely could hear Dad when he said the rest about Darla—that she died.

Chapter Twenty-eight

I HADN'T EVER BEEN TO A FUNERAL where I didn't wear my Scout uniform and bring my bugle, so it felt funny putting on my Sunday suit. Wayne already had his on and he sat on the bottom bunk, not watching me exactly, but just sort of there. He hardly knew Darla the way I did, but you could tell he was upset, acting real quiet, like the way I was when they wouldn't let me go to school and they thought I was the one that poisoned Moe.

I had trouble tying my tie even though I'd done it a million times, and Wayne finally got up to help me even though I didn't ask. "You got it all wrong," he said. He untied it and tied it back, and it wasn't much better, but I left it that way, or I would have except Mom saw it when we came out of the bedroom, and she made us redo it until finally it was about right.

Mom wore a black dress, which was what you were supposed to wear to a funeral, but it had gotten warm again and Tink had on her Easter dress, which was pink, with a pink hat and little white gloves. Mom tried to get her to change but Tink was stubborn, so Mom gave up and said, "You children hurry out to the car; we're going to be late." I'm not sure why Mom wanted us all to go. I guess she must have known Darla's mom from Dr. Rexroat's office, the way everybody in Sand Mountain knew everybody at least a little unless they were colored, but me and Wayne hadn't told her anything about either of us and Darla except that we knew her. Probably it was like visiting the shut-ins—Mom just thought it was the right thing to do.

Dad was out in his shed. Mom called him, once we got to the car, to come on, we were all ready. He smelled like a cigarette when he got in behind the wheel.

"Daddy smoked," Tink said.

I told Tink to shut up, no he didn't, and Mom said, "That's enough out of both of you. You should be thinking about others today, not yourselves, and you shouldn't be ugly to each other." That made me feel bad, that I wasn't acting right even when we were going to Darla's funeral, but that's just the way it had been for me since we heard.

Even the day before, when I made Wayne and David Tremblay go with me to where it happened, to the Old Bartow Highway out past Moon's, I didn't understand how I could be so curious instead of just sad. When Darla had died was Sunday, that second cold day of the canoe trip with the Scouts. She went riding on Bojangles by herself, and they said the last person to talk to her was Walter Wratchford. She rode the same direction we did that day I went with her, out the Old Bartow Highway, with the railroad tracks on one side and the old mines on the other that they never did reclamation on. The guy in the car that hit them said he saw Darla up ahead of him, on the side of the road, riding her horse. The train conductor of the phosphate train said he saw Darla, too, riding Bojangles, and he saw her pump her arm up and down the way you do to get a truck driver or a train engineer to blow their horn. He said at first he wasn't going to do it because he wasn't supposed to, but he didn't see the car, he just saw Darla riding old Bojangles and thought, What the heck, not having any idea that it would spook Bojangles and he would run out in the highway and suddenly the car would be there, too.

Me and Wayne and David Tremblay saw the skid mark. Where it stopped must have been where the car hit Bojangles, only it didn't kill Bojangles; it broke his legs, and Officer O. O. Odom, who was the one that came out after they got the report back at the police station, had to shoot him to put him out of his misery. Actually, the way they said it was that Officer Odom had to "put him down."

There was still the dried blood on the road, too, when we went out there. It was black instead of red, so it didn't look like blood. Somebody said they got a tractor and had to drag Bojangles's body back up to Moon's, where they buried him in one of the fields.

Darla got thrown off Bojangles when the car hit them. It threw her fifty feet to where she landed. We looked all over to find that place, or rather David Tremblay and me looked all over. Wayne just sat on his bike and said, "What difference does it make?" and could we please just go home? But I had to know exactly what was what, the way it always was with me with stuff like that.

We finally decided it was a place in the ditch where a lot of the grass was torn up and it looked like people had been walking around, and maybe a car, or the ambulance, or the hearse had pulled off the road. But it still didn't seem quite right. "Don't you think if she landed here it would of been soft and she might not of gotten hurt so bad?" I asked David Tremblay.

He said he didn't know. He said maybe she just died when the car hit them. I said that wouldn't have happened, because she was up on top of the horse and the car just hit the horse, so it must have been when she landed, maybe she hit her head, but there weren't any rocks or anything hard except the ground, but there was plenty of grass, and a little water in the bottom of the ditch, so it was even kind of muddy down in there. "I just don't get it," I said, and it bothered me for a long time that I couldn't make it make sense. I wished I could go out there with Officer Odom or at least ask him, but I was afraid to talk to him since that day we were in Mr. Straub's office and he wanted to put the handcuffs on me.

"Come on," Wayne said. "Let's get out of here." I could tell David Tremblay would have stayed if I wanted to stay longer, to try to figure everything out some more—probably because he still felt so bad for letting everybody think I was the one to poison Moe instead of him. But Wayne looked mad now and I hated it when he got mad at me, so I said, OK, we could go.

There weren't too many people at the funeral, and that was when I realized Darla and her family didn't go to any church. They didn't even have the service at a church or a funeral home but just out at the Peace River Cemetery, where I had played "Taps" that time at Mr. Rhodes's funeral.

I found out later that Mom had called Mrs. Turkel to see if she could help, and Mrs. Turkel asked if Mom could get Reverend Dunn to do the funeral at the cemetery. Also in that conversation Mrs. Turkel told Mom what a nice boy I was, and how good of a friend I was for Darla and Darwin, but Mom didn't tell me any of that at the time.

So Reverend Dunn was there, but you could tell by what he said that he didn't know Darla at all: "She was popular with her schoolmates; a gifted singer and dancer; a natural beauty; a spirited girl who greeted each new day with a song of hope and joy; a devoted daughter, sister, and granddaughter; a child of great faith in a better tomorrow; a young person who truly believed, to quote our late President John F. Kennedy, that you should ask not what your town can do for you, but what you can do for your town. How many of us will not soon forget her vibrant performances on the stage at County Fair with her brother, Darwin? Our hearts go out to Darwin, and to Darla's mother, Elaine Turkel, and to Darla's grandfather, Mr. F. N. Turkel, all of whom join us today for this graveside service on this glorious afternoon God has created. Blessed be the Lord, He has received unto Himself a new angel. Amen."

Reverend Dunn said a lot of this looking at Darla's mom and Darwin, who were the only ones sitting down except for an old man in a brown suit who kept doubling over and coughing and who I figured out must be the grandfather they were all so scared of, who I hadn't ever seen. I recognized him from the coughing. He didn't look anything like a general. He looked like he ought of have been the one whose funeral we were at, and I couldn't help wondering how somebody so old and pitiful like him could make Darla and Darwin and their mom so nervous all the time.

Reverend Dunn also looked at Mom and Dad and me and Wayne and Tink a lot, too. I guess he didn't know too many others of the few people that were there except Dr. Rexroat, who seemed like he might fall asleep standing up with everybody else around the grave. He winked at me once, or I thought he did, but it might have just been that his eye twitched. Another guy it took me a little while to recognize was Walter Wratchford. He stood just a little ways behind Mrs. Turkel's folding chair, and stepped up to hand her a Kleenex or a rag or something when she started crying the hardest. He had on a brown suit, with a brown vest buttoned all the way up the front, and his hair was still long, but he had put some oil in it and combed it straight back and even shaved. Like I said, I hardly recognized him and I also was pretty surprised to see him there with the Turkels like that, out in the open. The grandfather every now and then turned partway around to sort of glare at Walter Wratchford, but Walter Wratchford didn't even look back at the old man; he just stayed right there behind Mrs. Turkel, which I thought was pretty nice for him to do.

I didn't see anybody who might be Darla's dad.

The funniest thing—and it wasn't really funny, because nothing was funny that day—but the funniest thing, anyway, was Darwin, who didn't have a suit on like everybody else, but wore a Nehru jacket with a white turtleneck shirt underneath. I hadn't ever seen one before except in a picture in *Life* magazine of hippies. He wasn't crying like his mom, or barking out the coughs like his granddad, or looking over everything like Walter Wratchford. He was just sitting there staring at his hands, tracing the lines with his finger. Tink said he looked like a dentist, dressed that way, but she said that a lot later, after the funeral was over. Once, Darwin looked over at me for a minute until I gave him a little wave that I hoped nobody saw and he gave me a little wave back.

The cemetery was a mishmash of gravestones, some of them little white tablets like the one they had for Darla, which didn't even have anything written on it yet, and some of them big with stuff carved on them, like a lamb or a cross or a baby angel. Most of those were old and had green algae moss all over. In the middle of the whole cemetery was the oldest oak tree I ever saw—even older than the one down in the Boogerbottom. It wasn't tall, but the branches spread way out and some of them dipped down to the ground where kids could climb on them if their parents would ever let them. There was one mausoleum and that was all, a marble shed with a rusted door that I bet hadn't been opened in a hundred years. That place scared me, since I figured they just had the coffins sitting in there on big shelves. Wayne had told me that a boy got trapped inside one night and nobody heard him yelling for help, and when they opened the mausoleum the next day, they found him, dead. I knew it wasn't true, but it scared me, anyway, because you never know—it *could* happen.

I looked over at Darla's mom another time and Darwin must have been watching me, because as soon as I did, he waved at me again. Wayne elbowed me, but I felt sorry for Darwin so I waved back again, but then I didn't look at him anymore, just in case.

Reverend Dunn had said some more stuff that I didn't listen to very well, and then he read from the Beatitudes:

Blessed are the poor in spirit, for theirs is the kingdom of heaven.
Blessed are those who mourn, for they shall be comforted.
Blessed are the meek, for they shall inherit the earth.

Blessed are those who hunger and thirst for righteousness,
for they shall be satisfied.
Blessed are the merciful, for they shall obtain mercy.
Blessed are the pure in heart, for they shall see God.

For some reason he left out a couple of verses, including the one I always liked the best because I kind of thought it might be talking about me sometimes: "Blessed are you when men revile you and persecute you and utter all kinds of evil against you falsely—"

Instead, Reverend Dunn skipped ahead to the one about not hiding your light under a bushel, which was the last he read: "'You are the light of the world. A city set on a hill cannot be hid. Nor do men light a lamp and put it under a bushel but on a stand, and it gives light to all in the house. Let your light so shine before men, that they may see your good works and give glory to your Father who is in heaven.'

"Darla Turkel lit a lamp," Reverend Dunn said. "But she never put it under a bushel. She put it on a stand, and it gave light to all in the house." He rubbed his nose, which was a lot redder now than when he started, then he asked everybody to join him in the Lord's Prayer. Everybody did, or just about everybody.

Walter Wratchford's lips moved but I don't think he was saying all the right words, and Mrs. Turkel was still crying too hard. I didn't want to look at Darwin anymore, so I looked way off to the oak tree, and that's when I saw a colored boy over there behind the trunk, sitting on one of those low branches. I studied him even though I should have had my eyes closed for the prayer, but what the heck could he be doing there? I'd been around the Peace River Cemetery enough playing "Taps" to know he didn't work there. Plus he had on a white shirt, which anybody that worked there wouldn't ever wear, since they were always digging graves, filling in graves, planting sod, weeding, mowing. He looked like he was Wayne's age, and I wondered if maybe he was the colored boy that Darla got in trouble with down at the cemetery before I even started hanging around with her, the one that ran away when the police came because him and Darla were setting off fire-crackers. If that story was even true.

I wished I could ask Darla about it, and I wished I had asked her about it before, when I had the chance, when me and her were sitting on the Bowlegs Creek bridge one of those afternoons and moving our feet together through the dance steps her mom was trying to teach me.

Standing there thinking those things, that was when I got so sad about Darla myself. It was a hard, hard kind of sad I hadn't ever felt before, where all the ways you try not to let it get you— fretting about tying your tie right, trying like crazy to figure out how the accident could have happened, getting all the answers to all the stuff you thought were such great mysteries in your town, worrying what people think about other people, worrying what people think about you—

The kind of sad where all that dissolves, and you dissolve, too.

They finished up the Lord's Prayer and everybody just stood there for a few minutes with their heads bowed, not getting up, just a lot of sniffing, even Wayne, and that made me start sniffing, too. Dad put his arm around me and I let him. Mom put her arm around Wayne and he let her, too. Tink pulled at her little white gloves so they were way down on her hands, but since the fingers of the gloves were kind of stiff, it looked funny, like she had really long hands or something. She did prayer hands with them still long like that, but she wasn't serious about it; she was just messing around like little kids always do. I couldn't see what she was up to after that because I guess I must have been crying by then. I didn't want to get any tears on Dad's coat, or stuff from my runny nose, either, but he let me bury my face against him, anyway, and he kept his arm around me once everybody started leaving, and all the way back to the car.

Chapter Twenty-nine

DAD LOST THE ELECTION.

Some kids at school said it was because Dad liked colored people too much. Connolly Voss went on and on about that at lunch one day until Wayne pointed his fork and said the next guy to get stabbed at Sand Mountain High School was going to be Connolly if he didn't shut up—and it wasn't going to just be in the hand, either. But later on even Wayne said he guessed the colored-people issue was the main reason for how the election turned out. "Just look at the tire fire," he said.

David Tremblay said it wasn't about the colored people; it was about the annexation and Dad wanting to close down The Springs. I guess everybody had their own theory. I'd been so sad about Darla that at first it was kind of a relief to have the election to talk about, even though it did turn out bad. But then the more

I thought about it, the more I figured the reason Dad lost was because of me. If I hadn't stabbed Moe, Moe wouldn't have beat up Wayne, and David wouldn't have poisoned the roll, and I wouldn't have got blamed for doing it, and Dad wouldn't have got blamed for me.

One day after Dad came home from work, I followed him out to the shed and told him that. He listened real careful and nodded—not like he agreed with me, but just to let me know he heard what I was saying. He had a couple of pairs of old roller skates of mine and Wayne's on his worktable, which he was taking apart, and he held one of them and spun the wheel while I talked. I guess I thought he would tell me I was wrong to blame myself and that it wasn't my fault at all. That's what I wanted to hear, but at the same time I wouldn't have believed him but just known he was saying what dads are supposed to say.

When I finished, though, he stopped spinning the skate wheel but kept nodding for a second, then said he understood how I could feel that way, and that some people probably did hold that Moe business against us, but there were a lot of factors in how the election turned out and it wouldn't be fair to point to just one and say that was the reason.

"So I guess you don't get to take all the blame on this one," he said. "Sorry to have to tell you."

I kind of laughed when he said that, and him, too. Then he told me it was a lot closer an election than people thought it would be, and they even got out some of the colored vote, which was encouraging. After a while I asked Dad what he was doing with the roller skates and he said he was making us skateboards like he'd seen some kids riding on up in Bartow. He said I could help him if I wanted, and I said sure, and he let me do some sawing and sanding on the boards we needed before he attached the wheels.

Reverend Dunn came over to our house a couple of nights after the election to tell Dad that they didn't want him on the board of trustees of the Methodist Church anymore. Reverend Dunn and Mom and Dad sat in the kitchen drinking coffee and we couldn't hear what they were saying after that, but I did see them all three holding hands and bowing their heads while Reverend Dunn said a prayer. After Reverend Dunn left, me and Wayne followed Dad out to his shed again. We caught up with him right when he was unscrewing one of his nail jars, which I figured was the one where he was hiding his cigarettes again. Wayne asked Dad what happened, and Dad said they just wanted some new perspectives on the board and it was good to have that and he'd been a trustee for four years and change was good sometimes. Wayne said, "Did Reverend Dunn want you to be off of the board because of the election?"

Dad shook his head. "No, son. It wasn't Reverend Dunn. He was just the one who had to tell me about what they decided."

Wayne asked Dad why he hadn't been at the meeting, since he was still on the board of trustees before they voted him off. Dad said they must have just forgot to tell him about it, was all.

Later Wayne told me he didn't think what Dad said was true—none of it. I wasn't so sure, because I didn't think Dad would tell us a lie about anything but maybe was just confused a little bit. The phone rang a lot the rest of that night and it was people from the church calling to talk to Mom or Dad. I heard them talking about a petition, but nothing ever came of it that I ever knew about.

When we were lying in bed, I asked Wayne if he thought anything else bad was going to happen because of the election. Wayne said no, he didn't think so. He said people forget about stuff pretty quick, was how he saw it, whether it was good or bad. They just forget about it.

Something else bad did happen, though, which was that Mr. Ellis lost his job at the high school, the same as a couple of years before when he lost his job at the mine because of the strike. Another colored man I hadn't ever seen before showed up at the school, doing the janitor job one day, only nobody exactly realized it right away because I guess most people just didn't notice something like that, but I did.

Wayne told me it was because Mr. Ellis helped Dad on the campaign by trying to get out the colored vote—that that's why they fired him from the school.

Dad made me and Wayne go with him in the car to Mr. Ellis's house one night, which we were glad at least wasn't in the Boogerbottom but turned out to be one of the houses I saw that day of the colored soldier's funeral, down the long dirt road on the other side of the Peace River at the same place as the colored church. A couple of low dogs with long bodies and short legs circled the car as soon as we stopped. In the dark they looked liked sharks but Dad made us get out anyway. It wasn't too cold. Mr. Ellis was sitting on his front porch with his wife.

Dad walked right up to the porch and stuck out his hand to shake, and Mr. Ellis got up and shook Dad's hand but he didn't come down to the yard. Dad said he was so sorry for what happened, and it wasn't right, and he said he was sorry again and he wanted to help. . . .

Mr. Ellis waited until Dad finished, then he just said, "What's done is done, Mr. Turner. No used a man to cry over spilt milk."

Those low dogs swam around me and Wayne's legs and I wanted to get back in the car. Dad seemed to remember we were standing there just then and said, "Boys, you can introduce yourselves to Mr. Ellis." Wayne went first. He walked over to the porch and shook Mr. Ellis's hand, which I wasn't sure you were supposed to do with a colored person, even though your dad had done it.

Mrs. Ellis stood up at about that minute and frowned and walked inside the house without saying anything. The screen door slammed behind her and the dogs started howling until Mr. Ellis yelled at them to quit. We were all quiet then, and Mr. Ellis looked at the porch and kicked a loose board with his shoe. Nobody said anything for a real long time, even Dad. I stuck my hands in my pockets. Finally Dad pulled an envelope out of his pocket and handed it to Mr. Ellis. "I thought this might help a little, and I'll let you know if I hear of anything workwise I can pass along," he said.

Mr. Ellis took the envelope and stuffed it in his pocket like he wished he could make it disappear, which in a way it did. He nodded like he appreciated it, but also like maybe nodding was just something he did when he didn't have anything else to say. I remembered that night of the Rotary Club Minstrel Show when Walter Wratchford's dad called him "Mistuh Chollie" and how he nodded and nodded then, too. It was obvious he wanted us to leave.

Dad said good-bye, then him and Wayne went ahead and got in the car. But I held back for a second since I still hadn't shook Mr. Ellis's hand. I walked over to the porch and did that then. I don't know why exactly. I said I was sorry about everything. Once I got started telling him how sorry I was, I couldn't seem to quit right away and I said, "I'm sorry for doing my business in your grass at the high school, too. I just wanted to tell you that."

He didn't smile, but he nodded some. Then he said, "It's no need to speak about it."

I said, "Yes, sir," and he said, "Plenty of worse things than that," and I said, "Yes, sir," again.

"You love your mama?" he asked me.

I said, "Yes, sir."

"Love your daddy?"

"Yes, sir."

"Love Jesus?"

"Yes, sir. I try to."

"Well then," he said, "you going to be all right."

And he turned and went inside.

"Is he your friend, Dad?" I said after we'd been driving a little while.

"I like to think he is," Dad said.

Wayne said he was glad Dad was friends with Mr. Ellis. That kind of surprised me. Except for that story about Darla and the colored boy, I hadn't thought I knew anybody that was friends with anybody colored. But then I got thinking about what all Mr. Ellis had done for Dad's campaign, and how he lost two jobs from trying to help people, and how he never even mentioned to Dad about me peeing in the bushes at school, and I said I was glad Dad and Mr. Ellis were friends, too.

Then I said, "I don't think Mrs. Ellis liked us, though."

Dad was hunched over the steering wheel like he needed to get closer to what he was looking at to help him drive up the dirt road. It was so dark I could hardly see Wayne in the front seat ahead of me, even when I leaned way forward.

"Mrs. Ellis is upset about the situation," Dad said. "It doesn't have anything to do with us directly. Just the situation."

"It's a lousy situation, then," Wayne said.

Dad said that yes, it was. I wanted to say something, too, something like they were saying, but didn't know what.

I got lonely sitting there in the back by myself, so I asked Dad if I could climb over the seat to be with him and Wayne in the front. He said OK, but just be careful when I did. Wayne scooted way over so I wouldn't fall onto him, and once I got settled in the seat, he didn't even seem to care that our shoulders and arms were touching. We rode the rest of the way home like that all together—Dad driving, Wayne shotgun, me in the middle.

Chapter Thirty

I HAD DREAMS ABOUT DARLA. I couldn't remember most of them when I woke up except that she was somewhere and I was somewhere else and I couldn't get to where she was. Mom took me to see Dr. Boughner again, and I told him about the dreams. He asked me, "Can you remember more about where you and Darla were and what else was going on in these dreams?" and he even got a watch out and tried to hypnotize me. But it didn't work.

So he said, "Well, never mind, then, but what do *you* think the dreams mean, Dewey?" I said I didn't know, but couldn't he just tell me? It was probably in one of his books, like the phallus symbol he also kept talking about, and that I finally figured out, and now I saw those things everywhere I looked. He wouldn't give me the answer, though, so I said all I thought about my dreams was that I must just miss Darla and I guess I wished I could have been there and saved her from that phosphate train that blew the whistle and scared Bojangles, and from that car that hit them.

"Is there anything else?" he said.

"You mean like anything to do with my mom?" I said.

He nodded.

"No," I said. "I don't think so this time."

He seemed pretty disappointed, but he tried to be nice, anyway, and said he thought it was understandable that I missed my girlfriend and that I had the grief about it in my dreams. I tried to explain to him that Darla wasn't ever my girlfriend and I didn't know where the heck he got that idea anyway, but Dr. Boughner just smiled like he knew better.

After about another week I had a different dream, and this one I did remember. There wasn't much to it, just me and Darla tap-dancing on the stage of the Sand Mountain High School auditorium. That dream didn't make any sense, though, because I hadn't ever tap-danced with Darla or had a lesson in it from her mom or anything. When I woke up that night, I didn't know where I was. The room was almost as bright as the day and I went to the window and saw it was a full moon. Somebody was banging on something outside and I didn't even think about it; I just followed the noise even though I was in my pajamas—out the front door and down the steps and into the front yard, where the grass was wet from the dew, and I saw my shadow even though it was in the middle of the night. There was a woodpecker hammering on a telephone pole over by the street, and I watched him for a pretty long time, and the longer I watched, the sadder I felt about Darla not being there anymore, and someday Mom and Dad not being there anymore, and Wayne, and Tink, and even me. I got cold all of a sudden. Maybe it was the wind, or how wet my feet were, or how lonely I was. This sounds crazy, but I wished God would have been there—God or just about anybody—to pat me on the head and tell me everything is going to be all right. I went back inside and then into Mom and Dad's bedroom, which was something I hadn't done in a while but used to do all the time. I wanted Mom to wake up but couldn't make myself make her wake up, I don't know why. I just needed for her to know I was there, and for her to pull back the covers and let me crawl into bed with her and Dad. But she didn't, and Dad didn't, either, and for a second I got worried that they weren't even breathing and what if something had happened to them, but then Dad snored and Mom rolled over and I went back to my own bed.

I didn't sleep much, and the next day, after school, I did something that Mom had been trying to get me to do ever since the funeral, which was go over and play with Darwin. I thought maybe I had a guilty conscience, and maybe that was what was making me have insomnia.

When I got to their house, Darwin opened the door and said, "Hey," like he was expecting me. I said, "Hey," back, like it was just the usual thing with us, and then we went up to his room to find something to do. I was worried that he would want to play that Turn Off the Lights game of his, but he never even mentioned it. Instead they had an old chessboard he hadn't ever used, and I taught him how to play. Dad had taught me when I was about in first grade. I hadn't ever beat him, though, and one time he beat me in three moves, which I always remembered. Darwin learned it pretty quick, and since I felt sorry for him, I let him win. We didn't talk much, and when it was time for me to go, he said, "You don't have to come over here. I know you only liked Darla and not me."

"No, I didn't," I said, even though it was true. I asked him if he ever played cribbage, which my dad also taught me when I was little, and always beat me at, too. Darwin said no, and I said I would teach him next time I came over if he wanted.

"OK," he said.

Their mom was downstairs and she hugged me so hard when I was leaving that I couldn't barely breathe. Her voice was hoarse when she talked. She said, "You promise me you won't stop coming over here for dance lessons. Darla would have wanted you to keep practicing. She speaks to me in my prayers. Did you know that, Dewey?"

I didn't know that, and it scared me for her to say it, but I said, "Yes, ma'am," anyway. I hoped she wasn't going to turn into a crazy person. Darwin kind of rescued me from her. He pulled her hand off my arm where she squeezed so tight it left marks of her fingers on my skin. When I was finally actually leaving,

Walter Wratchford came driving up in his old blue Ford Fairlane. I guess Darla dying made it OK for him and Mrs. Turkel to be together and not just in the middle of the night on top of the Skeleton Hotel. He gave me a salute like we were both soldiers.

The granddad died in December; I think it was his cough that finally killed him, and it wasn't too long after that that Mrs. Turkel sold their old house and took Darwin and moved away to Tampa. Walter Wratchford moved over there, too, after a little while, at least that's where I heard he went, but I don't know if him and Mrs. Turkel got married or what they did. I didn't ever hear from Darwin, but one day I was watching TV and on the Tampa station they had a commercial for Del Webb's Sun City, where all the old people lived, and in the commercial there was a boy standing next to a shuffleboard with an old lady who was smiling at him. They were both holding shuffleboard sticks and he said, "My gramma has so much fun at Del Webb's Sun City, I wish I could live here, too." I couldn't believe it, and neither could anybody else, but the boy in the commercial was Darwin.

One night in bed I asked Wayne if he ever thought about Darla much. The mattress springs creaked like he was turning over on his stomach. Finally he said that he did, but he guessed he didn't want to talk about her right now. I said that was OK, and then I asked did Darla ever tell him that me and her went sneaking out one other time when Wayne was asleep and we discovered who the Howler was?

Wayne kind of laughed and said no, she never told him about that.

I said, "Well, we did," and I bet he couldn't guess who it was.

Wayne said he bet he could and I said how much did he want to bet? He said, "A buck-two-ninety-eight," which was this dumb thing he was always saying when you asked him how much anything cost, and then he said heck, everybody in town already knew who the Howler was a long time ago.

I said, "They did?"

He said, "Yeah. Walter Wratchford. When he drank liquor sometimes, he yelled and stuff up on top of the Skeleton Hotel. It was probably from being in the war and all."

I asked him why he hadn't told me and Darla that to begin with and he said he just thought it was funny us sneaking out like that to find out and he figured he would just go along to see what might happen. I didn't tell him about Walter Wratchford and Darla's mom up on the Skeleton Hotel. Except for Darla and me, I guess nobody ever knew about that.

One thing that bothered me for a long time was I hadn't ever given Darla one of my school pictures. Mom said maybe I should write to Mrs. Turkel and send her one; she said she bet Mrs. Turkel would like to hear from one of Darla's friends. So I did that. I wrote the letter and sent the picture. Mrs. Turkel wrote me right back a note thanking me, and she gave me one of Darla's pictures, too, from when we were in sixth grade. I guess nobody had burned them like Darla wanted.

At first I was happy to have it. But the longer I looked at it, the less it seemed like Darla to me, and more like just some other girl, until finally I put it in my bottom dresser drawer and didn't look at it again.

Our church had a live Nativity scene at Christmas and they set it up on the lawn of the high school, facing First Street, because there wasn't enough room at the First Methodist. The men from the church built a real stable that was open in the front facing the road, and a manger inside, and a pen where they had real animals from somebody's farm out in the county: a couple of donkeys, a couple of goats, a couple of sheep, a couple of cows. It was too bad there weren't any camels around for the "Three Wise Guys"—that's what Wayne called them—but people were pretty impressed anyway. The roof of the stable was chicken wire stuffed with palmetto fronds, and they built a little platform up there with a stool and sort of a cross where the Angel of the Lord could sit and put her arms on top of the cross so her wings spread all the way out without her arms getting too tired holding them up. On the programs they printed up, they wrote, "The *Angle* of the Lord," instead of the *Angel,* but nobody noticed in time to fix it.

Wayne was one of the Wise Guys and had a box he held with FRANKINCENSE written on the side. At least they were able to spell *that* right, even though David Tremblay kept calling it "Frankin*stein.*" I was never sure if he was joking around or if he

316 •

really didn't get it. I was supposed to be a shepherd. Wayne got a fancy costume that the church ladies made, but I just wore an old bathrobe, with a towel on my head and a rope tied around it. That was what was supposed to happen, anyway, except that on Christmas Eve the girl that was the Angle got sick, so they made me do it instead. "You're the only one small enough," Mrs. Ryland said, right in front of everybody. We were in the high-school office putting on our costumes and eating doughnuts, before they sent us out one at a time to replace the kids on the shift before ours, which was for an hour. Mrs. Ryland was the Burning Bushes Sunday School teacher and a boy named Skip Ryland's mom. Skip was a Wise Guy with Wayne and David Tremblay on our shift, and he laughed the hardest about me having to be the Angle, until his mom snatched his doughnut and made him apologize because it wasn't Christian to be that way.

I said I wouldn't do it, and some of the other kids said I shouldn't have to, too, including Boopie, who I had kind of been friends with lately and who was also a shepherd like me. But then Reverend Dunn showed up and you couldn't say no to Reverend Dunn when he wanted something, so they put me in the white nightgown with the gauze sewed all over it, and attached to the sleeves were the big wings made from goose feathers glued to cardboard painted white and gold, and the next thing I knew I was climbing up the back of the manger and sitting on the stool on the platform they had up there and spreading my wings out on the cross.

Once we got to our positions, we weren't supposed to move, even to scratch our nose if it started itching, so that's what I did. They had a record player with about a thousand feet of extension cord from the high-school office, and Mrs. Ryland put on the Christmas album that played through the loudspeakers they also had set up there: "We three kings of Orient are," "Oh holy night, the stars are brightly shining," "Silent night, holy night, all is calm, all is bright," "Good King Wince the Louse looked out on the feet of Stephen."

From where I sat on top of the stable, I could see everybody who came by, and it seemed like just about the whole town did during that hour we were there, either walking or sitting on a bench across the street or driving in their cars. At first I was embarrassed because I knew everybody would tease me about being a girl after the Nativity was all over, even though in the Bible the angel was a guy, not that my telling people that would make any difference. After a while I didn't think about it, though, I just liked being up there in the sky with my wings on, looking down on the whole world, or at least the whole world of Sand Mountain.

I saw David Tremblay's mom sitting on that bench across the street. She looked so tired but also looked like she could sit there forever instead of going home, which was nice and sad at the same time, especially when I thought about David's stepdad and how things were at their house. Boopie's mom came along and sat with David's mom and they started talking, and you could tell

David's mom liked that a lot because of the way she kind of turned toward Boopie's mom and didn't look so tired anymore.

My mom and dad came along, too, and Tink and that little friend of hers, Scooty. Tink and Scooty snuck over to the pen and tried to pet the animals. They got kind of loud, saying stuff like, "Here, cow. Come over here, boy," which I could hear all the way up on top of the stable until Dad told them to hush. I could see Mom studying the shepherds, wondering where I was, and then finally realizing it was me as the Angle. She pretended to reach up and brush some hair out of her face but really it was to give me a little wave that nobody would see.

I saw W.J. Weller, the kid that got his arm broke by Darwin that time. He went by with his family and their old dog, whose doghouse I hid in that one time for a while on the first day of school, back in August. And Mr. Juddy the dragline operator with his wife, who I hadn't noticed before walked bowlegged just like him. And Connolly Voss with his four sisters and his mom, who was taller than his little dad. And that colored lady who made the Sunday dinners, Miss Deas, with about a hundred kids piled in an old black Chevy like my grandmother had up in Virginia. And Officer O. O. Odom, also, all alone in his police car. He drove back and forth a bunch and I figured he must really like the live Nativity and the Christmas music and all, but Wayne said later he bet Officer Odom just wanted to see if he could get some of our doughnuts.

Of course I started thinking about Darla after a while—the real Darla, not the one from that sixth-grade picture—who more than anybody in the world would have loved to be the Angle of the Lord. She would have been good at it, too—better than me, better than Shirley Temple, better than anybody. All you had to do was sit on top of the stable in the costume for an hour and not scratch your nose, but with Darla you know it would have been a lot more than that; it would have been like in the Bible: "And an angel of the Lord appeared before them and the glory of the Lord shone round about them and they were sore afraid." Only I wouldn't have been sore afraid to see her there instead of me. I would have just been happy.

Chapter Thirty-one

I WAS SAD ABOUT DARLA FOR A LONG TIME, and just about stopped going to certain places like Sand Mountain and Bowlegs Creek because when I did I couldn't help thinking about her, which led to me missing her, which led back to me feeling so sad. I was always thinking about the funerals over the past year, too— Mr. Rhodes's way back in the early fall, and the colored soldier's when Walter Wratchford told me there was only one category for dead, and Darla's.

Maybe all that's why I didn't get upset or anything when Dad told us we were going to be moving. It was in the early spring. He had a new job lined up in Crystal River, which was a ways north of Tampa, almost on the Gulf of Mexico, and he said we would stay in Sand Mountain to finish out the school year and then pack everything up in June. He didn't tell us the other part—Mom did later—that they were having layoffs at the mine and they hated to do it but they had to let Dad go. Wayne said, "Who else did they let go?" and he bet there wasn't anybody else, or not any of the engineers, anyway. Mom said, "Never you mind. Your father says we're going and that's all there is to it. Sometimes things don't work out the way you planned, but we have a job to go to and I don't want your father to hear any of you children complain. Now, count your blessings and go set the table for dinner."

When Mom talked like that, there wasn't anything to say back to her except, "Yes, ma'am," which Wayne did and so did I and so did Tink. It seemed like David Tremblay and that girl Scooty just about started living with us after the announcement, and they both said they wanted to move with us to Crystal River, too. I wished I had a friend that liked me as much as David Tremblay and Scooty liked Wayne and Tink. Who I had had like that, or sort of like that, I guess, was Darla.

So I decided I was kind of glad about moving. It meant I would never get to be the Chattanooga Shoe-Shine Boy in the minstrel show, but I didn't want to do that anymore anyway. There'd been enough people making fun of me all year long, and making fun of Darla. I guess I didn't have the heart to want to be up there on the Mighty Miners stage making fun of anybody else, which was all they were really doing in that minstrel show: making fun of the colored people. I didn't want to be any part of that kind of meanness.

Besides that, I was thinking about calling myself by a different name when we got to Crystal River, and I was thinking that name might be Charlie, which was a name I kind of liked, I'm not sure why. It just sounded regular, I guess, and I thought maybe when we got to a new town I could let everybody think that's what I was—somebody regular.

A week after Dad told us about moving, Tink started crying late one afternoon and she wouldn't stop or couldn't stop, I didn't know which, for about an hour. Mom and Dad tried everything, but Tink just sobbed and sobbed. It turned out she thought we were going to have to leave Suzy behind when we moved, and when Mom and Dad found that out, they said, "No, sweetie, no— we would never leave Suzy," and they were so relieved that that's all it was, Mom told Tink she could choose anything she wanted for dinner that night, and she could decide what we would watch on TV.

Tink said she didn't care about dinner or TV, she just wanted to go to Sand Mountain and slide down from the top, which Mom and Dad hadn't ever let her do before because she was too little. Dad said it was still cold out—it was the end of March but it had been a long winter, especially February when frost killed off a bunch of the groves—and he also said it would be dark soon. But Tink looked like she was about to start crying again, so he said, "OK," what the heck.

For once David Tremblay wasn't over, but he came riding along on his bike just when Dad was backing the car out of the driveway, and said his usual, "Whatchyall doing?" so we took him with us, too. Dad was in a good mood, and him and Mom even sang a song on the way to Sand Mountain. Things were so lousy with the job and moving and all, plus the stuff that happened from the election, you would think Mom and Dad wouldn't be happy or anything, but for some reason it was just the opposite — when things got bad, they might be low for a while, but then they always kind of got better together.

I hadn't been to Sand Mountain since the last time I went with Darla, and I was dreading going now, on the way over, but it turned out not to be so bad once we started climbing. I even kind of liked thinking about the times her and me had gone there before.

It took us the longest time to get to the top of Sand Mountain because we practically had to carry Tink. Actually she wanted to be dragged *up* the mountain on the cardboard, even though we kept telling her to get the heck off, that wasn't how it worked. The sun wasn't even there anymore by the time we finally made it, but the sky was still light enough to see OK, and over the phosphate mines, it was streaked red and orange just like the last time I was there with Darla, which seemed like a really long time ago by then.

David Tremblay and Wayne hopped onto their cardboard right away and yelled, "Geronimo!" and disappeared over the side. I guess they didn't care about looking all around the way the rest of us did, especially Tink, since it was her first and, as it turned out, last time. The Tire Tower way over in the Boogerbottom next to the Peace River had flared up again about a week before —

a couple of months after they said they were sure it was done burning—and we could see a line of black smoke going straight up to the sky like somebody drew it there with a Magic Marker.

We watched the smoke for a while except for Tink, who was busy running from one edge to the other, to the other, and Dad said, "Oh, by the way," he guessed he hadn't told us yet, but the W. R. Grace Company was going to re-mine Sand Mountain.

"What?" I practically shouted when he said that, and Dad said, Yeah, they were going to reprocess the whole Sand Mountain because they discovered there was a lot of phosphate still left in the tailings, which is what the sand of Sand Mountain was, but now they had a new process that the chemical engineers had invented that they could get the rest of the phosphate out with. They figured there was probably ten million dollars' worth of it still in Sand Mountain once they moved it back over to the plant—kind of the opposite of how they made the mountain in the first place.

"And there won't be a Sand Mountain anymore?" I said.

Dad said, "That's right." Another two years and where Sand Mountain stood would be as flat as the rest of Florida. I guess Dad didn't think it was all that big of a deal, because he went over to get Tink so they could slide down together on their cardboard, which left just me and Mom the last ones standing on top. No more Sand Mountain. Dad could have told me the Russians just dropped the bomb or the Vietcong just won the war and I wouldn't have been shocked any more than I was. No more Sand

Mountain! I looked around in all directions, trying to memorize everything I saw.

West was the phosphate plants and the faded sunset and the torn-up land. South was the woods with Bowlegs Creek and probably that half man–half gator. East was the town with the Methodist Church, and Darla's house, and our house, and the high school, and the Skeleton Hotel, and the Boogerbottom, and the Tire Tower, and the Peace River, and that colored church— even though you couldn't see most of those places on account of the trees. North was the Pits, which Mom one time said looked like the four chambers of the heart, and Moon's Stable at the back side of the Pits, and the Old Bartow Highway. Where Darla . . .

Mom said we had to go now and there was just one more piece of cardboard, so we'd have to ride down together and did I want front or back. I guess I didn't move right away, so she put her arm around me and squeezed me. "Dewey Markham Turner, you're too young to look so sad," she said.

"But you're not old and you're sad a lot, too," I said back to her. It was true but I hoped it didn't sound mean.

Mom said when you're older, sometimes you have more you're sad about but that she had mostly blessings she was thankful for and I better know I was one of them. It was the second time she talked about blessings and how we ought to be thankful for them and count them, etc., which made me wonder if maybe she didn't really think we had all that many. But since it was my mom I didn't say anything. We sat on our cardboard, me in front, her in back, and I lifted up the front edge so it wouldn't get caught under the sand and flip us over. She said, "Look, Dewey, you can see the moon," and I did, a crescent moon already rising in the sky so close to the top of Sand Mountain that you could probably grab it if you had to.

Mom said, "Are you ready, Freddy?" I wasn't but said I was anyway, even though I kind of wanted to stay up there forever. Mom said, "Me neither," and then shoved us over the side. Everybody down at the bottom was waving at us and I wanted to wave back, but when you're doing something like that, going a million miles an hour down Sand Mountain, you don't want to mess around or anything. You just better hold on for dear life.

Acknowledgments

My profound gratitude to the "Angles" of the Lord who helped me climb Sand Mountain—not something I could ever do on my own: Bucky McMahon, Heather Montanye, and Pamela Ball; wonderful Kelly Sonnack and the Sandra Dijkstra Literary Agency; Candlewick Press and the gifted Kaylan Adair; my daughters Maggie, Eva, Claire, and Lili; and my wife and partner, Janet Marshall Watkins, who read, critiqued, edited, and reread with patience, grace, and love.

Can Iris Wight find a way to save both
the animals on her aunt's farm and herself?

What Comes After
STEVE WATKINS

After her father dies, sixteen-year-old Iris Wight is sent to live on her aunt's farm. Iris, a vegetarian and animal lover, immediately clashes with Aunt Sue, who mistreats the livestock and Iris. But when Iris frees two young goats to save them from slaughter, she discovers the brutal extent of her aunt's abuse.

www.candlewick.com